LEATHER BOUND

Shanna Germain

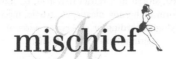

mischief

This novel is entirely a work of fiction.
The names, characters and incidents portrayed in it are
the work of the author's imagination. Any resemblance to
actual persons, living or dead, events or localities is
entirely coincidental.

Mischief
An imprint of HarperCollins*Publishers*
77–85 Fulham Palace Road,
Hammersmith, London W6 8JB

www.mischiefbooks.com

A Paperback Original 2013

First published in Great Britain in ebook format by
HarperCollins*Publishers* 2013

Shanna Germain asserts the moral right to
be identified as the author of this work

A catalogue record for this book is
available from the British Library

ISBN-13: 978 0 00 753335 0

Automatically produced by Atomik ePublisher from Easypress

'Keyholes are the occasions of more sin and wickedness, than all other holes in this world put together.'

Laurence Sterne

CHAPTER 1

Gorgeous green eyes. Blond curls. A perfectly trimmed golden goatee that highlighted a square jaw and delicious cheekbones. Thick, full lips just right for kissing.

It was the kind of face a girl could fall in love with.

Every girl but me, that is.

Oh, don't get me wrong. I had the lust part down. Kyle's face was so perfectly made, so sexy, that even when he was asleep, eyes closed tight to the world, just looking at him sent little flutters of want through me. And that was with most of his long, lean body hidden away beneath the covers. Sometimes I wanted Kyle with a fierceness that made me ache, even when he wasn't in the room.

Lust? Yes. But love? No.

We'd been having sex for about six months and our relationship was fun, hot and absolutely casual. Just like we wanted it. Which is why I found it weird that he was now asleep in my bed, conked out with my arm trapped beneath his head. In six months' worth of delicious sex, this was the first time we'd actually *slept* together.

While it was weird, I wasn't sure I minded all that much. We'd had a nice night –dinner on the back porch followed by giggling, groping, delicious sex on the living-room floor – despite the fact that Kyle had seemed preoccupied by something. He wasn't the kind of guy to keep things in, but he also wasn't the kind of guy to stay over. I wasn't sure what it all meant, but I figured he'd tell me when he was ready.

In the meantime, I needed a shower, something functional to wear to work and at least two cups of coffee. I'd let him find his way out of the apartment whenever he woke. He worked as a tat artist, which meant a lot of late nights inking customers. Something told me that mornings weren't his speciality.

I tugged my arm quietly out from under Kyle's head, trying not to wake him. He shifted, but didn't open his eyes.

Showering as quick as my own sleep-slowed body would let me, I padded back to the bedroom in my bare feet and opened drawers in the half-dark, trying to be as quiet as I could. Unfortunately, I'm a klutz in general and even more so before I've had my coffee. When I slid the closet open, it bumped against something with a bang. Kyle made a cute dreaming noise, and I stopped to look down at him half-buried under the covers. All I could see were strands of his dark-blond hair and one hand thrown over his face. He stirred, opening one green eye blearily. Even half-asleep and in the dim light of the bedroom, he was so very fuckable. It nearly made my mouth water.

'Mmm, you left me,' he said.

'I have to go to work,' I said. Unable to resist, I reached out to touch the soft curls that fell across his cheek.

'Not yet,' he said. 'Come back. We have warmth. And cock.'

'Cock, huh?' I was tempted. I was *always* tempted around him.

2

The bedside clock told me I wasn't late for work. Yet. I needed to open the bookstore, but since we showed up early to prep things, a few minutes wouldn't make too much of a difference.

'How much can you do in fifteen minutes?' I asked.

'I only need eleven to really blow your mind.' He was all grin and dancing eyes from his cocoon beneath the covers.

'Really? Eleven?' I said. 'I think I'm disappointed.'

'Get in here,' Kyle said, clearly more awake now, lifting the blankets to beckon me in.

I slid in beside him, scooting myself beneath the covers. He really was warm, his lean frame radiating heat. He ran a couple of times a week and his long muscles flexed beneath his skin as I settled against him. Running my hands over his body was a visceral pleasure. It was easy to get lost in the feel of him.

He touched his mouth to mine, sleep-soft lips parting with a quiet laugh. His morning stubble scratched my cheeks. He smelled like sweet chai, cloves and cinnamon, and I inhaled him deeply, lost for a moment in the sensations of touch and scent.

'I brought you a gift,' he said, whispering against my mouth, his hips moving forward to grind slowly against me. His bare cock nudged my thighs.

'Mmm ... what is it?' I couldn't help but giggle. He was always saying dorky but adorable things in bed.

'You'll have to see,' he said.

'A gift, huh,' I teased. 'Did you wrap it?'

'Not yet. It's like a reverse gift. First you get it, then you wrap it.'

'Funny man,' I said as I reached between us to stroke him. 'Oh, you did sleep well. That's some lovely morning wood.'

I loved the way he curved upward slightly when he was

fully hard, how he pulsed lightly against my palm. He had a beautiful cock, a smooth length that bowed into an impossibly soft head.

'Maybe I should stay over more often,' he said.

I only hesitated a second before he gave a teasing nip at my ear. 'Maybe you should,' I said. 'Especially if it means I get to do this before coffee...'

I was still speaking when he slipped a hand between my legs, parting them with the spread of his fingers. With a firming touch, he stroked me, wrapping his fingers lightly to tug at my dark curls. I felt myself open under his touch, already growing wet. It never took much around Kyle.

Kyle leaned in to kiss my neck, letting his mouth linger in the hollows, his tongue moving in time to his fingers. I couldn't help but buck my hips up toward his fingers. His touch was too soft. I wanted, needed more.

'It's almost like you want me or something,' he said, teasing with his tone as much as with his fingers.

'Kyle...'

Still he teased with soft strokes, refusing to give in to my low whimpers of want.

'Cruel,' I said. My voice stuttered with the sweet pleasures of his touch. 'So cruel.'

His grin was sharply wicked. His touch even more so, as he brought his hand back and then thrust forward, two fingers sliding deep inside me. I brought my hips up into the movement, letting my body welcome him. He curled his fingers against my g-spot, tugging forward until I felt small bursts of pleasure coil up through me.

So close. I loved that sweet moment when you can feel orgasm just over the horizon, can see it from the corner of your eye but can't quite reach it.

'More?' he asked.

'More, please,' I said.

He pulled away again, a gesture that left me emptied of pleasure and breath. With another thrust, he entered me again, more fingers, stretching me wider. I bucked against him, taking the lead to angle myself where his touch gave me the most pleasure.

His mouth found my nipple, tongue looping it lightly before he closed his lips to tug against the sensitive skin. I loved having my nipples sucked – sometimes I thought I could get off on that alone – and I arched into the pull of his mouth. He took more of me in, the pressure and release matching the movement of his fingers inside me. I groaned softly, unable to resist making the noises my body wanted me to make.

Kyle pulled away to look at me.

'How much time?' he asked.

'Five minutes,' I breathed.

'How do you know?'

'Internal clock?'

'I think you're full of it...'

'Listen,' I said, panting. 'I can use my mouth to argue about it or I can use my mouth to kiss you while you fuck me.'

He snapped his fingers in the air as if signalling someone. 'I need this gift-wrapped.'

Laughing, I reached out and grabbed a condom from the dresser. In the dark, I couldn't tell which side of the condom was up. Of course, I got it wrong the first time, trying to roll it down the wrong way over his head. I flipped it, got it wrong again, and then flipped it one last time. This time it worked perfectly.

'They should paint glow-in-the-dark arrows on these

things,' I groused, even as I slid the rubber down over his erection. Condoms were a necessary evil, but there was something I liked about rolling them down, stroking the length of him in the process. There was something he liked about it too; I could tell by the way he arched his hips, pressing his cock upward against my touch.

'It's like a USB plug,' I said, when I had it on.

'What?' He put his hand over mine, urging me to stroke him.

'Um. Hot man with beautiful cock, about to fuck me,' I said. 'Will explain technology later.'

'Geek,' he said.

'A geek you'd like to fuck,' I said.

'Isn't that a song?' he said.

'Don't know, don't care. Why are we talking about this when I could be riding you?'

I rose over him, letting my legs rest on either side of his hips. I loved being on top, loved that moment when I first started to lower myself down over his cock, that moment of connection, when I knew what was to come. He sighed beneath me, eyes meeting mine, his hands settling on my hips. He didn't pull me towards him, just let me ride myself slowly down on his cock, feeling it fill me, displacing the emptiness inside me with the lovely fullness of pleasure.

For all our playful banter beforehand, our actual sex was quiet. The only sounds we made were a lot of signs and groans, underwritten by the soft slap of our bodies coming together.

I leaned down and pressed my mouth to his, our hips rising and falling in unison, the strokes between us starting slow, a grind that left both of us groaning each time we came apart.

From this position, I could feel the way his cock curved

against the hollows of me. Every time I rose off him, his head slid against that sensitive bulb of my g-spot, making me gasp.

His fingers curved tighter around my hips, lifting me higher with each stroke, setting me down harder on him with each return.

'Touch yourself,' he said. 'Please. I want to watch.'

'I'll fall.'

'I've got you,' he said. He shifted his hands slightly, moving them down to cup my curves more fully, holding me up.

Leaning back slightly, I pressed two fingers to the sensitive tip of my clit. He watched me as I touched myself, green eyes lidded with desire. He lifted me in time to the circles of my fingers, matching stroke to stroke.

'You're so beautiful,' he said. 'I love watching you.'

His fingers tightened, nails digging into my skin, his breath as fast and ragged as mine. I couldn't stop looking at him looking at me. Getting myself off was hot. Getting myself off while getting fucked and watched by a beautiful man was so far off the scale of hot I had no words for it.

I tried to wait, to keep breathing through the pleasure that rose up through me, to stretch out that delightful moment before I came, but at the sound of Kyle's broken groan of my name, I couldn't hold off any more. He arched up under me, nails biting my skin, eyes closing. The pulse and clench of him brought my own orgasm, a quiet rippling sweetness that spread outward on threads of pleasure, until I could feel them all the way to the tips of my fingers.

We stayed like that for a moment, me still on top of him, our breaths catching and releasing, kissing softly. He felt different after sex, his lips softer and fuller, his touch gentler, and I relished the changes in him for a moment, knowing they'd been brought about by a pleasure similar to my own.

'You're awesome,' he said with a sigh.

'You're awesome too,' I said. 'But I have to run. Have a bookstore to run and all that.'

'We can't do this again? I'll be quick.'

'I wish,' I said, with a true sense of wistfulness. Maybe it was the fact that I was quickly approaching thirty or maybe it was just that my life had slowed down to a steady routine lately so I had more time to think about sex, but it seemed like my lust clock was always in overtime these days. My uterus didn't want kids, but my clit wanted sex. Pretty much all the time. Even with Kyle around a couple of times of week, I'd made pretty good friends with a whole community of vibrators in the last year. Turning down sex these days was akin to turning down coffee – something I only did with a great deal of reluctance.

I kissed Kyle's nose, with a sigh of regret.

'Sadly, if I stay I really will be late, which Lily will certainly hold over my head all day long if she can. Maybe longer.'

'You're afraid of Lily? Just threaten to mess up her hair.'

That made me laugh, as Kyle often did. My best friend did have perfectly coiffed hair. The kind that's so perfect you have to hate her, just a little, for having it.

'No go,' I said, as I pulled myself from the bed.

Getting dressed was me rushing and tumbling while Kyle watched me from his sprawl under the covers. Too late to do more than pull on whatever was closest, I grabbed a simple black dress from the closet and threw my dark hair into a messy ponytail. My store key on its red ribbon around my neck for pseudo-jewellery, my little librarian glasses, and I was calling it good.

When I sat on the bed to pull on a pair of knee-high boots, I caught Kyle's glance. He looked oddly serious for post-sex reverie, his usual grin replaced with something far more contemplative.

'Are you OK?' I asked.

He reached out and touched my arm. 'I just got fucked by a beautiful woman. How can I not be good?'

'Good.' I grinned at him before I kissed him, letting my lips linger against his for a long moment. 'You know how to get out, right?'

He nodded, reaching out to run his hand along my arm as I turned away.

I was at the bedroom door, mind already turning to work and the bookstore, before he spoke again.

From the depths of my bed, he said in that sexy, post-orgasm voice that never failed to turn me on, 'Janine. Marry me.'

The heel of my boot caught on the area rug, sending me sprawling against the doorjamb.

'Funny man.' Laughing, I turned to shake my head at him, at his impossible joke.

And in that moment, standing there in the doorway, I saw that he was serious. That he was, really and truly, asking me to marry him.

Shit.

* * *

Shit. Shit. Shit.

That was my refrain the entire fifteen-minute walk from my house to Leather Bound. What the hell was Kyle talking about, marry him? We had a perfect, lovely, sexy thing. Get together a couple of times a week, have dinner, get hot and heavy. Good fun sex on the kitchen floor. Or the couch. Or behind the couch. Then he went home and I curled up with a cup of coffee and a couple of books.

Lust. Not love.

Marriage. Was that why he'd been so quiet all night? Who the hell asked a girl to marry him from bed anyway? From *her* bed, no less. And, more importantly, why?

I was still turning a million questions over in my brain when I reached the bookstore. The door was locked – we didn't open for fifteen minutes or so – but the back lights were on, letting me know that Lily was already inside. Webster, the store cat, was snoozing in the big front window display, his grey striped tail tick-tocking, probably in time to some mouse-hunting dream.

I fished my skeleton key from where it hung on the long ribbon around my neck. Lily and I'd had them custom made when we opened the store, and I loved the heft of mine, the curled metal J of the bow.

Even when I was in a rush, even on a morning where I felt my world had just been turned upside down and carelessly shaken, unlocking the front door to Leather Bound felt like entering a far-away universe. Or someone else's story, right at that point where it all comes together and you know the ending is going to be fine. Everything dropped away in the seconds it took to slip the long metal key into the ancient lock and turn it.

As I stepped inside and shut the door behind me, I closed my eyes, inhaling the scent of paper and leather with a pleasure that I reserved just for this place. Yes, the bookstore was work, and sometimes it was hard and thankless work at that, but it was also a sanctuary. A little corner of bookworm heaven, made just for me.

'You, Miss Janine, are late,' Lily said.

I opened my eyes. From where I stood, Lily had her back to me so I couldn't see her customary smirk, but I could see the back of her legs, the black tattoo of the word *read* curled up the back of one calf, the red curlicues of the word *lips* scrawled up the other. She had lots of tattoos – most of them words – but I bet none of them got as many questions as that missing *my*. I'd seen it, of course. Kyle had done it for her. But I'd promised never to tell anyone just where that particular piece of lettering was situated.

'I'm sorry, Lil,' I said. I meant it. My co-owner worked her ass off at Leather Bound, maybe even more than I did, and we were supposed to share everything half and half.

Lil stretched to tuck a book into the upper shelf, tsking her tongue teasingly. As her black pumps lifted off the ladder, I caught a glimpse of one tan sole covered with hand-written book titles. Being book geeks was one of the few things Lily and I had in common, but it was a big enough thing that it had kept our friendship thriving for nearly ten years. Not to mention convince us to go into business together. It was a decision I'd never regretted.

While she finished shelving the books in her hand, I tugged at my buttons with cold fingers. My coat and scarf were collaborating to kill me, getting caught in my hair and glasses while I tried to get them off. 'I got stuck –' I started.

'Not stuck. Fucked. You got fucked, Janine.' Lily's laughter floated down at me. 'Don't lie. I don't even have to turn around and look at you to know.'

My cheeks burned hot all the way to my ears, the way they always did when I got busted trying to fib. I've always been horrible at even little white lies. I don't even know why I try. Especially not around Lily. She's like a genetically enhanced bloodhound when it comes to lies and falsities.

Still laughing, Lily made her way backwards down the ladder. Her cherry-red hair bounced against her shoulders in perfect ringlets. The one problem with Lily was that she was always picture perfect. Make-up. Outfit. Hair.

I touched my scarf- and sex-mussed ponytail, not even bothering to try and smooth it into something presentable. I'd had enough experience to know that, in some cases, attempting to fix things only made them worse, and gave you gigantic tangles in the process.

'How do you always know when I have sex?' I asked. 'I never know when you have sex.' Of course, Lily seemed to have a lot more sex than I did, so maybe that's why I couldn't tell. Or maybe I was just oblivious.

'I can smell it on you,' she said.

I sniffed myself. I smelled like cold wind and conditioner. Maybe a little like Kyle – he always smelled like chai and sometimes like those cinnamon candy hearts – but that didn't mean sex. And what did marriage proposal smell like? Would she be able to tell that too?

'You can not,' I said. I hoped.

Lily was still snickering when she hugged me, completely ignoring the fact that her gesture made it even more impossible to get my coat off or to keep my scarf from strangling me. 'You're right. It's just that you're never late for any other reason. Also,' she pointed out, 'you didn't bring coffee. And you always bring coffee.'

'Jerk,' I said, laughing.

'You love me.'

'It's true,' I said, as I managed to untangle myself finally from coat and scarf and stuff them under the front counter.

Then I took a minute to get my bearings. From the front counter, you could look out of the picture windows at the

12

world going by. But the worlds in here were what interested me most. Ancient books all shelved and labelled in their perfect little rows, just waiting for someone to adopt them.

Leather Bound was a lot of things to me, but mostly it was my second home. Sometimes it felt more like my first home. There were few things I loved more than being surrounded by books, especially old books. The scent of leather and paper and glue, the edges roughened by unknown fingers riffling the pages, the stories told black on white, permanent and yet ever changing. Different every time you read the words.

There were a lot of people who wouldn't understand that, who had moved on to video games, ebooks, videos, and argued that they were the same thing. Or, at the very least, that you could get the same enjoyment from them.

It wasn't that I didn't like new technologies. I did. I read ebooks almost as often as I read paper books. It was that it felt like the difference between masturbating and having sex. Masturbation was fun, but it was certainly not the same as having another warm, aroused body pressed against you.

Just the thought made me think of Kyle, and I shivered a little.

'Aha,' Lily said, pointing one ring-laden finger my way. Her bright-blue, perfectly kohled eyes flashed at me. 'You *were* having sex.'

'I said I was sorry.'

'You didn't,' she said.

'I'm sorry?'

'It's fine. I'm only a little jealous.' Lily handed me the change bag from the bank. I started counting bills into the register while she leaned on her elbows on the counter. 'Really,' she said. 'I mean ... who wouldn't want to be here opening the store we own together while you're off getting pinned to the bed? Me, I've run through every vibrator in my toy box at least twice in the last week, and I'm still bored out of my mind.'

'What happened to that –?' I gestured with my stack of bills. Apparently I couldn't think of names and count fives at the same time. 'The girl with the motorcycle. She was –'

'No,' she said, tugging one shiny red curl between her fingers. It sproinged back up perfectly when she let go. 'Just no. Don't even go there.'

Lily had the worst taste in women. Not physically. They were always hot as hell. But emotionally they were always just shy of bat-shit crazy. Some of them weren't even shy of it. I'd hoped the new girl would be different. She'd had a motorcycle, sure, which hadn't boded well for Lily in the past, but she'd also seemed nice enough. And she'd clearly been into Lily. She'd even come into the store and bought a book, some ancient tome on early motorcycles.

'Women suck, but I'm fine,' Lily said.

Despite her brave words, she was hurting. Lily believed in true love and happy ever after more than anyone I'd ever known. It sucked that she had such a hard time finding it. I wanted to offer her something. Condolences. Dating advice. The number of a totally hot girl who would be just perfect for her. But considering how screwed up my own relationship was at the moment – even the fact that I was suddenly thinking about Kyle in terms of something as serious as a relationship was a sign of things being way, way off-kilter – I wasn't in any position to offer her anything beside a heartfelt 'I'm sorry'.

She waved a hand at me, her nails perfectly polished in a blue-black hue that somehow matched her shirt exactly. Some days I dreamed I would wake up and have the kind of put-togetherness that Lily did. The horrible thing was I'd seen her get ready for things. What took her five minutes would have taken me five hours and turned me into a wailing mess with nail polish all over my bathroom and mascara smeared across both cheeks. She just had those skills somehow. I swear women like Lily are born knowing how to get their hair to behave perfectly just by looking at it sternly in the mirror.

An old boyfriend once asked me if I kept my face natural because I wanted to show off how I looked without make-up or because I was lazy. I didn't have the courage to admit that I kept my face 'natural' because I didn't know how to do anything else with it.

Lily raised her hand again and flipped off what I imagined to be a whole wall of former exes. The blonde biker chick. The beautiful volleyball player who'd had a penchant for threesomes. The teacher who'd shown up at Leather Bound in her glasses and her button-up cardigans, but who Lily said fucked like a wildcat in heat. And those were just the ones I could remember recently.

'Fuck love,' Lily said.

'Fuck love,' I said. Right now, I couldn't agree more. Love, or maybe the lack of love, seemed to screw everything up.

'Maybe you just need a quickie,' I said. 'A loving fuck to say fuck love?'

This time she flipped *me* off, her throaty laugh filling the front half of the store with sound. 'Seriously? Last time I did that, I almost ended up in Vegas saying "I do" to a vegan wiccan in front of a guy who didn't look in the least like Elvis. Worst. Quickie. Ever.'

I laughed with her, even though I felt my own throat close up a little as she went on.

'I mean, can you seriously ever see me getting married?

Little white dresses for both of us? House with a picket fence? Adopting kids or fighting over who gets to be the biological mom? Jesus.'

Can you see *me* getting married? I thought. Because I certainly can't. And, oh, Lily, my life is a little fucked up right now.

I'd never wanted to get married. I could easily give my entire life to a bookstore that was barely making ends meet, but couldn't seem to handle a relationship that required anything more than delicious sex and maybe dinner a couple of times a week.

I used to think I just hadn't met the right person, but now I wondered if something was wrong with me. Maybe I should think about getting married. Everything in my life was good, even if it was sometimes a little staid. Leather Bound was almost making enough money to keep us afloat. Lily and I worked well together. Kyle's work as a tattoo artist was getting recognition. Our sex was great.

'Actually,' Lily said quietly after a moment. 'Maybe that wouldn't be so bad.'

For a second I thought I'd been speaking out loud. My hands shook as they slipped the bills into their proper places in the register.

'OK, stop talking,' I said. 'Or I'll have to start the count over again.'

It wasn't entirely true, but I needed her to be quiet because my heart was thumping too hard in the hollow of my chest and, every time Lily said one more thing, I wanted to cry. Uncertainty and confusion do that to me sometimes. It's the little things that get me. When things are big and bad, I'm all strong and stoic on the outside. But when they're small and confusing and complicated, well, just bring on the tears.

16

When our friend Conrad died a couple months back, I didn't cry when he announced that he was sick, I didn't cry at his hospice bed and I didn't cry at the funeral. But when he shipped us a box of all the books he'd bought from Leather Bound over the years with a note thanking us for all the beautiful stories we'd given him, I fell down on my knees and wept until I'd ruined the letter with my tears.

Unwilling to think about that, I decided I'd tell Lily about my morning. Maybe she'd have more insight into the situation than I did.

'Hey, Lil,' I started. 'Kyle asked me to –'

At just that moment, the front door opened, and Lily and I both looked up in surprise.

My first thought was a very articulate 'I thought I locked that.'

My second thought was simply, 'Yum.'

* * *

Despite the fact that Leather Bound is a brick-and-mortar store, we don't get a lot of early-morning walk-ins. Probably because we only stock rare and old books. Obscure first editions and things signed by dead people are our speciality. So, things that people don't typically browse for. They call ahead, see if we have what they want and, if we do, they come by and pick it up. If we don't have what they want, I do my best to get it for them. It's something I'm known for, finding the obscure.

When we do get walk-ins, they're one of two kinds. The first is older men – book dealers, collectors, professors, the generation that still likes to fondle the books and eschew all technology, including the phone if they can. Lily calls them our Grounders, because she's afraid to get up on a ladder in her short skirts, in case she gives one of them a heart attack.

The other kind are the Velvets. Also Lily's name. They come in, usually looking either all sheepish or all professorial, and then they make their way, casual-like, towards the back of the store, like they're invisible lions sneaking up on prey.

We've got velvet curtains hung floor to ceiling back there. And behind them? A little room, not much bigger than a closet, the shelves stuffed full of delicious naughtiness. Not new stuff, though. Old stuff. Ancient versions of the Kama Sutra and Victorian-era sketchbooks and Sappho and Anon. You'd be surprised how much less repressed they were in years gone by.

So, Grounders and Velvets. Those are the kinds of walk-ins we get, on the rare occasions when we do get walk-ins.

What we most certainly never get are walk-ins who show up before we're open, sporting chocolate-caramel eyes and a lazy, dimpled smile that gave me a nearly irresistible urge to lick the corners of his mouth.

The guy in our doorway was beautiful, in that rugged, strong-jawed, day-old-stubble kind of way. Dark shiny hair that looked like it would tousle into perfect waves with a pair of hands in it. White T-shirt and grey button-down that brought out hints of gold flecks in his light-brown eyes.

I took hold of the counter while the air did that thing it does where it gets all thin and makes you dizzy for no reason at all.

Apparently Lily wasn't immune either. Which was odd, considering I'd never seen her go gaga over a male before. Except maybe a male puppy. And even then she was hard-pressed to admit it.

Not to mention, this was the longest I'd heard her be silent

18

in about a year. She was still standing in front of the door, pretty much blocking his entrance.

'Lily,' I hissed. 'Let the man in.'

'But we're not open yet.' Her mock whisper was all mock and no whisper.

'It's OK,' I said. 'Close enough.' Plus, hello, who cared? A man like that walked in your door, and I was pretty sure you opened for him … opened the door for him … any time of day.

I swallowed and tried to right myself so that I could put my professional face on. Thankfully Lily beat me to it. Sort of. Her social skills, as a general rule, far exceeded mine, a fact that I was ever grateful for.

'If you're looking for the sex shop,' she said, 'it's two blocks over and down on Mississippi. I can take you there.'

I tried not to gape at her. So much for that socially skilled thing. Why was she talking about the sex toy store?

She looked back at me for help and if I hadn't completely understood her distress, I would have burst out laughing. Even back here, I was having a hard time thinking. I couldn't imagine what it was like being so close to him. I wasn't sure if I was grateful to Lily for being on the front line or jealous that she was in touching distance.

The man's mouth was hanging open slightly, just like mine probably was. Somehow the expression didn't make him less sexy. I had no idea how that was possible, but it was. It sent me off in a small daydream, thinking about all the things that mouth could do. Beautiful white teeth that probably nipped at the edges of things just right. Thick, full lips with just a hint of sheen, as though he'd already been thinking about you and it had made him lick his lips in anticipation.

'The sex shop,' he said. Somehow he made it not so much

a question as a flavour. As though he was literally tasting the idea.

'I'm sorry,' Lily said. 'I just thought you might be looking for Lashes & Lace.'

'I know the place,' he said. His mouth had closed slightly, and now wore just a hint of a smile. Something hidden and teased in the half-curve.

'Well, people get us confused all the time,' Lily said. She was trying to recover, I could tell. But she was failing. Any time she absently fingered the yellow rose tattooed along the curve of her ear, she was either deep in thought or thoroughly embarrassed. Right now, she was scrubbing at it so hard it was like she was trying to wash it off.

'They do?' he was asking her. 'People come here accidentally to buy sex toys at ...' He looked at his watch. It was a beautiful leather and chrome piece, with what looked like a genuine antique face. The leather was old but so well oiled that I bet if you stood close enough you could smell it, animalistic and heady. I imagined myself leaning in to sniff his wrist, the place where the leather and pulse came together, that lovely heated skin.

Then I noticed the leather briefcase in his other hand, the copper clasps polished to a sheen. God, a man who looked this sexy who also appreciated old things? I was going to have to get a grip on myself.

'... at ten in the morning?' he finished.

I barely remembered what the two were prattling on about. Focus, Janine. Confusing us with a sex toy store at ten in the morning. Got it.

'You'd be surprised. It's an honest mistake.' I could practically hear the purr in Lily's voice as she got a hold of herself and started to turn on the classic Lily charm. She

20

surreptitiously wiped her palm on her skirt before she stuck her hand out. 'I'm Lily Marshen. Welcome to Leather Bound.'

He slipped his hand into hers. A shiver of want wiggled through me as their skin touched. I wondered what his skin felt like. How his long fingers would feel against mine. What he smelled like when his skin heated up.

I shook my head and focused. What was wrong with me? Yes, I was a sexual creature, and happily so. But I wasn't usually a drooling idiot around anyone, especially not around someone I hadn't even met. Besides, it wasn't like I didn't have enough lust and love trouble at the moment. I was not about to pile on even a tiny bit more. I had a feeling that this guy was a whole lot more, in both lust and trouble departments.

'Thank you,' he said. 'And while I'm a fan of a good sex store ...' Did Lily actually blush when he said that? I could have sworn I saw some pink flash over her perfect, pale cheeks '... I'm actually in need of a book.'

'Oh, you'll want to talk to Janine then,' Lily said. And bless her if she didn't sound just a little sad to let go of his hand.

For the first time, the man glanced my way. His eyes were the kind of thing you look at first and then can't stop looking at, the irises showing swirls of golden honey and caramel all rimmed in black. His lashes were so thick and dark, it almost looked like he was wearing eyeliner. Thank God he wasn't. Not that I minded guys in make-up, but having two people in the same room as me who knew how to use eyeliner better than me would have killed what little make-up ego I had.

He smiled at me. Watching him smile was like opening a book for the first time. That slow reveal, full of promise, just inviting you to come closer, to learn all the nuanced secrets that awaited within.

I tried to smile back, but my lips got stuck on my teeth somehow and I could just tell that I was grimacing at him instead. Lily cleared her throat. It was time for me to introduce myself, to be professional, to come out from behind the safety of the counter, but I couldn't quite remember how to make my feet do the thing they were supposed to do.

I remembered Lily's shoes with the book titles on them and imagined my own soles were covered in verbs.

Step, Walk, Move all too quickly became *Kiss, Suck, Fuck.*

I shook the mental image from my head, since it clearly wasn't helping, and forced my feet forward until I was standing before him. This close, he was taller than I'd thought. Even with my heeled boots on, I had to look up a little. From here, his eyes were more complicated, an overlay of honeyed caramel flecked with nearly hidden hints of green and gold.

I could hear Lily breathing somewhere near me, but I was having trouble focusing on anything beside those warm eyes and that dimpled smile.

Think of Molly Bloom, I told myself. Think of Hester. Think of Lolita.

No, wrong ones.

Thinking of literary characters was my usual trick in getting through panicky situations, but every time I thought of one now, it was a woman and she was not exactly doing innocent things in the recesses of my brain.

I had to break eye contact and look over his shoulder, to the street outside where normal people were doing normal things. A woman walked by with a white dog the size of a teacup curled in her arms. A couple stood arm-in-arm just outside the window and kissed briefly, his lips touching hers with a familiarity that made me feel like a voyeur.

Looking away, I forced my gaze to land on his, taking

in his unusual eyes, his attentive expression. After a long moment, the air righted itself so that I could breathe and then again so I could talk. Soon enough I could even stick my hand out, worrying only a little whether I'd been sweating.

'I'm Janine Archer,' I said, quickly, before he could take my outstretched hand and render me speechless yet again.

He spoke as his hand settled in mine. His skin was as warm as I'd imagined, a soft heat that seemed to sink into my palm. His fingers were firm, confident. He didn't shake my hand so much as hold it, tight and secure, as though it was an important package that had been given to his care.

He'd said something.

'I'm sorry?' I said. I hadn't heard him at all. What I did hear was Lily giving a quick, sharp laugh behind me and then trying to hide it with a cough.

'I said ...' He enunciated each word carefully, as though I was eight, but a smile played lightly at the corners of his lips as he spoke. And besides, I guessed I deserved it. I was certainly acting like I was eight. Or at least eighteen. 'I'm Davian Cavanaugh.'

'I'm Janine Archer,' I said. Again.

'I know,' he said. 'You told me.'

This time, Lily didn't even bother to try and hold her laughter in, damn her. Did I mention she's the world's loudest laugher? I wanted to turn around and pinch her earlobe or hide her away in the back room. Or something. It was impossible to be angry with her, though, once she started laughing. Shaking my head, I smiled apologetically at our potential customer.

'Please excuse us,' I urged. 'We're usually far more professional than this. It's just been ... one of those mornings.'

I fully expected Lily to make some kind of crack about

me smelling like sex. Then I *would* have to kill her and stuff her into the back room.

She was blissfully quiet. For once.

Davian lifted his brow into a high arch, his expression clearly stating his disbelief that we were typically more functional than this. I couldn't blame him. He hadn't exactly seen us at our best. The old me, or rather the young me, would have written this entire conversation off as a disaster and fled the room with her cheeks burning and tears threatening to fall. But this was the new me, the adult me, the me who had a business to run and bills to pay.

Think Scarlett O'Hara. ➤

That worked. I straightened my back and let go of Davian's hand.

'So, what book are you looking for, Mister Cavanaugh?' I asked. 'If it's rare, first-edition, banned or signed, I guarantee I can find it for you.'

He took a moment to look around the store, letting his gaze linger over the shelves before he turned slowly back to me. I was struck again by the caramel swirls of his eyes, the way they seemed to radiate heat.

'It's none of those things, actually' he said. 'The book I'm looking for doesn't exist.'

CHAPTER 2

I barely missed a beat.

'Luckily for you, books that don't exist are my speciality,'
I said.

If he'd expected me to balk or turn down his offer, he
didn't let his surprise show.

'I've heard that about you,' he said.

Which caught me all off-guard.

'What? You have?'

He shook his head, his smile turning slightly guilty. His
eyes flashed darker with amusement.

'No,' he said. 'I thought you were kidding. So I was
kidding too.'

'Actually, I *was* kidding.' At least I thought I was. Now
I was confused. Had I been kidding? Mostly. Hard-to-find
was my speciality. Doesn't-want-to-sell was also my speciality. Signed by a dead person in archival blue ink was also
something I'd found once, at quite a price to the buyer. Was
non-existent and completely bizarre my speciality? If this
morning was any indication, it just might be.

I took a quick breath in through my nose, trying to get
myself back onto a professional business track. I was well

aware that Lily was making noises of shuffling papers on the counter behind me, but what she was really doing was recording all of this for later with her impossible memory. I'd hear about every single nuance of this as soon as she and I were alone.

'In truth, I expected you to turn me down,' he said.

'I haven't said yes yet,' I countered. 'But I like challenges.'

I especially liked challenges from men with caramel-coloured eyes and more than a little wickedness in the pages of their smile. More importantly, I liked the kind of challenges that forced me to use my brain, the kind that could distract me from my current challenge, who was probably still sleeping in my bed, dreaming about wedding rings or something.

This guy would either turn out to be a crackpot – chasing down a book that didn't exist was one of the favoured pastimes of those with too much time, money or craziness, or all three, on their hands – or he'd turn out to be actually looking for something that didn't exist. Either way, it was something to keep my mind occupied and my field of vision focused somewhere other than my love life.

'You like challenges,' he mused. There was something in his gaze that implied so much, and yet managed to still remain above board. I liked that, the sexuality that seemed aimed just at me, while maintaining a sense of decorum. It made me wonder what he'd be like at an elegant dinner party, all dressed up and making small talk while fingering you under the table.

'Even impossible challenges?' he asked.

I still had visions of his fingers, and what they might to do to me. The idea lent my voice a low tease that I didn't mean it to have.

'Let's just say I've believed impossible things before,' I said.

'Even before breakfast?'

Was he ever going to stop throwing me for loops so I could get my brain in order? I felt suddenly and fiercely like Alice going down her rabbit hole.

'Did you just misquote Lewis Carroll at me?' I asked.

'Maybe,' he said.

Curiouser and curiouser. A lot of our customers covet books like fine art or hot women, but never actually read them. This man was not just looking for a book. He actually read books.

Could he possibly get any sexier? A better question was: could I trust myself to behave like a professional around him? I thought I could, but standing right here, right now, I had to admit I would have bet on anyone but myself to win that argument.

I figured I'd better get him into my office and put my work face on before I delved too deeply into questions I didn't really want answers to.

'Well,' I said. 'Come on back, and we'll see if I can help you make your unicorn of a book magically appear from thin air.'

From behind me, I heard Lily give another quiet snort of a giggle, but she suppressed it so fast I was hopeful that Davian hadn't heard. If he had, his face didn't change expression.

'I would appreciate that,' he said.

'Right this way,' I said.

* * *

While Davian followed me back towards the office, I kept wanting to turn around to look at him again. I resisted the urge, but barely. I could hear his fingers brushing the occasional book as he went by them, the soft whisper of skin to spines that you only hear in bookstores and libraries.

I wondered, as I often did, if books could feel us, if our very touch was enough to bring them alive. And I wondered, specifically, if they could feel Davian's hands on them, what the soft stroke of his fingers felt like to their bindings, to the edges of their pages.

'Here it is,' I said, turning to face him again, one hand out towards a wide set of built-in bookcases, full of oversized first editions.

Davian lifted that single eyebrow again, clearly confused.

Yeah, I'd felt that way the first time I'd seen my office too. Of course, it hadn't been my office then, but it was still a huge part of the reason I'd fallen in love with this space, long before we'd rented it and turned it into the store. Before Leather Bound was ours, it had been a bank, complete with a hidden swinging door for getting into the super-secret vault without attracting attention.

Friends had helped us turn the hidden door into a hidden bookshelf door for us before we opened.

I couldn't help showing it off sometimes. I kind of loved the moment of revelation. It made me feel all Nancy Drew.

While Davian watched, I slipped a book from the shelf to expose a single keyhole. We'd had it made to fit the same skeleton key that opened the front door.

Suddenly I realised that, in my secret joy at showing off the hidden door, I'd put myself in a dilemma. I had to either try and remove the key and ribbon from around my neck – an action that was sure to end up with my hair or my earrings caught in tangles and leaving me looking incredibly stupid in front of this man – or leave the key in its current place and bend down in front of him to open the lock.

After a brief hesitation, realising that he was watching me far closer than I would have liked at the moment, I chose the latter option. If he was going to look at my ass, that was fine, but I didn't think I could stand to look like a fool in front of him. Again, I meant. Considering I'd already done it once. Or twice. I couldn't quite remember.

I bent and slipped the key in the hole. The skirt of my dress suddenly felt too short and too flimsy to cover my ass, even though I knew it did. Please let this look good on me, I thought stupidly, selfishly. Not at all professionally.

Lily and I had secret codes for lots of things – 'I have a stone in my shoe' meant 'You have something in your teeth' and 'I need a raspberry lemonade' meant 'It's time for us to leave this party/bar/guy's house.' But we didn't have a secret code for 'the hot guy behind you is staring at your ass in that skirt while you bend over in front of him.' So I couldn't tell if he was or not. I also couldn't tell if I would have minded.

I stood, giving my butt a quick shake to make sure the fabric fell back into the right places, and then slipped the key back into its place between my breasts.

The bookshelf opened outward, exposing the small office hidden behind it.

'Nice,' he murmured, and I couldn't tell if he meant the hidden door, the office or my ass. Was it so wrong that I secretly hoped it was all three?

I held the door for him, noting that he was tall enough that he kind of had to duck to get through it. Thankfully, the ceiling was higher, and he could stand upright as soon he got inside.

I followed him, stepping into a room that, if anyone cared

to look, showcased more of my personality than any other place in the world.

A big ancient solid oak desk took up all of one corner of the office. I'd bought it at a garage sale and then paid all my and Lily's friends in pizza and beer to help me get it in here. It was so big we'd had to take the secret door off its hinges just to fit it. It had one leg shorter than the others, a flaw that our friend Conrad had fixed for me by stuffing an old book under it. I loved it like no other piece of furniture.

The desk's wide surface had nothing on it except my laptop and a pile of books I'd been using for another client's research. Normally, I was a clutter bug, but I'd spent a whole month sanding down and then re-varnishing my baby, and there was no way I wasn't going to look at it (OK, and run my hands over it, if I was going to be honest with myself) every chance I got.

I beckoned to the chair across from the desk, a double theatre seat that I'd scavenged from a dilapidated cinema a couple of years ago. Davian glanced at it before he settled himself into the folding seats. He could have taken up both, but he didn't. Instead, he sat on one, crossing his long legs to the outside as though someone was already sitting in the seat next to him. His jeans were dark, with just a hint of wear at the creases of his pockets. His grey shirt showed off his shoulders and the width of his chest.

While the seat next to him was tempting – oh, God, was it tempting – I knew myself better than that. There was no way I'd be able to sit that close to him and not touch him, accidentally or otherwise. Instead, I lowered myself to sit on a corner of the desk. I had a notebook in one of the drawers here somewhere, but I couldn't be bothered to look away from him long enough to get it right now. I'd just have to wing it.

'How did you hear about us?' I asked, mostly just to hear his voice. 'If you don't mind. Most people don't just walk in our doors looking for invisible books.'

'It's not invisible,' he said in all seriousness. 'It's non-existent.'

He opened his briefcase, the two copper toggles slipping with ease through the rich, dark leather. As he scanned the contents, I found myself scanning him, my gaze travelling the length of him, from the single dark curl that fell across his forehead to the open neck of his button-up shirt, to his broad shoulders and slim hips. I wanted permission to reach across the room and slip that very top button through its hole, just one, to find out what lay hidden underneath.

I liked the way he took up a space. The fold of his body had a presence that felt solid and real, without needing to make more of itself. Even his fingers, shifting the papers as he looked through them, contained a quiet strength that I found appealing.

Davian pulled out a small rectangle of vanilla-hued paper and held it out between two fingers. Even before I took it, I knew what it was.

What I didn't know was how he had got hold of it.

I turned it over, face-up, and stared down at it.

Leather Bound, handwritten in dark red with Lily's calli-graphic swirl. Another brilliant idea of mine that had turned out to be not so brilliant after all. Before we opened, I decided we were going to hand-ink all of our business cards, to give them a personal feel. I made one, realised my handwriting sucked, and then handed the project over to Lily, who'd studied art in college. She'd gotten through about twenty of them before we both decided it was my worst idea ever. Lily hadn't even offered her usual 'I told you so's. She just went out and had some real ones made by an actual printer.

We'd never given these handwritten cards out to customers and definitely not to strangers. Only to a few close friends and supporters, the people who'd helped get Leather Bound off the ground, financially or legally or emotionally.

I'm a bad liar and even worse at keeping my mouth shut. So I couldn't not ask the thing that was in my brain.

'Where did you get this?' I asked. 'We've never met.'

I'm decent with faces, but I'm not as good as Lily. I'm better with voices. I can hear one note from a singer and tell you who it is and how recent it is. But a face like Davian's? I would have remembered him. Without a doubt.

'No,' he said quietly. 'We've never met.'

'Then where did you get this?' It was an invasive question, but I asked it quietly, and he didn't seem put off by it.

'A ... friend,' he said. With a just-long-enough pause that I could almost read what he wasn't saying. Perhaps a former lover. Or someone he desired. Clearly someone he didn't want to talk about.

Despite my curiosity, I let it go. For now. I was good at digging. It's what I did. But privacy is privacy. Unless it became important in finding his book, I wouldn't pry any deeper than I had to.

'Well, tell your friend I said thank you for recommending us,' I said.

Something played across his features then, an odd darkness that pulled his caramel eyes slightly closed. His lips tightened a little, making his mouth seem drawn and concerned.

I waited to see if there was more, but he didn't say anything. I wondered if that meant I was right about it being a former

32

lover. A former love. Probably very recently former, from the look on his face.

Time to change the subject. As much as I wanted to know all I could about this man – including how he liked to be touched and what he tasted like and, oh, dear God, what he might look like beneath those perfectly fitted jeans – he was, first and foremost, a potential client. I didn't want him to feel uncomfortable. Or sad, which was what seemed to be slipping into his eyes the longer we sat there in silence.

'Why don't you start at the beginning, Mister Cavanaugh, and tell me everything you can about the book you're looking for.'

* * *

'Only if you call me Davian,' he said. 'I still like to pretend I'm too young and wild to be a Mister.'

Which, of course, made me wonder how old he was. He looked my age but since nearing thirty I thought everyone either looked really young, really old or exactly my age. Which could not have been true.

'I'm afraid to say you don't look particularly wild, Davian,' I said. I liked the way his name felt on my tongue. Devilish and yet comfortable, as if I was reading a new story in a very old book.

He didn't say anything to that. His smile, however, *was* a little wild. I caught a glimpse of the devil in that grin and I'm not afraid to admit that it ratcheted my heart more than a little. Smart bad boys wrapped in well-tailored shirts are on my fetish list. Along with leather, voyeurism, great nipples, pretty cocks and, well, any number of things that

I wasn't supposed to be thinking about while talking to a potential client.

Resisting the urge to say his name again just for the fun of it, I said, 'Tell me about your book.'

He leaned forward and rested his elbows on his knees. The dark edges around his irises made his caramel eyes even more like chocolate. It's weird to admit that I kept wanting to lick his eyeballs, but they just looked so much like a decadent dessert.

'What would you like to know?' he asked.

What I wanted to say was: I'd like to know why every time I look up at you, my whole body goes a little trembly. I'd like to know what your mouth tastes like. I'd like to know how your face looks when I very lightly touch the underside of your cock. Whether you're the kind of man who will hold my wrists down on this very desk while you fuck me.

What I actually said was: 'How about a title, an author and a publisher, for a start.'

'Well, that's the trouble,' he said. 'It doesn't have any of those. Thus the non-existent part.'

I nodded as if I understood what he was saying, but a bad feeling was forming in the pit of my stomach. We occasionally got crazies at Leather Bound, people who were obsessed with finding something that only existed in their own minds. I hadn't pegged Davian for that, but you never knew.

'Well, tell me what you do know,' I said.

From my semi-precarious position on the desktop, I grabbed my laptop and popped it open, then started taking notes.

'It's the only copy, because it's handwritten, and it's old,' he said.

After a hesitant pause, he added, 'Also, it's the manifesto of a secret sex club.'

It was only by the grace of some deity that I didn't fall off the desk. Or laugh out loud. My internal 'is this man crazy?' quiz-taker checked off another box towards a 'yes' answer. That made me sad.

'A secret sex club,' I said.

He had the decency to look slightly chagrined. 'I know how it sounds,' he said. 'And it's going to sound even worse when I tell you it's for a friend.'

He was flipping the copper closures on his briefcase, staring at me intently. It wasn't a fidgety gesture but one of intense concentration, as though he was trying to figure out something that was swirling around in his brain. I did that kind of thing sometimes when I was thinking, usually playing with an earring and a pen until Lily had to swat it out of my hand. Something told me it was way more irritating when I did it than when he did; on him, it reminded me of a lion studying prey, deciding on weaknesses before gearing up to pounce.

'It's called The Keyhole Club,' he said.

'The book or the club?'

'Both.'

While trying to type THE KEYHOLE CLUB, my fingers kept going to the s and x keys. I got SEXHOLE the first two times, but I finally nailed it. My ninth-grade typing teacher would have been so embarrassed.

'And it's a manifesto on sex,' I said.

He nodded. This time, my fingers still managed to find the wrong keys. KEY, I wrote. I backspaced three times and then wrote SEX.

'Anything else? Sex is pretty broad.'

He shook his head.

'Davian, if you're uncomfortable talking about sex...'

'No,' he said. 'I'm not uncomfortable talking about sex.

I'm not uncomfortable with sex at all.'

He shifted forward in the chair, his hands resting on his knees. Only half a foot closer to me, and the hair on the back of my neck lifted at his very presence. Despite how strongly he was falling into the crazy category, that honeyed gaze kept threatening to do me in.

I shifted back slightly and looked over his head at a blank piece of wall. Nothing to see here. Move along, libido.

He let me shift back, but didn't move away himself. I knew it was impossible to feel his breath from where he sat, or to feel the heat from his skin, and most of all it was impossible to feel that he was somehow hitching my lust up with every exhalation, and yet there it was.

'In fact,' he continued, although I was kind of hoping he wouldn't, 'I'm very comfortable with sex. I just –' and at that he did sit back, and my lust took a little tiny tumble down the stairs, my body sighing in both relief and disappointment at being released. '– haven't ever seen the book myself, so I don't actually know very much about it.'

You could just tell he was the kind of man who was used to knowing things. Being in a position where he had to admit his lack of knowledge seemed to put him on edge.

'So you're looking for a non-existent sex book for a super-secret sex club that a friend of yours, what, lost?'

Despite the lust that kept blooming in my body at every turn, I was definitely starting to think I was getting taken for a ride. Either that, or this guy had lost his marbles.

The potentially crazy guy nodded.

'That's really not much to go on,' I said.

He caught me with that gaze again, a tormented heat. I felt the weight of his want as solidly as if he'd pressed himself against me.

Why do I always have a thing for guys with complicated eyes? Never do I fall for a clear gaze, a simple, single colour. I'm a sucker for a little sadness behind the eyes, a fierce spark of defiance.

Kyle had that. Davian too. Probably, if I were to look back at every man I'd fallen in lust with, it was true of them all. There was some kind of warning sign in that, if I was smart enough to pay attention.

But Davian's gaze was on me, and I couldn't think beyond the needy lust that licked at my thighs.

'You know,' he said quietly, 'I walked in the door with this urgent need to find this book for my friend, but, since I got here, all I can think about is you.'

His voice carried both surprise and a sense of wonder. I had no idea what to do with either the shift in tone or the complexity his words carried. It was like Davian's sole purpose was to accidentally keep unbalancing me. It was certainly working.

'By which I mean,' he added, 'all I can think about is kissing you.'

More unbalance. Teeter-totter all the way down.

At that, my cheeks flushed hot and fast, damn them. In the process of bringing my hand up to my face to cover the red, I knocked an entire pile of books off my desk. He didn't bend to pick them up nor offer to help. Instead his gaze stayed solidly on mine, almost as if daring me to reach down and get them.

I left them where they'd fallen, waving my errant hand at them as if to say, 'No worries, they do that all the time. On their own. For no reason.'

'I don't … I, uh …' Get it together, Janine. Least professional bookstore owner ever. Least professional professional ever.

Professional. That's what I kept thinking. Be professional. I needed cheerleaders in front of me, doing that thing they do. Rallying me. *Gimme a B. Gimme an E. Be professional. B. E. Professional.*

Of course, it wasn't working. Davian had this presence about him, something dark and fierce, that made it hard to think. Maybe it was his contrast with Kyle's sweetness. Maybe it was because I was freaked out about the marriage proposal. Or maybe it was just my hormones, my pheromones, my lust clock, wreaking havoc with my usual held-together self. For whatever reason, my libido had become a tangible entity in the room, winding its way around my brain with its ridiculous and incessant needs.

I closed my eyes for a moment, forcing myself to stay in my seat. Or on my desk, rather. It was a skill I'd learned a long time ago, at my first job. Before I learned that I was a much better boss than employee. Sit still, breathe, don't speak until you already know what's going to come out of your mouth.

'I keep thinking about kissing you too,' I said.

Well, that didn't work.

* * *

'Well,' he said. 'Now that that's out of the way.'

'Gah,' I said. My usual articulate self. 'I'm so sorry. This is why I usually let Lily do all the talking.'

'I'm glad she's not talking now,' he said. His gaze just kept melting the edges of me. Like licking a lollipop, until bit by bit you got to the sweet, juicy centre. I flexed my thighs together, tight, willing the pressure to quell the beating pulse between them.

'I kind of wish she was,' I said, even though that wasn't true.

Somehow we'd gotten closer together, although we hadn't moved. Or rather I was pretty sure *I* hadn't moved. And yet I was sitting on the very edge of my desk, as though every cell in my body was working hard to bring me closer to Davian.

'I'm sorry,' he said. 'I don't mean to be vague, and I certainly don't want to hinder your work. I just –'

'Have trouble trusting people?'

It came out more biting than I meant it to, and I clamped my teeth on my tongue, hoping it would keep me from talking for a while. If I wasn't trying to fuck the customer, I was trying to poke him with the sharp stick of too much honesty. Nicely done.

'I won't deny that,' he said. Thankfully, he laughed a little as he spoke, easing some of my embarrassment.

'Look,' he said. 'Can we take this slow? To be honest, I'm not entirely sure what I'm doing here, and I don't want to screw it up.'

That sounded more like the beginning of a relationship than a business proposition. Still, I understood where he was coming from. I'm the kind of girl who jumps too quickly into business relationships and painfully slowly into anything that so much as smacks of love. Maybe he was just the opposite.

'Slow is fine,' I said, not at all unaware of the odd role reversal that was happening. 'But I still need to know as much as you can tell me so that I don't walk into this blind.'

Sighing, he nodded. 'Fair enough.'

He settled back into the chair and crossed his legs.

'My friend wrote me a letter, asking me to find a very important book that he, to use his words, "accidentally misplaced,"' he said. 'Which is very unlike him, but I wasn't able to ask too many questions.'

After a pause, he added, 'And that's pretty much the whole story.'

I didn't think that was true. There was more going on there, behind those complicated eyes. But he'd asked to take it slow, and I'd said yes.

'This is a very unusual job,' I said. 'In truth, I've never had anyone ask for something like this. My rates for this kind of thing would be ridiculously high.'

'I know,' he said. 'Money's not a problem.'

'You do know that you sound more than a little crazy? That this whole thing sounds suspicious.'

He smiled, sending my heart into another pitter-patter of yum.

'I know,' he said. 'And trust me, if it wasn't this particular friend asking, there's no way I'd even be here.'

I had a moment to wonder if this mysterious friend was really Davian. Had he misplaced his own book during some moment of stupidity, too embarrassed to admit it, but wanting it back? He didn't really seem like that kind of person. And the darkness had come back into his eyes as he spoke, a sadness that I couldn't place. There was more here than he was letting on, but I didn't think he was lying about his friend. Or about the book.

'I'd like a list of his potential friends, then,' I said. 'People I can talk to. And all of the information you have about the sex club.'

I impressed myself with my own straight face at that.

'Here's the thing.' He leaned forward, so that we were the kind of close you see in movies, the kind of close that's reserved for your best friends and the people you really, really wanted to kiss. And lick. And fuck.

I tried to focus on his eyes, but their caramelly heat was making things worse, so I lowered my gaze to his neck, watching the place where his pulse thrummed beneath the skin. Nope, that was no better.

'I can't talk about the sex club,' he said. 'I've already said more than I should have.'

I sighed, and the breath leaving me was almost painful. There was no way I could take this job. Not that the idea of playing super sleuth didn't appeal to me, but the holes were starting to show in his story. Big, big holes. He clearly thought he was part of a *Fight Club*-esque novel or something.

The crazy thing was that, even with all of that, I almost believed him. I certainly wanted to believe him. Hot sexy well-read guy with just a little crazy to offset the good stuff? That wasn't too far on the wild side, was it?

Yes, sadly it was.

We sat in silence. My office got smaller and smaller with every breath, until I swore I could feel the heat shimmering off his skin, until I felt like all I had to do was reach out my hand and it would brush along his thigh.

I knew I couldn't take this job. No matter how much I wanted to. No matter how hot he was. It was a wild-goose chase. A blind alley that led to a dead end filled with nothing but lust and failure.

Slipping down from the desk, I smoothed one hand down the front of my dress and prepared my professional voice, which was pretty much my bitch voice wrapped in some sweet coating.

'I'm sorry, Mister Cavanaugh,' I said. 'I don't think I'm the right person for this job. But I really appreciate you coming to see us. I wish you the best of luck with finding someone who can help you.'

41

Even as I stood up, he hadn't moved back. I was closer to him than I had been before. So close I could feel his body heat, and catch the slightest hint of pine on his skin. It made me feel a little dizzy.

He took my hand. It was a gesture that seemed as natural to him as breathing, and yet he looked utterly surprised that he'd done it.

'Please reconsider,' he said. There was so much sincerity, so much yearning, in his voice that for a moment I wondered if I was making a mistake.

Then I thought about the conversation that had just happened. There was no way I was going to find this book, even if it did exist, and I wasn't about to take on a client who was this sexy and this close to being clearly crazy. As much as I wanted a diversion from my current life, there was no way that saying yes to him was not the worst idea ever.

'I'm sorry,' I said again. 'I just can't. I can, however, recommend some other places to try.'

I meant to say something then, or ask something, but he stood, moving closer to me in the process, never letting go of my hand. He reached into his pocket with his free hand and dropped a simple cream-coloured card on my desk.

'I don't want someone else,' he said. 'Please call me if you change your mind.'

He picked up the Leather Bound card. 'And I'd like to keep this,' he said. 'In case I need to find you.'

For some reason I was loath to give the card up again. As if I'd hoped to use it to find some clue about who'd given it to him, how he was connected to my life or to Leather Bound.

I wanted to make some crack about how he knew exactly where to find me. Here, mostly, with my nose tucked into books.

42

But of course I merely nodded and watched as he slipped the card into his jeans pocket. It would have been unprofessional to do anything else. And I was trying damn hard to stay professional.

Despite the fact that he still holding my hand and that his eyes were a creamy caramel that seemed swirled full of dark thoughts and even darker desires. Despite the fact that my life was falling apart around me and that I had an impossible question I couldn't answer and a non-existent book I couldn't find.

CHAPTER 3

After Davian left, walking out of the office while I stood there and refused, refused, refused to look at his beautiful ass in those dark jeans, I dropped my head into my hands. It felt like time for either hysterical laughter or panicked tears, but my body just couldn't seem to move past the arousal state into something new.

It didn't take long for Lily to poke her head in, her already arched eyebrows raised another notch.

'Oh. My. God,' she breathed. 'I thought you were going to fuck him right here in your office for the whole world to watch.'

Lil dropped herself into the chair Davian had vacated. Her stockinged legs were just long enough that she could rest her feet on the corner of the desk. 'And by the whole world I mean me, of course.'

Fuck. Yes, that was just what I'd wanted to do to him. Or rather, have him do to me. His presence had dredged up desires I hadn't had in a long time. Since long before Kyle, who had made it clear early on that kink wasn't really his thing. I'd agreed, thinking it wasn't that important. Our sex was vanilla, maybe, but it was good vanilla.

Now I couldn't get images of leather and submission out of my mind. I kept thinking about how Davian's hands would feel capturing my wrists, holding me down. About him fastening a collar of leather about my neck and holding it while I sucked him.

'No,' I said, unsure what I was even saying no to.

'No, what? Janine, you were practically puddling into an ooey gooey mess of melting chocolate in here.'

I gave her the look. She was used to that look. It was a look that said *please stop talking before I come over there and sit on you.*

It was a threat that clearly didn't hold as much weight as it used to, because she just kept going.

'OK, fine,' she said. 'But at least tell me the rest. Is he looking for some ancient Egyptian script? Some musty old academic bible? Or something juicier? Please say juicier.' Her tongue flickered out, playing around with her ball piercing.

'No,' I said. 'It's not juicy. In fact, I turned him down.'

She quit playing with her piercing and her mouth dropped open just a little. 'What? Why? Huh?' She was pushing her point to the max, playing up the confusion to show me that I'd made a mistake. 'He's hot as hell. He wants a book that doesn't exist. It's absolutely perfect for your little sleuthing brain.'

I started to say something, but she wasn't finished. 'If you're going to set up a no-client-fucking policy, this is the wrong time,' she said. 'Fuck him *and* take the job. You can totally do both.'

Suddenly, I realised that even as Lily was friend-yelling at me, I couldn't take my eyes off her legs. The sound her stockings made against each other as she shifted her calves was seriously distracting me. How was it possible that I never realised what fantastic legs she had? It wasn't that I didn't find girls sexy. I did. It was just that I usually found guys sexier. Besides, Lily was my best friend and the co-owner of my business. There was no way I was going to get involved with her in that way. Again, I mean.

But watching the way that Lil's legs were sliding over each other was focusing all of my brain on the heat between my legs.

What was wrong with me? It was as though since Davian had walked in the front door, I'd been nothing but a single ball of need, rolling around in lust gardens, snorting sex flowers. My own sex-filled version of the foolish lion in the poppy fields of Oz. Except I wouldn't fall asleep. I'd be so filled with lust that I would kill myself with want.

'Janine?' Lil poked me with the toe of her shoe.

'Hm?'

The silence that ensued from her was full of unasked questions. I dragged my gaze from Lil's legs to her expectant blue eyes.

'You were talking about fucking the sexy dark-haired man who landed on our doorstep a few hours ago,' she prodded. 'Or rather talking about not fucking him. No blow job, no book job, neither of which are decisions I understand.'

I got a hold of myself, shaking my head and focusing on the least sexual thing I could find, a blank spot of wall behind Lily's head.

'*You* were talking about fucking him,' I countered. 'I was talking about not taking him on as a client.'

'Because you want to fuck him.'

'Lil, you are not helping what is already a very bizarre situation here.'

Even though I wasn't looking at her full on, I could tell

when she grinned in that sly way she had, letting me know that her intention was the exact opposite of helping.

'Um, hello, he was hot as hell,' Lily said. 'And you, my friend, have quite the rampant little libido. If all your little buzzers weren't going off, I would have been worried about you. Besides, I know Kyle's awesome, but you have the look of a woman who's bored to death. So please please please tell me you're going to go out with this gorgeous hunk of a man.'

Kyle. Was it awful of me to realise I'd almost forgotten about Kyle and his proposal while I'd been busy with Davian? Probably. But it was true. That was some kind of sign, wasn't it? And what did she mean, 'the look of a woman who's bored to death'?

'All my little buzzers weren't going off.'

'Liar.'

'He had one of our promo cards,' I said casually, knowing her well enough to know she'd follow the swerve in the conversation. I only felt slightly bad about using her curiosity to my advantage. 'Our early ones.'

Those eyebrows went up again. 'Our disaster cards?'

I nodded.

'Odd,' she mused.

'Very.'

'From where?'

I shook my head. 'He didn't say.'

Lily nodded, tracing the outline of the book she had tattooed on her forearm, the way she often did when she was thinking. It was one of her first tattoos, and was lightly faded, looking more like a natural part of her skin than a hand-drawn piece of art. Kyle had offered a couple of times to redo it for her, give it some more life, but she'd declined, saying it was a reminder to her. I didn't know of what.

'You know, I feel like I recognise him from somewhere,' she said. 'But I have no idea why. Or where.'

I waited to see if she had more. Like I said, Lily's fantastic with faces. If you give her a couple of minutes, she'll usually come up with the connection.

When nothing else came, I said, 'If he was really looking for something, which I doubt, it wasn't something I could have found. It was the right thing, turning him down.'

'I trust you,' she said. In a way that said she actually did trust me. Which I was grateful for, and was feeling like I didn't really deserve. 'Now, why did your face do that funny thing when I asked about Kyle?'

'What funny thing?'

She made a face, scrunching her expression up so that it was all soured. 'This funny face,' she said, which came out as *dish funny fashe*.

'I don't ever look like that,' I said.

'I let you segue me with the disaster card bit,' she said. 'That was my one freebie. You're not getting out of this one.'

Have I mentioned that Lily and I have known each other a long time? And once Lily had something in her craw, she didn't let go of it very easily.

Caught under her stare, I relented. 'Kyle and I are –' I started, and then didn't know how to finish.

What? Engaged? Unengaged? Not at all engaged? About to break up? That last one felt the most true right now. But I was afraid to voice it out loud, lest it become true when I didn't want it to.

Lily didn't ask what, but she'd dropped her feet to the floor, and was sitting straight up, watching me like a cat watches prey. Which meant I was pretty much the prey. For at least the second time this morning.

It was turning out to be that kind of day.

'Kyle asked me to marry him,' I spit out.

'Whoa, wait. Back up, please. When did I miss this? And how? I thought you were just, you know ...' She made the universal sign for fucking with her fingers. Leave it to Lily to offset her perfect appearance with the regular use of vulgarity.

I told her the story, the down and dirty version, leaving out this morning's laughter-filled sex, since she'd clearly already figured that part out when I walked in the door.

'He asked me as I was leaving for work this morning.'

'As you were leaving?'

I nodded.

'That doesn't bode well for anything,' she said. 'And you said...?'

'I didn't. I came here.'

'Oy vey,' she said. Lily's Jewish upbringing comes out at the oddest times, considering that most of the time she's the least Jewish person I've ever met. But this time I had to agree with her.

'Yeah,' I said.

We sat in silence for a moment. I refused to look at her legs. Or at her face. Or at the half-curve of a smile that I was sure was resting at the corner of her red-painted lips.

'Did we have any other customers?' I asked. While I was in here – what had she said? – puddling like warm chocolate.

Lily snorted softly. 'It was someone actually looking for the sex toy store. Can you believe it?'

'Today?' I said. 'Today, I can believe almost anything.'

* * *

Thankfully, we were busy the rest of the day. But even with customers and orders to keep my mind occupied, I felt antsy and restless.

Kyle. Marriage. Davian. Lust. A sex club. Mysterious non-existent books. All of these unanswered mysteries were eating at my brain.

All day, my fingers beat an odd rhythm across book covers when I checked people out. I found myself shifting from one foot to the other for no reason.

An hour or so before closing time, I actually snapped my gum so loudly I startled myself. Thankfully the store was empty of customers at that point, but it was the last straw; I'd broken myself of gum snapping when I was nineteen. I had to find something to do before I made myself crazy.

I came storming out from one of the aisles where I'd been trying to organise books. Lil was behind the counter, drawing something. It's what she did when she got bored. Mostly she drew her own tattoos. Sometimes tats for other people. Sometimes she drew Webster stalking dust motes or secret caricatures of our regular customers.

I keep telling her she could make a good career of it, but she keeps telling me that she has a good career. Which, of course, is exactly what I want to hear. She's smart like that.

'Why don't you knock off early?' Lily asked, watching with a raised brow as I tried to throw my gum into the garbage while it was still stuck to my fingers.

'Because, because, because ...' Of all the wonderful things he does, my mind finished, stupidly. A string of quiet swear words followed while I finally managed to get the gum into the garbage can.

'Go take care of –' she waved her drawing pencil through the air, not being dismissive, but generally telling me she understood there was far too much going on for it to be summed up in a few short sentences '– things.'

'I'm OK,' I said. 'I just need something to do. Maybe I'll change the window display.'

'We just did the display,' she said. It was true. Our front window was big enough to set up a whole scene in. It was one of the things I loved best about the place. We changed the decor for each new season, and we'd just done the fall version of a reading room, adding a couple of chairs, a fake fireplace and a big maroon cushion for Webster to curl up on. No display then.

'Maybe Webster needs his nails trimmed,' I ventured.

We both glanced at Webster, who'd forsaken his big cushion for one of the chairs, where he snoozed, stretched out, his belly to the sky. Clearly, he didn't need my help either.

'Go do something,' Lily said. 'I've got nothing, and I mean nothing, going on outside this place right now. Besides, I like to have you in my debt.'

'But –' I started.

And then I stood there, uncertain what else I wanted to say.

The truth was I didn't want to be here, because I kept thinking about Davian with an urgency that scared me. Every time his face flashed in my brain, I got wet. Every time I saw his hands touching his briefcase, or my desk, or the tickets, my lizard brain, the part of me that was all sex all the time, woke up, aching for something I couldn't name.

I didn't want to go home because I'd think about Kyle. Kyle, and his proposal. And then I'd have to think about what was wrong with me that I didn't just say yes to this smart, funny, gorgeous, talented guy who wanted to spend his life with me. Wasn't that what every girl dreamed of?

I definitely didn't want to go to Kyle's, because I wouldn't just think about Kyle there; I'd actually have to talk to him. And probably come up with some answers that I didn't want to give.

The only other places I ever went – did I mention I was an introvert? – were Cream, the coffee shop that our friend Stefan owned, and Cock's Tail, the bar that our friend Jay owned. Both of those places offered comfort, but they also meant someone who cared about me offering sympathy and a listening ear. If I knew anything right now, I knew that I didn't feel like talking.

I felt like hiding out in a dark room where no one could see me, and letting all of this go for a little while. Somewhere that I could hide in the dark and think and make some of this stupid sexual desire disappear. Somewhere that I could –

Suddenly, I knew just what I needed. And I knew just the place to get it. Dark. Quiet but not too quiet. Solitary but not too solitary. I grabbed my coat and practically ran to the front desk, where Lily was still hunched over her sketchpad, chewing on an eraser shaped like a robot. A mostly headless robot.

'Hey, Lil, did you mean it when you talked about closing up?'

'Nope,' she said. 'I changed my mind. You must stay here for ever and ever.'

She must have seen something in my face because she started laughing almost instantly and flapped her hands at me, headless robot included. 'Go, please. I love you, but you're starting to make me crazy.'

I leaned across the counter to kiss her cheek, and as I did so, I saw what she'd been sketching.

It was Davian's face. Almost. Just a little off, although I couldn't tell how. I tried to puzzle out what it was. The eyes, slightly off-kilter? No. Not the mouth either. Something else. But it was definitely him.

'Guess I'm not the only one with the hots,' I teased, tapping the edge of the drawing with my finger.

'No,' she said. Her tongue stud flashed silver between her teeth. 'It's just that I do remember him from somewhere. But not here, I don't think. I don't know.'

'Well, if you do think of it, let me know, 'kay? And I'll open tomorrow. On time, I promise it!'

'Mm-hm' was her only response as I slipped out the door.

* * *

Leather Bound is in a part of town that most people, locals and tourists alike, just call the Sweet Spot. It's this little area – two streets, maybe six or seven blocks long, of mixed business and residential – that's known for being a bit risqué. It's not a gay district per se, just a sexy district.

Most of the smart businesses play up the theme, giving themselves double-entendre names, like ours. And it works. It's safely naughty. So if you want to bring your best friend somewhere for her bachelorette party, you'll probably head here. Maybe stop by Cream for a cup of coffee, then head to Lashes & Lace for toys, then on to Cock's Tail or one of the other half-dozen nightclubs that offer a naughty ambiance.

I asked around before we opened Leather Bound here, but no one seemed to know why this area is here, or where it came from.

It's a good place for Leather Bound. Although we're not specifically focused on sex books, we definitely do our fair share of sales in that direction. Plus, the rent is cheaper than anywhere else, we get more walk-in sales and it's easy to get to almost anywhere from the store.

Like to Lashes & Lace, which was just around the corner a couple of blocks and down the street. I practically ran there. Now that I had a mission, I had someplace to put all my nervous energy.

I slipped in the front door, the little bells tinkling to mark my entrance. As far as sex toy shops go, Lashes & Lace is high-end, deluxe and very, very lush. The walls are painted in a lovely crimson, and the lights are kept soft and dim. There's more a sense that you're walking into someone's home. If that someone owned a couple hundred sex toys and had a fetish for leather paddles as wall art.

A woman I didn't know was behind the front counter, her ample curves tucked into a leather corset dress.

Perfect. Anonymity was the key thing I was craving at the moment, and that made things so much easier. And sweeter.

Walking past her, I caught her eye and gave an 'I'm heading to the back' gesture with my hand. She nodded. Sometimes I loved wordless exchanges.

A wide black curtain hung at the back of the store, and I parted it to step through. Here, it was even more dimly lit, soft cream walls and flickering electric lights that guided you down a long hallway. Doors opened off either side. I wasn't surprised to find many of the doors marked FILLED, even in the middle of the day. L&L was known for catering to couples and tourists who wanted a clean, safe place to act out their fantasies.

I slipped down the hall until I found a door that read EMPTY. I swiped my credit card and, when the door clicked open, I stepped inside.

The room was small but cosy. Three walls were covered

with long roll-up shades. I knew from experience what lay behind the fabric: floor-to-ceiling windows. On either side, the windows were two-way. If you opened those, whoever was in the room on the sides could see you. Along the wall opposite the door was a one-way window. You could watch the action, but they couldn't see you.

I know a lot of exhibitionists, those people who get off on fucking in front of people, and I'm thankful for them because I like to watch, but I'm not one myself. The thought of being in front of people, of having sex in front of someone else, makes me feel breathless and weak, as though my legs won't hold me.

At a basic level, I'm afraid I wouldn't be able to let myself go and enjoy it, knowing that someone was watching. It's more than that, though. I just don't know exactly what. Maybe it's the introvert thing. Or a trust thing. Trusting them, trusting myself.

But to sit in a dark corner and watch someone else get off? Yes, please. When I was little I wanted to be Harriet the Spy or Nancy Drew, looking through people's things for clues, watching through keyholes, discovering the forbidden. That desire has changed over the years, it's grown up from secrets and clues to sex and lust, but it's never gone away.

I pushed the button on the wall facing me. As the shade began to slowly rise, I settled into the chair that smelled slightly of antiseptic, anticipating the view.

L&L doesn't advertise what shows are coming up or send out event listings, so you never know what you're going to get. Sometimes it's a couple, clearly into exhibitionism, loving every second of being watched. Sometimes it's famous porn stars, working a whole room full of bodies, orgy-style.

Once Kyle came with me and we watched a threesome, two laughing, giggling women lovingly suck off a man on his knees. It was fun to watch, and we'd fucked on that fantasy for days, but at that time I'd realised something about my voyeuristic tendencies: I like it best alone.

Last time I was here, there was a gorgeous man lying on his back, bound in cream-coloured ropes that contrasted with his ebony skin, his cock beautiful and erect. No one came in or out of the room while he was there, and he never moved or opened his eyes. He was like a statue, a bound, breathing man of stone, only his cock twitching, tiny movements that were almost impossible to see. It was one of the sexiest things I've ever seen.

This time when the shade slipped up, giving a small clunk as it hit the top, I sucked in my breath at the view. In the larger room, silhouetted by a single lamp that showed off her body but hid her face in the shadows, a woman sat in a small folding chair. Her long brunette hair fell about her shoulders in waves, and her hands were held, possibly bound, behind the back of the chair.

A tiny tattoo – the small shape of something dark that I couldn't make out from where I sat – rested in the hollow of her throat. She wore a black button-down shirtdress that hugged every curve. It was open from her upper thighs down, showing off a pair of old-fashioned garter clips attached to seamless black stockings. Her chin was lowered, but her green eyes were raised, her gaze apparently resting on the man who stood off to her side.

He was mostly outside the halo of the light, but I could see he was fully dressed in an impeccably pressed pinstriped suit, the cut accentuating his wide shoulders. It was all very 1950s, right down to the hat he wore. The space he took up was larger than his actual body, a presence that was incredibly sexy even through the window between us.

He held a pair of long-handled scissors – the only shiny thing in the room – his hands already settled into the large black handles. As he brought the scissors closer to her, I realised that the reason her dress was open at the bottom was because he'd cut the buttons off; they lay littered about her feet on the floor. This time, he started from the top, aiming for the button that held the dress closed over the curve of her breasts.

My hand was already under my skirt, toying with the edges of my panties as I watched them. The suspense of his slow movements, her breath rising and falling as he opened the scissors over the button thread and held them there without closing them all the way, was making me feel breathless and on edge.

Slowly, slowly, he closed the scissors all the way, a sound I could hear in my head, the small snick of steel meeting steel. With a delay that seemed to take for ever, the button fell away, rolling and tumbling down the fabric and against her stockinged thigh to finally land on the floor.

Her dress had bloomed open, showing the paleness of her skin beneath the black, an alabaster hollow that was flanked by two beautiful curves. Her chest heaved softly as he guided the scissors to the next button, the movement arching her back just slightly so I could see her nipples peaked against the fabric.

The sight made me bring my free hand to my own chest, fingers slipping under my bra, tweaking one nipple softly. I tugged my panties to one side and slipped one finger along my cleft, stroking myself softly with my fingertip. My clothes were suddenly too restrictive, too cumbersome. I wished I'd taken everything off before I'd slipped the shade up. I wanted full access to myself, to pinch and tug as I pleased. The room smelled of my arousal, sweet and urgent, and I wondered what she smelled like, in that other room.

On the other side of the window, he brought the scissors to the next button, and he must have said something to her, because she looked up suddenly and shuddered, her legs pulling together just slightly. The button was quick to fall, letting the fabric slip away further.

Carefully, he tucked the closed scissor blades between her thighs, waiting until she brought her legs fully together before he let go. The scissors stayed there, upright, their sharp point buried between her thighs.

He ran his fingers over the points of her nipples, sending visible shudders through her with every contact. I sensed that this was a game of power, of how much pleasure he could give her before she opened her legs in want and pleasure, before those scissors went tumbling to the floor.

I closed my own legs, mimicking her, keeping one hand between them. The pressure angled my fingers into a new place and I moaned softly at the unexpected pleasure.

Bending down, he put one hand on each side of her dress, where the fabric had fallen open. In one easy movement, he pulled outwards. Under the strain, the buttons didn't stand a chance. They went flying, tumbling to the floor, and the dress opened fully to reveal all of her, from her large, pointed nipples down to her lovely V of dark curls. The garter belt fitted the swell of her hips perfectly. I couldn't take my eyes off the pale strips of her thigh that showed above the stockings, the way the nylon rolled just slightly as if at some point she had begun to roll them off and had been distracted. The scissors between her thighs were the only hard-edged thing about her.

His fingers played along both nipples, causing her to squirm and arch in her seat. My movements echoed hers, as though, by watching, I was gaining a synthesis with her. He held one nipple tightly between his fingers, almost pinching it, and then tugged it, elongated it until it was thin and tight. I could almost hear her gasp, the way her mouth fell open at the sensation. He did the same with the other until he was tugging both nipples as far away from her body as they could possible stretch. The muscles of her thighs clenched, shifting the scissors. He kept his stance until she was panting, uttering words I couldn't hear.

I feared for a second that she would lose control and drop the scissors. I didn't know what that meant for her, but I knew it wasn't what she wanted. She wanted to be very, very good for him. And at that moment, with my own hand clenched between my thighs, my clit pulsing hard and fast against the movement of my finger, I wanted her to be very, very good for him too. I wanted her to get her reward, whatever it might be, so that I could have it too.

He released her nipples, and they sprang back against her body, flushed and rosy. He touched each one again, a tender touch, a finger-kiss, to soothe the ache. Then he pulled the scissors from between her thighs. She shuddered again and let her legs fall open.

I was close to coming, but I didn't want to, not yet, so I stilled my hand for a moment, watching. He slipped the scissors between her skin and one of the stockings, slicing down the front in irregular patterns. Then he did the other. The torn-open dress and the gashes in the material combined to make her look like she'd spent the night being well fucked, even though I got the feeling that the couple had just begun playing shortly before I arrived. The look was sexy on her, and when he let the scissors drop to the floor so he could catch her hair with one hand and pinch her clit with the other, I felt the first pulse of pre-climax slip through my body.

He stroked her, hard and quick, with two fingers, and I caught his rhythm, echoed it with my own, until an orgasm rose inside me, impossible to resist. I let the pleasure pull my eyes closed, let it pull forward the loud moans that rose from somewhere in my chest and sank into the walls. There was a calm in allowing the orgasm to wash over me like that, in allowing all of the stress of the day to slide away. The pleasure was lovely, but almost secondary to the release of tension that I'd been carrying in my body. I relaxed a moment, hand wet between my thighs, letting my whole weight rest against the chair.

When I opened my eyes, I saw that the man had turned around to stand behind the woman with his hands on her shoulders. Now that he was inside the halo of light, I could see him more clearly. Those hands. That build. And most of all, those impossibly coloured eyes.

It was Davian. And I could have sworn he was looking right at me.

* * *

Now grateful that I was still mostly clothed, I tumbled out of the tiny room as fast as my orgasm-wracked body would let me, breathing heavily, feeling confused and off-balance. The only thing I knew for certain was that I needed to get out of L&L before he saw me.

So much for my respite, for my chance to hide away and recover. Whatever moments of peace I'd experienced mid-orgasm slipped away as I hurried outside and then down the sidewalk, feeling incredibly exposed by the late-afternoon light.

It wasn't until I was on the street, blocks from L&L and at the very edge of the Sweet Spot, that I let myself stop and breathe and think. I clung to the wall with one hand, panting, trying to wrap my mind around everything.

OK, so it couldn't really have been Davian, right? That was just too much of a coincidence. That was just too … weird.

And even if it was, there was no way he could have seen me inside the room. L&L was known for its discretion, for its customer safety and privacy. If they said a window was one-way, I believed them.

Why then had it seemed like he'd seen me somehow? Why had it seemed like he'd looked right at me at my moment of orgasm? It was a fever dream born of lust, I was sure. My oversexed mind had cooked up the image of him to add to my pleasure. That's all it was.

I walked home, still tumbling everything over in my brain. What a day it had been. First Kyle. Then Davian. Then … whatever that was at L&L. People said bad things happened in threes. I wondered if that was true about really weird things as well. I hoped so. If it was true, at least it would mean all the odd things that were going to happen to me were over for a while.

Kyle, thankfully, wasn't at my place, although there were a number of voice messages from him on my cell when I pulled it out of my pocket. I didn't listen to them. I promised myself I'd call him in the morning, when I was feeling less Alice in Wonderlandish.

A hot bath. Some food. And sleep. Those were the things I needed, and in that order.

As it turned out, I didn't make it to either of the first two. To my complete and utter surprise, I got as far as undressing, and then crawled under the covers and slept. Tomorrow is another day.

Just call me Scarlett O'Hara, I thought, as I lost myself in dreamland.

CHAPTER 4

I kept my promise to Lily. I wasn't late to Leather Bound the next morning. I even hauled my ass out of bed early enough to stop at Cream for coffee. I saw Stefan in the corner, but he was captured by an overly enthusiastic customer, so I left him to his fate and headed to Leather Bound, armed with a caramel mocha for me and a cinnamon latte for Lily. I smelled like Christmas, all wrapped up with a coffee bow.

I'd slept fine, but I'd dreamed of sex all night long. Some of it was sex with Kyle and Davian, sometimes both of them at once. Sometimes the woman in the shirtdress was there, and sometimes Lily and sometimes even one or two of my exes. But mostly it seemed I'd dreamed of having sex with a faceless stranger, who then kept turning into Davian or a Davian lookalike. I was never sure.

Lily hadn't arrived at Leather Bound by the time I got there, so I set her coffee on the counter, hoping it wouldn't get too cold, and spent some time giving Webster chin scratches and breakfast before I headed back to my office.

I needed to tackle two things this morning.

One, call Kyle.

OK, wait, three things.

One, figure out what I was going to say to Kyle.

Two, call Kyle.

Three, research Mister Cavanaugh and find out as much as I could about the mysterious man and his equally mysterious book. Yes, I'd turned him down, but I supposed I was like Lily in that way: once something caught my interest, especially something as shiny and intriguing as this, I didn't let it go easily. Not to mention that I thought I saw him cutting the buttons off a hot girl at the sex store. Yesterday he'd responded to Lily's comment about L&L with a knowing smirk. 'I know the place,' he'd said. If it really was him I'd seen, then he certainly did.

But first, I should decide what to do about Kyle. Second, I should call him.

So I sat down at my beloved desk and got ready to do a little research. Because clearly the best way to do the thing you don't want to do is to tackle something else instead.

I popped open my laptop and give a couple of light strokes over her keyboard for good luck. Lily says she's ancient and just needs to be put down, but she's seen me through a lot of thick and thin, and I get her upgraded every couple of years. She might not even have any original parts by now, but she works like a charm. Mostly.

'Come on, Clementine,' I whispered. 'Gimme something good.'

The internet is everyone's friend when it comes to finding information, whether you're trying to find rare books or stalk strangers. But the truth is that most people don't know how to use it properly, or they find a bit of surface information and figure that's good enough. My skill is digging deeper, poking into all the little corners of the web to find the hidden books and the dirt that most people don't even notice.

I figured it would take me five minutes, maybe ten, to find out everything the world knew about Davian Cavanaugh and his non-existent book.

Turns out I was wrong.

I was still digging when Lily showed up twenty minutes later, just in time to open Leather Bound, and I hadn't found a thing. Not a single mention. These days almost everyone on the internet leaves a trail of some sort, even if it's accidental. In fact, it's near impossible to *not* have at least something about you. Especially with a name like Davian Cavanaugh. If you're alive in the world with a name that unusual, then the internet knows about it.

Except that it didn't seem to.

Which meant that he'd either given me a fake name, which was seeming more and more like a possibility, or was a super secret spy. If he was a super secret spy, I was definitely changing my mind and taking him as a client. And I was definitely fucking him.

But I was betting more on the former.

Curiouser and curiouser, cried Alice.

'Hey, thanks for the coffee.' Lily poked her head in, holding up the drink I'd brought her. As always, she was impeccable, right down to her swingy skirt and her purple toenails peeking out of a pair of black sandals. It was way too damn cold for that. I was in a long wraparound dress, striped tights, and black boots and I was still freezing.

She looked me over. 'No sex this morning, I see.'

'No sex,' I said. 'Thanks for finishing up yesterday. How did it go?'

'Steady.' She draped herself in the theatre chair with a tired 'oof'. 'I'm glad we're almost at the weekend.'

We close Leather Bound on Mondays and Tuesdays, which

gives us a sort of weekend without killing our business too much. Our only other option was to hire employees, which got all kinds of crazy and expensive. And no, it has nothing to do with the fact that I'm slightly anal and slightly OCD and I'm not about to turn the store over to a bunch of people I don't know.

'Yah, weekend,' I agreed, although I didn't feel that way. Mondays and Tuesdays were the days Kyle and I usually spent together. He kicked off at the tat shop early on Monday and took Tuesday as one of his days off. It was something I usually looked forward to, but now it made my chest feel tight. I realised I hadn't even listened to his messages as I'd promised myself I would, much less called him. I was beginning to feel like a horrible, horrible person.

'Did you talk to Kyle?' Lily asked. 'About the whole marriage thing?'

As if there was something else I needed to talk to him about. Sometimes I hated her knowing me quite so well.

Clearly she saw the answer in my face because she quickly said, 'Never mind. I'll go flip the sign.'

I heard her turn the sign – it was wooden and it clunked against the glass storefront every time you moved it – and then I heard her talking to someone. Her voice carried back, but not her words. Probably a customer, from her tone. That made two early-morning walk-ins back-to-back. What an odd week it was turning out to be.

I pressed Clementine's lid shut on my myriad disappointing searches, forcing myself to let go of my desire to spend time researching a man I knew nothing about and didn't need to know anything about. He probably wasn't the man I'd seen at L&L. He was just some guy – some very sexy guy, granted – who was either looking for a little thrill to fill his boring days or was two eggs short of a sanity dozen. Either way, it was a hassle I didn't need.

It would have been easier to convince myself that was true if I wasn't thinking about him constantly. The sexy mystery of him was clearly doing bad things to my brain.

Well, I'd turned down the job, and we were rid of him. I was going to excise him from my brain once and for all.

A second later, Lily rushed into the office, carrying a piece of paper, her blue eyes wide.

'Janine,' she said. 'They want to kick us out!'

* * *

'Rewind,' I said. Lily sometimes got overly excited about things and jumbled her words. I had no idea what she was talking about, but I was hoping this was one of those occasions.

'They want to kick us out,' she said, a hundred times more slowly. It didn't help. Her words still didn't mean anything to my brain and I tried to place them in some sort of context.

'Some guy just delivered a letter from the landlord.' She shoved it into my hand, and before I could read it she said, 'They're saying they're going to double our rent.'

I looked at the letter she'd handed me, but I couldn't read it. The letters were fuzzy, as if typed with a really old typewriter. Then I realised it wasn't the letters; it was because my hands were shaking so much it blurred the type. I took a deep breath and tried to steady myself. Read it for real this time.

Lily wasn't kidding; they wanted to double our rent. We could cover it, maybe. Just maybe. If we were willing to go mac and cheese and live in cardboard boxes – or the back room – for the next year.

Some of which I did in college, and I was so not willing to do that again.

'What the hell?' I said. 'I don't think they can do this. Doesn't our lease go for at least another four months?' I tried to count backward, to when we'd opened the place, but my head was doing funny things. Numbers usually liked me, but right now I couldn't think.

'Two,' Lily said. 'Two months. They're trying to raise it with the next lease.'

'So we have two months to either talk them out of this, find a new place or start making a whole lot more money.'

Lily chewed her perfect lower lip and nodded. 'Yeah,' she said.

'Well, that sucks.' I dropped my ass into my desk chair and let the letter fall into the recycling box. 'Fuck-fuckity-fuck,' I said.

Lily didn't say anything. She just leaned against the doorway, staring down at her painted toenails.

When we moved in here three years ago, we got lucky. Our landlord was a book-lover who quickly took us under his wing. Conrad was the only reason we'd been able to afford the place. He'd rented it to us for way less than it was worth, and he'd made us a rent guarantee, with the promise that he'd keep the rent low as long as we promised to visit with him and to give him a discount on books.

Neither promise was hard to keep. First, he was easy on the eyes. He was just getting to that stage men have where they're going grey at the temples, and the phrase 'tall, dark and handsome' described him perfectly. More importantly, he became a friend. Someone I trusted with every bone in my body. Conrad quickly became a fixture at Leather Bound, and his sense of humour and kindness made it easy to spend time with him.

But Conrad had died two months ago, leaving a hole in lots of places. Sometimes it felt like our entire little community was still grieving for him. I knew that I was. And Lily too.

Our new landlord was no Conrad, but he'd mostly been hands-off. Or at least he had been until now.

'What a jerk,' I said. 'I'll have to go talk to him. What's his name? Walter? Weiner?'

'Wes,' Lily said. 'And I think maybe I should be the one to go and talk to him.'

I realised I'd been swearing, rather loudly, and kicking the leg of my desk repeatedly. Trying to let go of the rising anger and panic I felt, I inhaled big and let it out with one last 'Fucker'.

'Rar?' Lily said, which always made me laugh.

'Fine, rar. You're right. You should probably be the one to talk to him.'

'I'll just show him my tattoos,' she said.

'That's a great idea,' I said.

I closed my eyes. My head was thumping hard, a tiny headache making its appearance known behind my eye. We didn't bring in enough money to pay double rent, but I wasn't sure we had the money or the ability to start all over again either. Behind my eyelids, I saw Leather Bound slipping away.

'What are we going to do, Lil?'

'Stop turning down potential customers, for a start,' she said, all business. 'Call Davian up and tell him you'll take the job.'

'I already turned him down,' I said.

'Then turn him back up,' she said.

'I think he's a little crazy. I don't even think there is a book,' I said. 'There has to be another way.'

Even as I said it, even as I considered taking on Davian's job, I felt my heart speed up, knocking against my chest in its excitement at seeing him again. Stupid traitor, that lustful heart of mine.

'Not that I can think of,' Lily said.

I sighed. No matter how crackpot crazy Davian might turn out to be, it turned out that we might need him. At the very least, we needed his money.

'People suck sometimes,' I said.

'And not in the good way,' Lily said.

CHAPTER 5

Stupid things make me feel stressed, I'll admit it. When I was in college, if a professor scolded me or even gave me a disapproving look for something I'd done, or even something I hadn't done, I would feel sick for weeks. A former boss telling me that she wanted to see me in her office would sometimes drive me to tears.

My life was falling apart, someone wanted to steal my dream store from me, but the thing that really made me feel like throwing up was that idea of calling the man I'd just turned down and asking him to reconsider.

The man that I'd said no to. The man that I still wasn't entirely sure I hadn't just watched cut the buttons off a woman and bring her – and, if I was going to be honest about it, myself – to orgasm. The man I couldn't stop thinking, or even dreaming, about.

His card was still on my desk. I picked it up and ran my thumb over it. Letterpress from the looks of it, and expensive. It had his name and a phone number, and beneath that, right in the centre, the shape of a keyhole pressed into the paper with black ink. The black keyhole was indented, the letters of his name and number raised.

Taking a deep breath, I forced myself to dial the number on the card. I didn't exhale until I heard the answering machine's mechanical voice, asking me to please leave a message at the tone.

I did just that, mostly stumbling all over myself to try and say what I needed to say without sounding like a complete fool. I'm pretty sure I didn't succeed in the latter part, but somewhere in there I managed to convey the idea that if he was still looking for someone to find him his book, I'd like to talk with him about the possibility of such a thing. And then I hung up and tried not to throw up.

I couldn't put off calling Kyle any longer. It was time. Long past time. Especially now that I'd seen how many messages he'd left. I listened to all of them. It was far less penance than I deserved for just running away like a scared little rabbit.

The first message was his usual sweet and funny self, still upbeat, laughing at himself a little and apologising for the way the proposal had slipped out.

'Wow, I didn't expect that,' he said. 'And I bet neither did you.'

I could almost laugh with him at that point. But the others became more serious and sad, asking me to please call him, and saying he hadn't meant to scare me off, and he would gladly take it back if I'd just let him know how I was feeling.

'I am feeling like an asshole,' I said aloud.

I really was. He was a nice guy. What was I doing, avoiding him like that, just letting him hang in the wind? An asshole and a coward.

I hit CALL BACK and put my ear to the phone.

Kyle answered on the first ring.

'Janine,' he said, before I could say anything. 'I was getting worried.'

74

'I know,' I said. 'I'm an asshole.' I meant it more than I'd meant anything in my life.

'Yeah,' he said. 'Me too. I never should have thrown that on you like that.'

Somehow it didn't make me feel any better to hear him try and apologise when I was the one who'd run away. Still, at least he didn't sound angry or hurt, just confused. God, he really was too nice. Maybe that's why I couldn't fall in love with him. I didn't want to be one of those women, you know the ones, who only go after the men with a little miniature asshole inside them, but it seemed like I always turned away from the nice guys. Maybe Kyle was the right person for me, after all. If I gave him time, maybe love would just happen. It did that sometimes, right?

'Janine?' he said.

'Sorry. I'm here. Can we talk? Would tonight be OK?'

'I have a full tat tonight,' he said, and I could tell that he'd thought about saying yes to my question despite that. 'How about tomorrow night?'

I swallowed hard. On one hand, it bought me a reprieve of a day. On the other, it stretched things out for both of us.

'Tomorrow night's good,' I said.

'Your place?'

Did I want to do my place? I didn't know. This wasn't the kind of conversation to have in public, but I knew that if Kyle came to my house, we'd end up naked. Which was going to colour my decision in all the wrong ways and make things much harder.

No, I definitely didn't want to do my place.

'How about Cream?' I said.

Kyle didn't verbally agree, but he did hang up the phone with a quick goodbye, which I figured was close enough.

* * *

Just as I hung up on Kyle, my phone rang. Stupidly, since it was apparently my morning for stupidlies, I answered it without thinking.

'Thanks for calling Leather Bound. This is –'

'Janine. I know.'

It was Davian. This time, unlike at L&L, I was sure it was him. Now that I'd heard that voice once, I would recognise it anywhere. It sent little electric sparks through my ear into the back of my brain. There must be some kind of pleasure centre back there, reserved just for men with sexy phone voices. Clearly mine was underused because with every word it sent a few more little zaps through my body.

'Thanks for calling me back,' I said.

'My pleasure,' he said.

Through the phone, his voice sounded slightly deeper, just enough to give me a vision of him, calling from what I imagined to be his bedroom. Of course, in my imagination, he had nothing on, and was stretched out on the bed, his long legs muscled, one arm behind his head while he talked to me.

I was only a little embarrassed at myself for how my body reacted to his voice. He made me want to put my hands on my desk and bend over for him. To go down on my knees surrounded by books and put my mouth on the length of his cock. Even though I'd never seen his cock. Crazy, this lust thing.

He has the silliest-looking cock ever, I told myself. You don't want it.

That didn't work. Now all I could think about was his cock, and what it actually might look like.

'So, what changed your mind about taking me on?' he asked.

Did he always have to use language that was just bordering on suggestive without ever crossing the line? That was part of the seesaw effect he had, making me uncertain about the meaning of everything he said. Hell, he made me uncertain about the meaning of everything *I* said.

'How do you know I changed my mind?' I said. Oh, for the love of God, was this man's presence, even his phone presence, always going to make me say such stupid things?

'Because you said as much on your message,' he said. The laughter in his voice was evident. I wanted to crawl under my desk.

I cleared my throat and continued.

'Right,' I said. 'If you're still interested, I was hoping we could meet briefly, so I could gather some additional information.'

'More than you could gather in, say, a conversation over the phone?' His question took me aback.

'We could do it over the phone,' I admitted. 'Sometimes it's just better to talk face to face.'

'So, what you're saying is you want to see me?'

Why did his voice always sound like it was suggesting at least eleven things and all of them dirty? Or was that just in my brain?

B. E. Professional. Go.

'I'm saying that I'd like to talk with you further about taking you on as a client,' I said, all proud of myself for managing an even tone.

'Nothing else?' he asked.

No, nothing else. Not at all that I thought I saw you slowly stripping a woman naked at the local sex shop. Not at all that I'd dreamed of you last night. In one particularly vivid one, I'd been down on my knees in front of him, his hands in my hair, guiding the tip of his cock over the point of my tongue again and again.

'Nothing else,' I said. 'Could you meet some time this week?'

'How's tonight? I can stop by before you close the store.'

'Tonight's fine,' I said.

'I'll be there with bells on,' he said.

There was no more. Just the click that told me he'd hung up. Well, what had I expected? An 'Oh, by the way, I also forgot to tell you that I want you, Janine, and you should come over to my place where I'm naked, stroking myself, just waiting for you'?

Well, yes, actually, that would have been nice. But even though I kept the phone pressed to my ear a little longer, I didn't hear him say anything like that.

* * *

I was pretty sure Davian wasn't going to show.

Lily had left early for a date – 'She's a musician, with a guitar!' she had crowed before she ran out the door – and it was almost closing time.

I'd spent most of the last very slow hour trying to occupy my thoughts by flipping through a naughty Victorian finger-puppet book. It showed you how to hold your hand so it came through the cut-outs. Your fingers became legs. The curve of your fist became a pair of buttocks. Some instructions even recommended that you squeeze your hand to 'create a sense of movement'. It was one of my favourite books, and I was always surprised that no one bought it.

I had two fingers through one of the cut-outs, creating a Victorian woman's up-skirt image, when I heard the front door open. I slipped the book back into its proper place and stepped out from behind the velvet curtain.

And stopped short. Davian was dressed in a grey wool coat, wooden toggles up the front. Dark slacks. Same briefcase. A pair of chocolate-brown glasses that matched his eyes so perfectly it almost made me want to cry.

He was probably one of those people, like Lil, who could put that look together in five minutes. Even as I hated him a little for that, I also wanted him. So fiercely that I was forced to capture Webster as he walked by, just to have something safe in my hands. Or semi-safe. Webster, unused to being snatched up by his owner, wriggled in my grasp, demanding an end to the indignity.

'Thanks for coming by,' I said, holding the cat between us like some kind of spine-bending, claw-wielding force field. 'Do you want to come back to the office?' I said, and instantly regretted it. I didn't trust myself to behave around him. At least, out here, I was mostly safe.

'I'm afraid I can't stay,' he said. 'I'm running late. I wanted to see you though.'

He let that hang in the air for a moment.

'And I have something that should help you get started on your search. Well, two things.'

He reached into his briefcase. I watched that beautiful hand enter the folds of polished leather and I swear the space between my legs practically sighed with want. He pulled out an envelope and held it out to me.

I had to put Webster down in order to take it.

Davian didn't let go.

'Are you sure about this?' he asked. 'I don't want you

to take on this job if you're unsure.'

'No,' I said. 'I'm not sure about anything right now.'

I kept my hand on the envelope, waiting. Leather Bound needed the money. And, if nothing else, having something to sink my teeth into, something complicated and confusing, would keep my mind off Kyle and the rent issues and whatever else the world seemed determined to throw at me.

I took the envelope as he released it, careful not to touch his hand, careful to not even brush one tiny piece of his skin. I couldn't imagine how I'd shaken his hand the first time I'd met him, how I'd actually touched the man and hadn't pushed myself all over him with wanting.

Once the envelope was safely in my grasp and away from his potential touch, I looked inside. A cheque, the amount of which instantly made my breath come a little easier. And two tickets.

'That's more than my normal rate,' I said.

'This is clearly more than your normal job,' he said.

Any other time, I might have argued with him. But not this time.

I pulled out the tickets. On one side, they were printed with an image of a woman in cat ears, swirling her long, striped tail. The cat woman was naked except for her appendages. So naked that I thought I caught a glimpse of a clit-piercing in the image. A tattoo across her bare stomach read THE CAT HOUSE.

I looked at him in confusion.

'The Cat House?' I said.

'It's a dance place.'

'A strip club.' I wasn't against strip clubs. In fact, I liked them, liked sitting in the dark, watching. But I'd definitely never been to a strip club as part of my job before. 'Usually

I just sit at my desk and do google searches,' I said. 'Which is kind of the same thing now that I say that.'

'It's not a strip club,' he said. 'At least not as you know it. But this is the woman you'll want to talk to.' He pointed at the woman on the ticket. She had eyes so bright blue it reminded me of kittens when they're still at that stumbling-around stage.

'Kitty,' he said, as if giving voice to my thoughts.

'What?'

'Her stage name is Kitty.'

'Kitty,' I repeated. Unimaginative name. So many good names in the world, and so often people pick boring ones.

'It's not very original,' he said as if he'd heard me yet again. 'But she manages to own it.'

Be still my heart.

'What is this for again?' I asked. Kitty and the Cat House aside, I had no idea how this was going to help me find anything.

'In order to find the book, you're going to need to become part of the club. And in order to get into the club, you're going to need to go through initiation. That means interacting with Kitty.'

'There are two tickets here,' I said. 'Does that mean you think you're coming with me?'

I didn't know if I wanted the answer to be yes or no.

It was no.

'As much as I'd like to,' he started, drawing a slow gaze over my body in a way that made me hot and cold all at the same time, 'I'm afraid I wouldn't be welcome. Take someone you like. Not Lily, though. Kitty likes redheads. I'm afraid you won't get a word in edgewise if you show up with her on your arm.'

81

'Not welcome,' I echoed. What did that even mean? 'Davian, is there more to this than you're telling me, anything else I should know?'

'Isn't there always?' he asked. 'Isn't that how stories work best?'

It was that line that caught me. I'm a sucker for boys with books. Men who read. Men who understand stories. It wasn't bad enough that he was complete and total eye candy. He had to keep throwing book stuff at me. As if he knew without even asking where my secret love and lust sat in the space of my chest.

Still I had to ask. 'Right. But there's nothing that's likely to end up with me getting, I don't know, killed? Injured? Strung up by the wrists?'

His brow went up again, the almost hint of a grin, wolfish and wanting.

That wasn't what I meant, that last one. I was thinking more torture and less bondage. Well, I *had* been thinking more torture. Now I was thinking about him holding my wrists tight in his hands, circling them with strips of leather.

He caught hold of his smile before it had a chance to fully bloom, and tightened his lips back to seriousness. 'No,' he said. 'But if that changes, I would certainly let you know.'

Oh, great.

'There's no time, no date, no address,' I said. 'How do I know where to go? Or when?'

'Tomorrow night, ten o'clock,' he said.

'Tomorrow?' Gods, was I going to repeat everything he said? Clearly I was.

'Is that bad for you?' he asked.

I was supposed to meet Kyle at eight. The show was at ten. If things went poorly between Kyle and me, I'd go and see Kitty by myself. If they went well – although I wasn't sure what that meant right now – Kyle might want to go with me. He liked pretty women doing artistic things, especially when they were naked. As he'd once said, 'Who in the whole world doesn't like boobs?'

'Tomorrow's perfect,' I said. 'Just tell me where.'

'That,' he said, 'is something of a test.'

'A test.' Yes, Janine, you've shown him how well you can play the repeat-after-me game. Say something original now, please.

But nothing would come.

Tucking his finger beneath my chin, Davian raised my face until I looked him in the eye. The pressure of his finger made my pulse go wild, a thumping beat of want that swam in my ears.

'Yes?' he said.

What was I saying yes to? It didn't matter.

'Yes,' I said.

I barely got the word out before he leaned in and kissed me.

* * *

It was a kiss unlike any other I'd had. His closeness threw my balance off, my body wanting nothing more than to lean into him as hard and fast as I could, my mind trying to back off from something so unexpected. Thankfully, I didn't fall over in my attempt to reconcile the two parts of me.

Instead, I welcomed his lips against mine. The musky male scent of him, the heat of his mouth, the way he captured my lips greedily, all of it sent my head spinning in a million directions. Client, I thought. Potential client. Leather Bound. Job. Business. Not pleasure.

But all of those mental moans of protest were overshadowed by that other, louder, fiercer voice in my head, which was not using words at all. It was urging me to lean into the kiss. To do far more than that. To put my hands in his hair, as I'd been aching to do. To pull away his tie, unbutton his shirt, run my palms across the width of his chest. And worse, oh so much worse.

When he slipped his tongue between my lips, parting them, entering me, all thinking stopped. Sensation blossomed along every exposed part of my body, aching for his touch. I moaned, a low sound of want that was neither controllable nor comprehensible.

At the sound, he cupped the back of my head with his hand, capturing me into the kiss. He bit my lip softly and I couldn't help but release another sound, this one urgent and demanding.

He laughed against me, the sound muffled against my lips. It was a delicious laugh, one that promised all kinds of things in the future. Pleasure. Maybe a little pain. Definitely more than a little power.

Power. For some reason, the word brought me up short. Jesus. I was supposed to be in charge here. Of myself, if nothing else. I was the professional. Davian was my client.

Despite my desire to do nothing ever again except continue to kiss this sexy man in my office, I put my hands flat on his chest, on his absolutely wonderful chest, and pushed myself away from his touch.

He let me go without protest, his hand falling away from the back of my head. His eyes were deep and still, his expression unreadable. I couldn't hear anything except my own soft, quick breaths and the thrum of want that ran through my body like a strummed guitar string.

I knew I should say something, apologise maybe, but I didn't know what to apologise for. And I truly didn't want to.

'You can get there from here,' he said.

Because I was thinking about kissing, about being kissed, about Davian putting his lips to mine again and prying my mouth open with the tip of his tongue, his comment only went as far as my lizard brain. The number of dirty, sexy things that flashed in my brain between the time he said that and the time I realised he'd moved back to talking about business was very, very high.

'What?' I said.

He cocked a grin at me. Loaded, I thought. Loaded and damn dangerous. But fine too.

'That's your first clue,' he said. 'You can get there from here.'

I just stood there and stared at the fine form of him as he walked out the front door. As if daring one more thing to pop up and hit me with a surprise today.

Nothing did. Maybe that in itself was the surprise.

* * *

As soon as he left, I retreated to my office and pulled out Clementine, gearing myself up for some serious sleuthing.

Davian had said I could get to the Cat House from Leather Bound. So it had to be somewhere in the Sweet Spot. I closed my eyes and tried to imagine a place big enough to house a strip club. I'd been up and down those streets a hundred times and had never seen any indication of it. And it certainly wasn't new; there were a couple of strip clubs around, but I was pretty sure that none of them had closed down or changed ownership. And, thanks to Conrad's nudging thumb,

I'd joined the business owners' association, so I mostly kept abreast of any new businesses.

The internet gave me nothing. It was starting to hurt my ego that I was having such a bad search week. First Davian and his book. Now this.

Well, when the internet didn't give you what you wanted, it was time to turn to more traditional methods.

I called Cream and asked for Stefan. It took only a few seconds for his Tennessee drawl to make its way to my ear.

'Come and get some cream and sugar for your coffee, sugar,' he purred.

'Stefan, how did you know it was me?'

'Who's "me"?' he asked. I couldn't tell if he was kidding or not. 'I always answer the phone like this.' Still couldn't tell.

'It's Janine, from Leather Bound.'

'Jah-neen,' he drawled. 'Where in the hell have you been?'

'I'm in your shop every morning, Stefan. Where the hell have you been?'

Truly, I saw him almost every day, but he was usually entertaining other customers with some story that involved rapidly flying hands and his imitation New Jersey accent, so I often slipped in and out without saying hello.

'Ah, you know me, darling. Always on the swoon.'

'Truly,' I said. My voice was droll, but I was already smiling. Stefan always makes me smile. It's in his nature to make people feel good just by being around them, like helium or ice cream or something.

'So, if you don't want my cream – and take no offence at this, lovely, but I don't really want to give it to you – why are you bringing me your voice on this infernal device instead of in person where I can feed you sugar and caffeine?'

'I need some information.'

He lowered his voice a notch, rolled into a deeper note. 'Is this classified?'

'I don't know yet,' I said. Neither of us was serious, but this was a game we played from time to time. He liked to tease me for my book sleuthing, calling me Darling Nancy Drew. Or sometimes just Darling Nancy. Mostly, he liked to tell people that he was the caffeine assistant to the world's most famous book sleuth.

'Hit me, sugar,' he said.

'Have you ever heard of the Cat House?'

His laugh. One of the things that I like best about people is their laughs. Stefan's got a throaty chuckle that goes against everything else you know about him. It's even throatier through the phone.

'Only about seven bazillion of them, scattered across the entire southern US. Any one in particular? Because I've tried them all, except for, of course, the ones in Texas. You know how those wild wildebeests are.'

'Stefan, sometimes I have no idea what you're talking about.'

That laugh again. Making me laugh too. Introvert is me, but the people I like? I really, really like. I'd keep them around me for ever if I could.

'Me neither, sugar, me neither,' he said. 'But I'm serious now. Tell me what you need.'

'Have you ever heard of a place actually called the Cat House, somewhere in the Sweet Spot?'

'Tell me more,' he said. Not as if he needed information, but as if he liked drawing it from me.

I told him what I knew. Which wasn't very much. That I was looking for the Cat House, which was something like a strip club, and that I had to go there.

'A moment,' he said.

The phone clicked in my ear. Not a hang-up, but a set-down, probably on a counter somewhere. Through the line I could hear the steam of the espresso machine and the clank of cups. A couple of voices talking and laughing. Typical background noises of a coffee shop. It was oddly comforting for not actually being there. More businesses should have this as their on-hold music.

Very soon, he was back. 'Sorry. Eleven times a day I tell that woman the perfect shot is exactly twenty-one seconds long and every day she flibbergibbits it up.' For as long as I'd known him, Stefan had complained endlessly about his employees. Also for as long as I'd known him, Stefan had had the exact same employees. They were good at what they did. Which, I got the feeling, entailed handling coffee and handling Stefan in equal, loving measures.

'First, tell me how you know about this place and why,' he said.

'I have tickets.' I waved them in the air as if he could see them on the phone, and then was glad no one could see me do that.

'You ... have tickets.' He mulled this over for so long in silence I would have thought he had hung up, except I could still hear the sounds of coffee being made in the background. 'Pray tell, how did that happen?'

'It's a very long story,' I said.

'And one that I'm sure I'm going to hear very soon.' It wasn't a question. It was a very sweet, very Southern form of blackmail.

'You are?' I agreed hesitantly. 'But where exactly is it?' I had so many questions, but that seemed like the one I needed an answer to first and foremost.

'Promise me you'll come and have some coffee before you go and I'll tell you everything you want to know. Bring that boy of yours, the cute blond one.'

'I'm –' I was about to say '– planning to come there tomorrow anyway and the cute blond one is not really very happy with me,' but Stefan cut me off.

'OK, I'm going away now to save the coffee shop from –' here his voice raised, clearly not meant for me '– the scoundrels and bandits who are running it into the ground, yes?'

'Yes,' I said. 'Thanks, Stefan.'

'Love, thank me with something besides words.' Which pretty much meant, 'Promise to come in and spend some time with me when you don't actually need me for something.'

I hung up, and felt slightly better for having a plan. Tomorrow, work all day, go to Cream to meet with Kyle, talk to Stefan while I was there, go to strip club ... no, wait ... find strip club, then go to strip club, then discover whatever it was Davian was sending me there to find out by talking to some chick named Kitty.

What a horrible plan.

* * *

Any week that starts off like this week did is just bound to keep getting weirder. And that's pretty much what happened.

The next morning, a regular brought his first-edition book back, citing that it had stains. Which it did. Because it was a first-edition book and about a million people had owned it before him. Then I mixed up the shipping time on someone else's book, so it didn't arrive when I said it would. Lily was cranky because her date had gone badly. I had Kyle and Davian and some chick called Kitty on my mind.

All in all, it was one of those days.

By the time I got home, I was stressed, on edge and later than I would have liked. I had less than twenty minutes to dress and get to Cream to meet Kyle. Hopefully I could figure out what I was going to say to him before I got there. You know how you have those conversations in your head and everything sounds fantastic? Well, I hadn't had a single one of those yet. So far I'd been alternating between 'You know I really like you, but marriage isn't something I'm interested in' and 'Can't we just have sex?' Neither of which was even close to what I really wanted to say and both of which just sounded stupid.

I also wanted to get to the show at the Cat House early so I could have some time to scope the whole thing out. Maybe, in retrospect, it wasn't a great idea to go with Kyle, either way. I was supposed to be doing research, supposed to be paying attention and, I don't know, getting some woman I didn't know to talk to me about a man I barely knew. But Davian had given me two tickets.

Ugh. What had I got myself into? Some days I longed to be a person in a novel instead of a person in the real world. They always said smart, funny things. And didn't run away from the man who loved them. OK, maybe that wasn't true all the time, but they usually had it figured out by the end. I wasn't sure I was ever going to figure it out.

Either way, I needed to be out of my work clothes and into something with a little more oomph. Standing in front of my closet, I hemmed and hawed over what to wear. Sexy? Slutty? Did I even own something that qualified as either of those?

I'm bad at the dressing, have I mentioned? I wished suddenly and fiercely that I'd had Lil come home with me. She'd be sprawled on the bed right now, chomping the grape-flavoured gum she loved so much, but that I wouldn't allow in the store because it made all the pages smell like grape for ever. She'd be directing me on exactly what to wear, and not to wear. 'That one makes your ass look scrumptious,' she'd say. Or 'No, no, no, no. Not those. Hell no.'

I missed those days of our friendship, those days when we did everything together, with a sudden fierceness that ripped through me more strongly than it should have. When had we lost that? I couldn't remember. In fact, I wasn't even sure I'd felt like I'd lost her until the question had popped into my head just now. It had been recently, surely. Sometime after we'd opened the store. Was it when Kyle and I had got more serious? Whatever that meant. Or something else? And now I needed her, needed to hear her tell me everything was OK, that I'd make all the right choices, and she wasn't here. Which was my own damn fault.

What would Lil do? I thought stupidly, staring at my closet.

A little red dress caught my eye as I scanned the fabrics. Red dress, black stockings, black boots, my hair up in a bun with some long earrings. I could do that. And it wouldn't look out of place no matter what the event was like. I hoped.

I dressed quickly, throwing a scarf around my neck for good measure. Despite my hemming and hawing, I would almost be on time to meet Kyle. That meant Kyle first, then talk to Stefan, then Cat House. Or WC. Whatever it was.

On the way out the door, I grabbed the tickets. OK, things were looking better. Stop being a coward and face Kyle. Get through tonight. Learn some things about my new client. Good. I could do this.

I opened the door and practically fell over Kyle, who was on his knees on my welcome mat.

CHAPTER 6

OK, 'practically fell over' isn't quite the truth. I actually did fall over him. Because I am a klutz. A cute klutz, if the rumours are to be believed, but still a total and complete klutz. I tried to stop myself, and if he'd been standing up, it would have been easy. He was tall enough that he would have taken my weight, even at my breakneck speed, and we would have wobbled, but not fallen.

But he was kneeling to pull his phone out of his bag and I didn't see him until way too late. My legs went bent-knee right into him. The tickets flew out of my hand to flutter down the hall, and I did the most awkward and unsexy air-flying routine ever invented. I'm pretty sure everyone within a mile got a flash of my underwear.

At least I'd worn something sexy. Which also meant something that covered far too little.

I tried to sigh and all I could do was utter a little half-squeak.

'Janine. Holy – are you –? What the hell? I'm so sorry.'

Kyle was clearly as confused as I was, and maybe as out of breath. He'd scrambled up from his kneeling position to loom over me. From my floor-sprawled position, he was like a really tall, skinny giant holding down one big paw.

I gently waved his hand away for the time being. I looked like a fool, but I wasn't going anywhere just yet. My ankle throbbed like I'd just fallen off of a pair of high heels, some part of my head had thunked against something with a sound loud enough that I could still hear it somewhere inside my teeth, and I was pretty sure an elephant was sitting on my chest.

I'm not that tall; why does a fall from my own height end up with me so banged up?

'What?' I was trying to get my words out through my gasps of breath. 'Are you. Doing here?'

'Um.' Kyle looked as confused as I felt.

'We were supposed to meet at Cream,' I said. The air was coming easier now and my head didn't actually hurt where I'd bonked it. Only my ankle continued to whine about being twisted. It was the same ankle I'd broken when I was in college, during a particularly stupid bike-riding incident that we won't talk about, but this time the pain wasn't nearly as bad. Hopefully, I'd just pulled one of my usual dumb moves and hadn't actually broken anything.

'Are you OK?' he asked.

I nodded, but didn't get up.

Kyle, clearly realising that I wasn't going to get up anytime soon, plopped himself down beside me.

For the first time I really looked at him. I mean, other than the look of 'Holy crap, what's he doing there, I'm falling on him.' He was dressed in dark jeans and a black T-shirt, topped with a grey suit jacket. His blond hair was brushed back so that it fell in long strands across his forehead. I always forgot how beautiful his eyes were, green like perfectly ripe olives.

And, at the moment, they were very very confused olives.

'I thought you said to meet you at your house at seven,' he said. 'I'm a little early, because we hadn't talked and ...' He stopped, shaking his head. I knew him well enough to know that meant he was trying not to get upset. My heart did a little tug of guilt and sadness.

'Not my house,' I said. 'The Cat House. Cat.' As though that made it so much clearer for him. Considering I'd never even heard of the Cat House until today. And hadn't actually said the Cat House on the phone.

'You wanted me to meet you at the Cat House?' he asked.

'No, but I thought you might come with me. Wait. You know the Cat House? How?' Because even though Stefan had been keeping a tight lid on it while we'd talked, I'd heard the surprise in his voice when I asked after the Cat House, and something beyond surprise when I said I had tickets. So why wasn't Kyle looking confused?

'I –' he started.

'Wait.' We were still sprawled on the ground. I rotated my ankle and was rewarded with nothing more than a small blip of pain. Awesome. 'Help me up first?' I asked.

He took my hands in his and pulled me up. I took a tentative step on my aching ankle, and found it held me surprisingly well.

'Inside,' I said at his inquisitive look.

The door was still open, of course. It wasn't like I'd found the time to lock it, or even shut it, between leaving and making my flying leap-fall over Kyle.

I wanted to talk about the Cat House, about why everyone seemed to know about it but me, about what he was doing there, and about a million other things. But what I didn't want to talk about was probably the very thing that Kyle did want to talk about.

As he helped me into the house and shut the door behind me, I figured that was exactly what he was going to ask and I steeled myself against it. He had every right to; I'd practically run away from him and hadn't looked back. I still didn't know what I'd say, but it was time to face it, to stop running away from it, whatever the consequences. He deserved that, and probably much more. Definitely much more.

I turned as he locked the door from the inside, my shoulders square, prepared. Instead of being met with a question, I was met with a surprisingly close view of Kyle's face. His green gaze was raking me, taking in the red dress, the stockings. I could feel the cold of it, not faraway cold, not angry cold. Not even really cold, but it was the only way I could think of to describe the intensity, the laser-focus with which he was looking at me.

'What?' I asked.

'I want to know,' he said. 'why you have a client that takes you to the Cat House. I want to know why you're dressed the way you are, because it's hot as hell. And I want to know if your ankle is OK. Mostly, I want to know the answer to the question that I asked you days ago.'

'I have some questions, too,' I started, but he put one finger to my lips, silencing me, clearly not finished.

'But right now, what I really really want to know is why you aren't kissing me.'

He leaned in and kissed me, deep and hard, bringing me towards him with a single clasp of his hands around my ass. He tasted of sweet milk and honey, his tongue a welcome and gentle explorer of my mouth. His kiss was totally different from Davian's.

And yet I wanted him just as much.

* * *

'I don't,' I gasped, forcing myself to pull away from the kiss. 'I can't. I mean, I want to, but I feel –' God, why did I always have to feel so bad about things? Why did everything have to have so much weight?

Kyle held my face in his hands, the heat of his palms. 'I know,' he said. 'I know what you're going to say. I know you can't. I know it was stupid. I know. I know. I know. So shut up for now and kiss me, OK?'

I did. I kissed him. It was hot and sweet and a little sad, but I closed my eyes and I knew I wouldn't cry. He tasted like cinnamon and sugar, a sweet spice that let my mind go momentarily silent. His hands in my hair, so familiar, so desired. The way I anticipated his moves, his fists tightening in my loose curls, the soft push of his tongue. His sigh was a remembered pleasure. I'd missed it, even though it had only been a few days.

I swept my fingers down and dragged them over the front of his dark jeans. I found the hardening length of his erection with my palm and cupped it, swirling my thumb over the tip until he groaned and pushed into my hand.

'Come with me,' he said. He tugged me towards the bedroom and laid me down on the thick green spread. Same colour as his eyes. You'd think I'd have noticed that before. He lowered himself down beside me, one hand tracing the curve of my hip down over my thigh.

'One of my favourite places,' he said.

My hand found his cock again, harder now, lengthening beneath the fabric. 'One of my favourite places,' I said. Which almost made me burst into tears. I was tangled in guilt and confusion and something else that I couldn't identify.

'Stop,' he said. 'Save it for later.' He clearly meant it, and I let myself trust what he was saying.

'OK,' I said. And I went back to kissing, to touching, to getting lost in the feel of him. His lips. His fingers brushing over the fabric of my dress. The push of his cock against my hips.

He tugged the neck of my dress open as far as it would go, tucked two fingers beneath the fabric and circled them over my nipples. I groaned, pushing against his touch, asking for more. Needing more.

'I'm going to have to take this off you,' he said, voice so close to a growl that I shivered involuntarily.

'Please, please, please,' I said. We fumbled getting the dress over my head, leaving me in nothing more than a bra and stockings. I was bare beneath the black nylons, and he drew in his breath.

'Oh,' he said.

His gaze was enough to send me tilting, to make me arch my hips up towards him.

'Touch me,' I begged. It was as though agreeing to let the questions between us stand, at least for now, had opened me back up to the lust that was heating every part of my body in tiny pulses. I gave in to it.

When he touched me, it wasn't what I ached for, the press of his fingers to my wet centre. It was to pull the stockings down over my ass and hips in the slowest move I'd ever seen. Watching me being revealed. Funny how I can't stand to be exposed out in the open, but having one person watch me with such fierce desire nearly brought me to my knees.

'Oh, my God,' I said. 'You're killing me. Killing.' I was almost gritting my teeth, the desire to be touched was so strong. I fumbled for him, to show him what I wanted, touch upon touch upon touch, but he interrupted my gesture by sliding one finger ever so slowly along the outer edges of my pussy. I bloomed at his attention, my wet lips opening, granting access, asking for more.

Without waiting, he thrust a finger into me, curling it, a tap-tap-tap against my g-spot that I couldn't resist answering. I squirmed, slipping into the perfect position, letting his touch against me roll through my body.

'You're so wet,' he said. Still thumping my g-spot, he leaned down and caught my clit in the suck and pull of his lips.

'Aurr,' I said. Nothing at all like a word. He laughed against me, the heat of his breath on my clit contrasting with the cooler air. Another finger. Or two. It was hard to tell from up here. All I could tell was I was wet and filled, aching to be taken fully, to be taken over the edges of whatever Kyle was about to offer.

He suckled harder, pulling the tender bump of my clit into his mouth before tonguing me. His fingers curled and curled, drummed and drummed. Every touch a sensation higher, a little more pleasure, until they ran together, all those zings of yum, into one big shudder. My orgasm stood on the cliff, just waiting for the right moment to jump and fly.

Kyle knew it. He caught my gaze, those gorgeous green eyes drilling into me.

'Come for me, Jae,' he said. The sound of my name, his name for me, caught up with the rolls of pleasure, and I came, jumped over the cliff, pleasure and noise and ohmygods and him groaning as my body tightened around his fingers. It was delicious and quick, and then I was panting and giggling.

He waited until I was nearly still, my breathing falling back into itself, then he slid his fingers from me, the slick sound of my pleasure loud in the room.

'I seriously want to fuck you,' he said.

'That's funny, because I seriously want you to fuck me.'

A second later, 'Need,' I amended. 'I need you to fuck me.'

Laughter from us both as he reached for the condom box I kept on the dresser. And a twinge of sadness too. He was the one man in my life who knew where I kept the condoms. No one else in the world knew that right now.

The deep thoughts slipped away as he rolled the condom slowly over his erection, his cock filling the rubber sheath. It was a beautiful sight. A sight that I wanted. I rolled a finger along the soft hang of his balls, watched his erection respond to the touch with a jump.

I tugged my stockings all the way off and dropped them on the floor. He positioned himself over me, giving me a gorgeous view of his beautiful hips, his sheathed cock, the long muscles of his arms. Then he was in me, my pussy so open that there was no moment of pause, just first I was empty and then I was filled with him. His tip hit my sensitive g-spot, slid over it so that I mouthed a low groan.

Cupping his ass in my hands – who could resist that warm skin, the way the muscles bunched lightly as he thrust into me – I pulled him tighter against me, as if he could actually go deeper than he already was, and he uttered a low 'fuck, Jae' that nearly sent me over the edge.

Then he stopped moving. The lack of friction made me feel crazy, needful, edged.

'Givegivegive,' I begged, pulling him inwards, trying to bend his body to my needs.

'If I move, I won't last,' he said.

'Don't care.' My voice was all breath, a drumbeat of want in the back of my head.

He shifted, moved away from me, then plunged back in.

I wanted to wrap my legs around him, tight and capturing. But he was already moving, driving me back against the bed. Every time he backed away, he was almost completely out of me, some part of him hitting my clit with each withdrawal until it was a maddening ache.

'Come for me, Jae,' he snarled, his words caught between his teeth, ending with a soft grunt of pleasure. 'Come for me so I can come for you.'

He shifted once more, slid out of me and in, my clit coming fully alive. I came with a low keen that rose and rose. Kyle joined me, his voice lower, and I felt him pull away from me, his ass flexing beneath my grip as he came, saying my name.

He lowered himself against me and we stayed that way for a long moment. This is the last time I'll lie beneath this man, I thought with an odd, sudden certainty, although I didn't really know why. After all, we might stay lovers. Or whatever it was that we were. Right?

Then he sighed and shifted, giving me a kiss on the cheek before he rolled away, onto the bed beside me. That moment was coming, the one I'd been avoiding. I could feel it barrelling toward us.

'You don't want to marry me, do you?' he asked.

God. That was one of the things I always appreciated about him. He spoke his mind. But sometimes it felt like a steamroller.

I shook my head, afraid to open my mouth because I knew tears would come. I didn't want to cry. I would not cry.

'It's OK,' he said. 'I shouldn't have asked. And not like that.'

The tears came anyway, despite no words, making his face a watery blur. I tried to stop them but, as soon as I blinked, they cascaded down my cheeks.

He reached out a hand and wiped them away. Which somehow made me cry more.

'I'm not crying. I just have allergies,' I said, an old joke, waving my hand in front of my face as though it would help.

'Well, stop it then,' he said. 'Before your tongue swells up and you choke to death.'

He wrapped his arms around me, and pulled me close. We were still sex-sticky where our bodies came together and I was tear-sticky where my face rested on his shoulder. When I knew I could speak without crying, I said, 'I just wasn't expecting it. And … I don't know. Isn't what we had enough?'

'Had,' he said. Musing. My heart panged hard in my chest. I was fucking this all up.

'Sorry,' I said. Tears threatened again, but I swallowed them back. Stupid eyes.

He ran a hand through my hair. 'I know,' he said. 'I just thought, I don't know. That we were moving someplace else. Toward a future. I don't want a casual thing any more. I want a serious thing. A forever thing.'

He pulled away slightly so he could look at me, running his gaze over my face. 'With you.'

'I'm sorry,' I said again. Wishing I had something better to say.

I could tell from his eyes that he heard everything I meant to say in that phrase.

'You're a good guy,' I said. I meant it. 'Far better than I deserve.'

'Nah,' he said. 'We're just different. We need different things.'

I watched him while he got dressed. He turned away to put his pants on, and I got thinking how weird it is to go from being lovers to people who have sex to … whatever we were now. People who turned away to hide their naked bodies from each other.

I pulled my dress back down over my head. 'Do you want to talk some more?' I asked.

'Not right now,' he said. 'I'm kind of all talked out. Besides, you need to get going if you're going to make the show.'

A quick glance at the bedside clock told me he was right.

'Shit,' I said. I'd completely forgotten about the Cat House. It wasn't like I was going for fun. I needed to be discreet, or at least professional. What I didn't need was to show up late, looking like I'd just been well fucked. Or maybe that was the perfect way to show up. Who knew?

'Do you want to come with me?' I asked. 'It's work, but it also might be sexy. We have to hurry, though. I have to stop by Cream on the way.'

'Well, get dressed then,' he said.

I jumped out of bed, only remembering the ankle too late to be careful of it, but it didn't even let out a tiny twang.

I dressed fast. The only difference is that this time I pulled on a pair of boots without heels. They didn't look quite as good with the dress, but they'd protect my ankle, and that felt more important at the moment.

'Ready?' I asked. Kyle was back in his jeans and jacket, his hair only slightly less sexed up than mine. It looked good on him. Sandy-coloured, a little mussed and, as always, falling across his eyes. Fuck, he was hot.

Even as I looked at him, I got an odd feeling in the bottom of my stomach. Something was wrong with me, wasn't it? That I didn't just say yes to this beautiful, smart, kind man. That I didn't want what everyone else in the world seemed to want. That a marriage proposal sent me into dithers instead of making me all warm and fuzzy. Jesus. Was I broken somehow?

'Ready,' he said. 'Let's go.'

I opened the door, reflexively looking to make sure there weren't any more surprises on my doorstep. When I was certain the coast was clear, we stepped out and I locked the door behind us.

We walked fast. Well, as fast as I dared. I didn't want to tweak my ankle, but the boots I had on seemed to do a great job of keeping everything in place. The sun had set and the tiny streetlights entwined in the trees lit our way.

I was still all tingly from good sex, the insides of me all melty and warm, the outsides buzzing with leftover pleasure and arousal. But that softness was mingled with confusion. Had we made some kind of decision? Were we still together? Was Kyle really as OK with all of this as he said he was?

He walked comfortably beside me, not seeming at all concerned that we hadn't talked more about the marriage thing, and that made me feel better. I slipped my hand into his and grinned when he squeezed it lightly.

Sometimes life was good enough that you had to bask in it for a little while. Especially at those times when you can hear bad coming around the corner, its little footsteps making their way toward you.

We were almost at Cream when something occurred to me.

'Wait, Kyle, how did you know we'd be late? Did I tell you what time the show was?'

He didn't hesitate with his answer and he didn't falter in his step, but that was a Kyle trait. If you wanted to hear the truth, he told it to you. He wouldn't tell you things you didn't want to know. But he'd told me right from the beginning that if I asked something, I should want the truth, because he was going to give it to me. It's like he had the truth brimming in him all the time, and, if you so much as made a little hole for it to escape, it was likely to explode all over you.

'Cat House shows are always on the same day of the month and they always start at the same time,' he said.

Now I was the one to stop walking. 'How do you know about this place when I don't? I mean, not that I don't expect you to know things that I don't, but I've never even heard of it and I've lived in this city way longer than you.'

He stopped as I did, still holding my hand. 'Some of my clients go there.'

There was more. There was always more with Kyle. One of the reasons I liked him so much was that he was complex and deep, always had a million things on his brain, even when he was making me laugh. Or making me dinner. Or making me come.

But just this once I wished I could get him to say everything that was in there, everything that I wanted to know without prompting.

As though he'd read my mind, he nodded. 'Your eyes are so full of questions they're about to explode. How about this? I promise I'll tell you the whole story after the show, OK? Everything I know. And I won't even make you ask all the questions. Deal?'

I traced the love line in his palm with my thumb, or at least what I thought was the love line, feeling its deep length. Feeling bad, but also hopeful.

'Deal,' I said. 'And I really am sorry.'

'I know,' he said.

His kindness was breaking my heart into little bits.

'Why do you have to be so nice about it? Why can't you just be a big fat jerk so I can hate you?'

For once, he didn't answer. He just kissed my forehead.

105

'OK,' I said. 'Let's go find us a Kitty.'

He lifted his eyebrows at that, about a second before he burst into laughter.

'You don't have any idea what we're about to experience, do you?' he asked.

'Purr?' I responded.

'Yeah, we're in so much trouble,' he said.

CHAPTER 7

From the outside, Cream was the kind of place that looked like any other coffee shop. Almost. If you didn't notice that, on the sign over the door, the font of the word CREAM was made up of naked people curved into letters.

Or if you didn't look through the windows and see the erotic art that lined all the walls.

'I'll be fast,' I said. 'Want coffee?'

Kyle shook his head. He still looked a little dazed about everything, as though he was a man who'd expected a punch in the jaw and then got a kiss instead. Which, now that I thought about it, was pretty close to what had actually happened. But he was clearly still waiting for the other punch. So, it seemed, was I.

'I'll wait here,' he said. 'It's nice out.'

'Back in two shakes,' I said.

I stepped inside the shop and was instantly inundated with the scent of fresh baked goods and well-made coffee. Almost as good as the smell of paper and leather.

Cream was tiny, just room for a couple of tables up front and the long counter behind which two of Stefan's baristas worked. A new art show featured black and white photos of body parts. Nipples tightened between clamps. The corner of an eye with long false eyelashes. The very tip of someone's erect cock. The natural wood floors and walls, combined with the beautiful, sexual artwork, did a lot for the place.

The tables were always filled with couples and singles. Every table had a sugar bowl, a napkin dispenser and a coffee cup filled with free condoms. Off to the left, a library shelf was lined with sex books, some of which I knew they'd picked up at Leather Bound. Another shelf offered more books, these for sale, along with a glass case filled with leather whips, blindfolds and other sex toys.

You could always tell who was coming to check it out; they were the giggly ones. Tonight, two young women sat at the farthest table, their mouths open just a little, watching everything. Their gazes followed me as I made my way to the counter. The table in the corner was full of the local cops, as it always was. A couple of them gave me a nod as I went by.

Behind the counter, two women worked to the sound of steam and espresso. A huge blackboard was handwritten with drinks and prices, mostly offerings with a sexual slant. Asking for a Red Hot got you a cinnamon mocha and a kiss from the barista if she was wearing red. Their drinking chocolate came in matching nipple cups. Here, even a vanilla latte had double meaning.

I didn't recognise the woman working the register. She was young, bleach-blonde in a way that made her look punk and tough, with hoop piercings in both eyebrows. Sexy in a very ass-kicking kind of way.

'Welcome to Cream,' she said. 'What's your dream?'

Before I could respond, she pursed her lips. 'Hm. I was trying that out, but I think it's a flop. What do you think?'

'The guys will like it,' I said.

'Yeah, girls are harder. Ain't that the truth?' She shook her head, laughing. 'What can I get for you?'

Stefan came around the corner from the back at just that moment.

'I'll have one of him,' I said. 'And a cup of coffee to go.'

'Everyone always asks for the exact same thing,' she said, shooting me a smile. I do like people with a quick wit.

'Sugar,' Stefan said.

He was one of the few people in the world who could get away with calling me that. I think it's because he gives the impression that you're the only person he's ever called by that nickname, as though he'd just tweaked your given name slightly into this new form.

He came around the counter and gave me a hug. He was at least six inches taller than me and at least that many inches wider. Getting inside his hug was like being enveloped in a coffee- and sugar-scented blanket. A very strong, very masculine blanket.

'Her coffee's on me,' he said.

'Thanks, Stefan.' Normally I pay. And I tip. Which means that on the rare times I do run into Stefan and he offers to pay for me, I don't feel bad about it. I stuffed a couple of dollars in the tip jar and gave the bleach-blonde a nod of thanks when she proffered my coffee.

'Tell me all,' I said, once we'd grabbed ourselves a small table in the corner.

'First, I don't know how you found out about the Cat House, but watch yourself.'

OK, if he was playing assistant to my Girl Friday again, I could play that. I leaned in conspiratorially, lowering my voice. 'Right, because the book buyers are dangerous.' I looked around, as if to make sure no one was listening to me or watching our conversation. 'And they might –'

'No, I'm serious, Janine.'

I'd never heard Stefan use my given name in my whole life. It brought me to a complete stop, my coffee cup halfway to my mouth.

'Wait. What? Are you being serious?'

'Did I not just use the word "serious" in the previous sentence?'

'Yes, but ...' I started.

Then I sat back and rephrased my question. 'What do you mean? What do you know? Why am I the last one to know about everything?'

Everything at this particular moment being Kyle's desire to get married to me and this whole Cat House thing. And possibly something about Lily and something about Davian and what the hell was up with our rent being raised anyway. So, yeah, turned out I really was the last to know about everything.

'I don't know very much, to be honest,' Stefan said. 'As long as I've owned Cream, I've never gone. Too cult-like for my taste.'

'Cult-like?' I echoed.

He nodded. 'Sure, they have a leader who makes all the decisions. Some kind of initiation ceremony. Secret sex stuff that happens underground and that you can't talk about.'

'Are you pulling my leg, Stefan? Because I really need to know this stuff.'

'Sugar, I never kid about sex.'

He must have seen my look because he took my hands in his. He had featherlight hands, his skin far softer than it had any right to be.

'Look,' he said. 'It's not dangerous to your life or anything. It's just very underground. And there is sometimes talk of people getting sucked in.'

'Sucked in? Sucked into what?'

He waved a hand over my coffee as if to cool it.

'You'll be fine,' he said. 'You're smart and strong, Sugar. And you don't have a crazy libido, do you?'

I felt my eyes go wide.

'OK, scratch that. Try to keep that sex lust of yours in check and you'll be just fine,' he said. 'Do you have someone to go with you?'

I pointed out through the window to where Kyle stood on the sidewalk, talking into his cell phone.

'Right, of course,' Stefan said. 'Your cute blond boy. And you trust him?'

'What?' I said.

He shrugged. 'I'm just making sure. I don't want you to wander off and get mugged by some invisible Cult of the Nine Nipples or something. Also, don't drink the Kool-Aid.'

I nearly snorted coffee out my nose. Unpleasant, but totally worth it for the laugh.

'I'll be fine,' I said. 'How do I find this door?'

'Go around the back.'

'The back of what?'

He made a gesture towards the back of the building we were sitting in.

'You're saying this place is at the back of this building, the building that houses your own shop?'

He nodded.

'And you've never seen it?'

'Sugar,' he said, 'I've seen the door. And that is enough for me.'

I looked at Stefan for more answers.

'That's all I know, Sugar,' he said. 'But come back safely

111

to me and tell me everything you can.' He made his eyes big at me. 'I mean all the dirty nasty fun bits, of course. Even an old settled guy like me can dream.'

Then he hugged me like I was going off into the wilds of the African jungle, never to be heard from again.

When I walked back outside, the world kind of returned to normal. Kyle finished his call and gave me a smile. People were strolling back and forth on the sidewalk. Everything was as it should be.

Except that nothing was. And one of my favourite people in the world had just bolted like a scared rabbit and warned me against a place named after a pet shelter. Or a bathroom. Or a wine room. Whatever.

All I had to say to that was: What. The. Hell?

* * *

The door was surprisingly easy to find. It really was at the back of the building as Stefan had said, and it was clearly marked THE CAT HOUSE. Despite the obvious, I'd certainly never noticed it.

The truth of all truly hidden things: they were right in front of your face all along.

A tug on the door handle revealed that it was locked.

'How do we get in?' I asked.

'I haven't a clue,' Kyle said.

'I thought you knew all about this?' I said.

He cracked me a grin. 'I know about it. But I've never been here.'

I tugged on the door again, realised it was silly and then looked around for a buzzer or a camera or something that would let us in.

I was poking at what was probably just a lump on the wall when the door opened.

A bald-headed man stood in the doorway. His eyes were cold, so dark they were nearly black. His stance was that of someone guarding treasure, like a knight or a dragon. The bald-headed version of Smaug the dragon. Everything about his presence screamed doom. Or dom. I imagined him with a leather crop in one hand and a ball-gag in the other. The vision seemed perfect.

'Yes?' he said. His voice was higher than I imagined, which created an odd sense of dissonance about him.

'Uh,' I said. Because clearly that's what one says when faced with a big dude who scares the crap out of you while also maybe turning you on.

'The coffee shop's out front,' he said. He waited for about half a second, and then made as if to shut the door.

'We have tickets,' I said. 'For the show.'

He looked me up and down, clearly waiting for me to produce the tickets.

I pulled them from my pocket and held them out. My fingers were shaking; the tickets bounced slightly in the air, giving me away.

He eyed them and then ran some kind of penlight over their corners before nodding. 'You're late,' he said.

'I'm sorry?' I said.

'Yes, you are,' he said.

I'd had a lot of weird exchanges in the past few days, but that was one of the weirdest. I looked at Kyle but he was clearly as confused as I was.

'Come in then,' he said. 'And quickly.'

Suddenly we were inside a long, well-lit hallway and the door was closed behind us.

'Tech?' he asked.

Once again, I was utterly at a loss. I was going to say 'Uh' again, but I got the impression that you only got to say that once around him without him breaking into a snarl. So I managed an 'I'm sorry?' then realised I'd already said that too.

He sighed, shaking his head. It was a big head, and I had to bite my lip not to snort at the slightly bobblehead image it gave him.

'Newbies,' he sighed. 'Don't you do your homework before you come here?'

'Hey, I tried –'

He silenced me. 'No cameras allowed. No recording devices. Do you have anything?'

'Just my cell.' I dropped it into his outstretched hand. Kyle did the same with his.

'We'll have it here for you when the show's over,' he said.

He looked Kyle and me over slowly. Whatever he saw he did not approve of, but he seemed willing to let us go in anyway.

'Three things to remember,' he said. 'If you're chosen, you'll know what to do. If you're not chosen, that's that. No whining about it. You can come back and try again. Come back a million times if you like. Long as you have tickets. And if you have no idea what I'm talking about –' he looked me over specifically this time '– and it's clear that you don't, then just enjoy the ride.'

'Ride?' I said.

'In you go.'

Then we were through a double door that opened into a dim room. It looked like a small, old, high-end theatre, dominated by a huge black curtain across what must be the stage. The chairs were large, linked in semi-circled rows that faced away from us. Small candles flickered against the walls. In the semi-dark, it seemed like almost all of the seats were full, and yet there didn't seem to be more than two dozen people in the audience. I couldn't tell if they were men or women, young or old. Just that there were dark heads in seats.

A shadow moved against the wall and then I saw two eyes through a dark mask.

'Your tickets,' the shadow said in a soft, feminine voice.

I handed them over. The shadow ran a small light over them, then nodded. 'This way,' the masked woman said.

We followed her. Kyle reached for my hand in the dark and squeezed. His eyes looked huge in the half-light. She led us to the last two open seats together, right in the front row. Every time I show up late to a show and there are seats open in the front row, it makes me nervous. I wondered if I should have brought a raincoat or something. Well, too late. I was here now. If I was going to get drenched by something on stage, I'd just have to deal with it.

I smiled at the dark-haired man on the other side of me as I took my seat. He didn't smile back.

'How did I not know about this?' I whispered into Kyle's ear. My voice was too loud, even at a whisper. No one else was talking or whispering or even opening a piece of gum. But I couldn't stop talking. 'I come to Cream all the time. How does Stefan not even really know about this? Also, choose us? Choose us for what?'

He shrugged. 'I told you. I have no idea. Exclusive.'

'I don't know what that means,' I said. It hurt my pride a little, I think. I thought of myself as a good researcher, as someone who knew what was going on around me. Especially around the Sweet Spot, which I considered my home. To get a glimpse of this secret sex world hurt a little. To know that people in my life knew about it and had never mentioned it hurt more. Which was stupid, I knew. If I didn't know to ask, how would they know to tell me?

I leaned in towards Kyle to ask more questions but, as I did so, half a dozen more shadows, clad in dark suits that covered everything but their eyes, seemed to materialise out of the walls. One by one, they made their way through the audience, moving more like flickering blackness than humans. It was spooky and mesmerising all at once. A shadow went to each of the candles and silently put it out.

The theatre went dark.

Not a sound. Not a rustle. No one opened a cough drop or sneezed or even moved. I wasn't sure people were even breathing. I couldn't hear or see Kyle next to me. If not for the heat of his leg where it barely touched mine, I would have wondered if he was still there.

It was so quiet and dark, it felt like what I'd always thought a sensory deprivation chamber would feel like. On one hand, it made me want to cough, or snort, or laugh. Pound my feet against the floor. Pull out my iPhone, which of course I didn't have. Kiss Kyle loudly and with lots of tongue. Make some kind of noise.

On the other hand, I wanted to settle into that silent blackness, to let it envelop me. Isn't that what sensory deprivation did? Gave you time and space to float and think.

The lack of stimulus didn't make me calmer. It made me hyper aware. My ears seemed to be actually turning this way and that, searching for sound. My eyes strained against the blackness. I needed something, anything to latch onto, to find my bearings. But nothing came.

I sat. I breathed, inhaling and exhaling too loudly. Time stopped or expanded or speeded up. Something began to shift.

My eyes and ears accepted their fate, stopped searching so hard for something to grab hold of. Instead my skin became alive, sensitive to every movement of air, to every change in temperature. My pulse thrummed in my veins, so fierce I was surprised I couldn't actually hear it. The heat of my body overtook everything else.

Every time the air changed, it was the stroke of a lover's hand along my skin. The back of my neck dotted with sweat. I thought I could feel each droplet forming, teasing my skin with cool liquid. Someone somewhere breathed, and the hair along my face tickled my cheekbones.

A touch brushed the side of my arm, a barely-there sweep, an almost-not-there feathering, something so light that it almost didn't seem real. It could have been just another wisp of breeze, a mote of dust in the air.

The way my body reacted was the only indication I had that this was something different. All of the hairs on my arm stood up as if to follow the touch's trajectory. My skin went cool and then hot. Deep inside the centre of me, my pussy pulled tight in reaction to the touch. I almost gasped at the strength of the sensation, but resisted by biting down on the insides of my cheeks.

Another soft brush along the edge of my neck, pushing my hair aside. The intensity of such light contact made me shiver. I couldn't tell if it was skin or gloves or something far from human, like a feather. But with every touch my entire body responded, yearning for more, my insides opening up.

My clit pulsed soft and tentative, asking for more. I refused to groan or shift or even make a noise. If no one else was falling prey to their arousal, I wouldn't either.

Then I had a horrible realisation: maybe this wasn't part of the show at all. Maybe this was just someone in the audience touching just me. Maybe everyone else was just sitting there waiting for the show to start.

And I realised it didn't matter. My whole body hummed, alive and wanting. If I was the only one being touched, so be it. I liked it.

Next to me, I heard a sigh, a quiet, barely-there sound that I knew instinctively was Kyle. I'd heard him sigh just like that the first time I brushed my tongue along his cock. Or trailed a damp finger around his nipple.

The sound made me smile. It didn't take long before I could hear soft sighs and breaths from all around, a kind of chorus of pleasure, as though the unseen people were playing us like instruments. The more I listened, the more it became just that, a perfectly played song of desire, sighs and moans and bodies shifting in the dark.

The next time my touch came, I didn't hold back. The brush of fingertips across my chest, landing just lightly at the edges of my nipples, made me sigh in want and pleasure.

The song rose around us for a few more minutes, and then, without any kind of finale or last chorus, it just stopped. Everyone went silent. The touch against my skin didn't come back.

I sat in the dark and silence again, my body hyper aware, my clit throbbing so hard it was all I could do not to reach between my legs and touch it.

A huge sound rolled through the blackness. The curtains in front of us were whispering open, revealing two men, oiled and naked, in a pale, flickering light. They were entwined, their bodies coiling together as if in time to some silent music. One was lean and thin, with a body like Kyle's, the muscles of his legs pulsing with his movement. The other was taller, wider, his skin dark and shiny.

They writhed, kissing, touching, grinding their bodies together, until I had to shift in my seat, the sexual tension unbearable. I drew in a breath, caught by their utter beauty, their lack of concern for anything but each other. It was the best and worst kind of tease, wanting it to go on for ever, but also wanting them to do something, anything, more. To find their way into each other, to move toward climax. Simultaneously, each one reached down and took the other's cock in his hands, stroking so slowly, so leisurely, I could feel my own hips respond.

The thin man went down on his knees, looking up at the other. You could see the lust in his gaze, in the way he leaned into the man's touch at the back of his neck. With a single, long stroke he buried the man's cock in his mouth. They thrust together as one, mouth and cock, the two bodies with it. I couldn't stop watching, couldn't stop imagining it was me with that beautiful cock, that a man was on his knees before me, sucking the length of me into his mouth, bit by bit.

It wasn't hardly enough. Even as I was straining my eyes to see more of them, every nuanced muscle and movement, they parted, a wholeness become two halves and then they were gone off the stage.

The lights went up, just a little. Enough so that I could see Kyle's expression as he turned and mouthed 'Holy fuck' at me.

Kitty walked on a moment later. Where the men had been silence and truth and bareness, Kitty was everything that was the opposite of that – a black and white striped vinyl cat suit, complete with tail and ears, a blonde wig that added at least six inches to her already tall frame. Her smile was as big as her hair, ruby-red lips, perfect teeth, a glittery piercing in each of her dimples.

She cut the sexual tension as soon as she walked on stage. A song came up, the kind of beat you could clap to, stomp your feet to. You could almost hear people settle back into their seats, breathe sighs of relief, prepare themselves for the change of entertainment.

I leaned over to Kyle. 'I could never do that,' I whispered.

'What? Wear a cat suit?'

'No,' I said. 'Well, yes, but that's not what I mean. I mean that. Get up on stage.'

'Sure you could,' he said.

I just shook my head. No way I was ever doing that.

Sitting here in the dark, watching? Good. Up there, dancing? Or worse yet, showing my sexual self? No thank you times ten. No literary heroine in the world was going to give me enough chutzpah to do something like that. Nor did I want her to.

Kitty strutted around the stage, moving to the upbeat tempo, shaking her body inside the vinyl suit. Despite, or maybe because of, her over-the-topness, she was hot as hell. Embodying everyone's fantasy woman, part cat, part pin-up girl, part pole dancer. My tongue went dry. I found myself wanting to lick the slick vinyl that curved over her breasts, her hips, the cleft between her legs.

She stripped slowly as she moved to the music, lots of coy moves. Pulled off her gloves inch by inch until she could catch the end of them in her teeth and tug them all of the way off. Seemed to toy with the idea of removing her tail, then thought better of it and left it on. Tugging her ears out of her big wig and throwing them into the crowd. She was down to her vinyl suit and her tail when the music changed, something slower, sensual, the background beat of drums echoing the pulse at the base of the throat.

Kitty came down off the stage, the lights moving with her to catch every curve, every jiggle. She made her way across the front row of seats, touching a few people here and there, her movements showing a connection with them, a familiarity that surprised me. She stopped at a man near us, leaned down and whispered in his ear until he released a low groan.

When she got to Kyle and me, she stopped a long time, eyeing us both. Her eyes were the neon blue of coloured contacts, the pupils slitted like a cat's. A tiny black mole, a shape I couldn't put my finger on, rested at the corner of one eye. I couldn't stop staring at the contrast of her pale skin with her unreal eyes.

Finally, she held her hand out to me. I thought she wanted to shake it. Or, I don't know. What do you think in moments like that? You think, 'I should do this thing.'

So I did.

And then she pulled me out of my seat and started to drag me onto the stage with her.

* * *

I flailed, like the dork that I am, forgetting that there was a whole theatre of people watching the two of us. I planted my feet and dug in my heels and windmilled my arms like a wild thing. There was no way I was getting up there on stage.

Kitty was stronger than I expected; she held her ground easily, but when she realised I was panicked, she stopped pulling me. Her face near me, she lowered her voice.

'I chose you,' she said.

I shook my head. I had no idea what that meant. My heart was thumping so hard in my chest I thought it might break a rib or something. My face was hot. I just wanted to crawl back into a dark corner and hide.

'Isn't that why you're here?' Her voice was so low against my ear I could feel the vibrations.

I realised I was supposed to go up there on stage with her. I was supposed to talk to her about Davian. I was supposed to save my store and my friend and my job. I was supposed to say yes to her.

But I couldn't. I just stood there, shaking my head, my whole body planted and trembling. I couldn't step forward. I couldn't get up there on that stage. Not clothed. Not naked. Certainly not in a sexual context. No way.

Kitty looked at me for a moment longer, her neon eyes expressionless. Then she carefully placed me back in my seat.

'Take me,' I heard Kyle say, and without a pause she pulled Kyle up onto the stage with her instead.

The whole thing must have taken less than thirty seconds, because most of the crowd seemed not to have even missed a beat. If they'd seen the exchange, they didn't react to it.

Kitty and Kyle were already up on stage, the lights back down to nearly nothing, the music slowing yet again to a slow dance song, something I remembered from high school. It would have seemed like the silliest thing ever, them slow dancing up there with Kitty's big hair and vinyl suit and Kyle's dark jeans and sex-rumpled hair. But somehow the way they moved together made it wildly sexual, as though they were just filled to the brim with the kind of lust that could barely be contained. I shrank down into my seat, watching them dance together, hip to hip, his arms around her. Their bodies pressed and released, a fluid movement that seemed to work its way even through the pounding of my heart and the heat of my face.

Facing me, Kitty beckoned Kyle down on his knees. I expected him to turn and look at me, to run off the stage, to protest somehow. He did none of those things. Slowly, he slid down the front of her, his hands on her hips, then her thighs, lowering himself to the floor. Kitty spread her legs in front of him, pulling the snaps of her vinyl suit open to expose her shaved pussy, the piercing glinting among its folds.

She said something to him that I couldn't hear, and he bent forward. Her hands went to his hair, her body gyrating in time to the music as she held him there.

I couldn't see his face, only hers, but I knew what that tongue felt like, that mouth. My body responded with the memory of him sucking me, tugging on the point of my clit, lapping at me with the flat of his tongue. I remember how he liked to drag his teeth ever so softly along my labia, and then slide his tongue deep into me, to fuck me like that until I came.

I was wet beneath my dress, but I didn't dare touch myself. I needed to pay attention, to catch every nuance. I'd screwed up, but maybe there was time to fix all of this.

Kitty didn't put on a fake show for the crowd; there was no lip-biting or orgasmic screaming. In fact, she closed her eyes. A whole room of people watching her and she closed her eyes. Went inwards. I caught my breath, watching. Her body gyrated against Kyle's, again and again, her fingers seeming to guide his movements. They stayed that way for a long time, the music rising and swelling, Kyle on his knees before her. She reached one hand down between them, leaning her upper body back.

And opened her eyes. She looked right at me, those odd cat eyes, bright in the low light.

When she came, I saw it in her eyes first, a tiny flare of

pleasure. Her face tightened and released, her back arching tighter as she ground against Kyle. With a long, low cry of joy, she brought both hands into the air, her final, grand gesture.

The theatre went black. The music died. There was no more sound from the stage. Around me, the ragged breaths of those who'd been watching.

If Kitty had been trying to tell me something, I'd missed it.

I sat and waited, waited for the touch of someone, for the arrival of someone. For Kyle to come back. Even as I heard other people leaving, shuffling out in the darkness, still I sat. The people on either side of me left, and still I waited.

Finally, Smaug came and found me. He looked less intimidating now than he had when I'd arrived. He dropped my cell phone into my hand without a word.

'Please,' I said. 'I need to talk to Kitty.'

'You can't,' he said. 'Sorry, kid, but you screwed up. She chose you, and you said no. It's all over.'

'But you said I could come back. A million times, you said.' I was babbling. I could feel it, and yet I couldn't help myself.

'No,' he said. 'I said if you didn't get chosen, you could come back. If you get chosen and you say no, there's no second chances. You're just out.'

He looked me over, much as he had when we'd walked in, which seemed like lifetimes ago now. 'Still, never seen no one say no to Kitty before. You've got balls, you have. Or you're really really stupid.'

I suddenly felt lost and angry, like a child who'd been abandoned and then scolded. Or maybe pouty was the right word. I was pretty sure my lip was sticking out.

'What about Kyle? The man I came with.' What about Kitty, the woman I was supposed to talk to? What about all these million things that I didn't have a grasp on?

'Kyle's not coming back. At least not tonight. You should go on home.'

Everything about his voice said, 'You're out of your league, kid.' And I probably was. I'd never felt so off-kilter, so uncertain and out of place, so nervous and yet so utterly, thrillingly aroused in my whole life. I had no idea what was going on.

I nodded and stood, not knowing what else to do. He led me out of the theatre and down the long hallway where we'd come in. When I stepped outside, it was like the night had stopped. It was still and quiet; the only thing that was loud was all the stuff going on in my head.

'Thank you,' I said, not even sure what I was thanking him for. Maybe just because he'd been nice. He nodded, and turned, letting the door begin to close behind him. As he turned, I caught a glimpse of the side of his neck beneath his shirt collar. There, almost at its base, a tiny tattoo. I knew that shape. I'd seen it … where?

It clicked for me then. On Davian's card. That dark keyhole. That wasn't a mole at the corner of her eye. It was a tiny keyhole tattoo.

'Wait,' I said. 'Can I –?' But the door was already falling closed behind him, and I was pretty sure that no amount of hammering on it was going to get him to open it back up.

CHAPTER 8

So there really was a sex club. And it had apparently eaten my boyfriend. Ex-boyfriend. Date for the evening. Whatever it was that we were now.

As I walked away from the club, I called Kyle and left a message asking him to call me and tell me he was OK.

I couldn't get the image of Kyle down on his knees out of my mind. It was so sexy, and yet I wondered why it seemed so easy for everyone else to show their sexuality in front of other people. I could barely breathe at the thought, and yet Kyle had gone willingly. He'd actually volunteered. 'Take me,' he'd said. That simple.

I walked around the block and the next block, carrying my thoughts with me, until I found myself in front of the Cock's Tail. Even from outside, I could hear the live music, a thumping beat that seemed to start at my feet and work its way up to my brain. A little loud music, maybe a little dancing; it didn't sound perfect, but it sounded way better than going home alone to my cold, dark house.

I stepped into the bar, the live music swelling around me. It was something that defied genre, a little bluegrass, a touch of dance beat, a thread of big band, well played by three enthusiastic men and accented by a woman's clear, true voice. The tables around the dance floor were packed, as was the floor itself. The bar was pretty full too, but I saw a spot at the far end, between a couple and a man who was paying too much attention to his phone to glance at me twice. I hoped.

I slipped in between them and took a seat. I'm not tall, but the barstools at the Tail always made me feel like I was. Clambering onto them was a task, but I liked the result.

Part of it was that the floor behind the bar was lowered by a couple of inches. Which made even Jay, the bar owner who was currently playing bartender, look a little shorter than what I guessed was his actual six-feet-something height.

Jay gave me a smile and an elbow wave, still pouring a pint in the process. Even in the low lights and looking slightly frenzied by how busy the place was, he was a beautiful man. Olive skin that was accented by his dark hair and dark eyes, plus that wide-shouldered slim-hipped physique that was hard to ignore. He knew how to dress too, even for a bartending shift. His jeans hugged his ass perfectly, and his short-sleeved button-up was a dark green that set off his skin perfectly.

Seeing him made me realise how long it had been since I'd been in. When we'd first opened Leather Bound, Jay and his employees had been some of our biggest supporters. We'd even had our grand opening party here. For a long time, Lily and I had been here almost every night, and then at least once a week, and then, well, now I couldn't remember the last time I'd been here.

'Janine,' he said, wiping his hands on the bar towel tucked into his belt. 'I thought you'd dumped me.' He leaned across the bar to kiss my cheek, making even phone guy look up briefly.

'You didn't get my Dear Jay letter?' I asked.

128

'I get so many,' he said. 'Hard to keep them straight. Your usual?'

I was surprised I still had a usual. But then again, that was probably why Cock's Tail was such a popular bar. Sure, it had a great atmosphere and Jay brought in the best unknown musicians around, but it was also that he remembered everyone. And, apparently, their usuals.

Even if I didn't. I was mostly a gin and tonic girl, but sometimes went for the oddballs.

I gave him a smile and a nod. 'That would be perfect.'

Then I sat back to wait and see what he would bring me.

As I watched the crowd and, beyond them, the musicians, my mind kept rolling over what had happened at the Cat House. I felt in way over my head, and I wasn't even sure why.

'Long day?' Jay asked. He set a drink in front of me, a martini glass full of creamy chocolate-coloured liquid. I leaned forward and sniffed it. Chocolate and coffee. Oh, right. I'd been drinking coffee martinis while we finalised Leather Bound. That made sense. I'd needed all the alcohol and caffeine I could get back then. In some way, I supposed that was still true.

'Very,' I said.

He leaned in so that I could hear him beneath the music. 'It's nice to see you, either way,' he said.

'Thanks, Jay.'

He returned to his other patrons while I sipped my drink, scanning the crowd, realising that I didn't know a single face. Either tonight's crowd was unusual or the patronage of the Tail had completely turned over while I'd been gone. I turned my attention to the band instead, captivated by the woman who sang lead. She shimmered in a flowing purple dress that seemed to be made of sequins, her voice a clear high beckon that flowed through and over the music. I envied both her voice and her hair, short blue curls that framed her head like a rare flower. No one noticed me in the fray of people, and I liked it that way. I just wanted to sit and watch.

I let the warmth of the drink and the sounds of the music wash over me, feeling some of my tension slip away the longer I sat there. Jay caught my eye occasionally and threw a smile my way.

When the band announced they were done for the night and that the next band would be coming on shortly, I realised I'd been sitting there for nearly an hour and was on my second drink. If my tension wasn't gone by now, it wasn't going. It was time to go home. I gave Jay the settle-up sign and he brought my cheque.

'Don't be such a stranger,' he said.

'Promise,' I said. I meant it. I'd missed being here, the music and the life that always filled this place.

'Good,' he said. He turned away, trusting I'd leave the money on the bar as I always did.

As I was digging out cash, the lead singer slipped between my stool and the man next to me, offering her apologies as she did so. Closer up, her hair was neon blue, like looking through sapphires in the sun, her skin the colour of pure milk. I caught a whiff of her, the sweet scent of maraschino cherries, as she leaned across the bar.

'You have a fantastic voice,' I said.

She glanced at me, canting her head sideways. It was an oddly shy gesture, almost birdlike. Her eyes were huge, a denim hue that matched her earrings.

She lifted her hand to her throat, a fluttery movement that I recognised. Shyness. Something slightly submissive. Her throat was bare of jewellery, but at the very centre, in the hollow of her neck, a tiny black tattoo beat with her pulse. A keyhole. It was a simple shape, but the shading somehow made it seem as if you could put your eye up against her throat and see through to the other side. It was the kind of work that Kyle would appreciate for its simple complexity.

I knew that shape. It seemed like I was seeing it everywhere lately. Like when you buy a certain make and colour of car and every time you go on the road after that, that car is all you see. Keyhole tats were my new Honda Civic.

'I know that –' I said. But she didn't wait for me to finish. She leaned forward and kissed me on the mouth, the scent of cherries washing over me like a breeze. Her lips were soft, barely touching me, and yet I could feel her breath in the hollows of my mouth.

When she pulled away, all I could see were the big blue saucers of her eyes.

'Thank you,' she mouthed. She turned away and started to slip through the crowd.

'Wait,' I said. I wanted to ask her about her tattoo, about keyholes, about cat houses, about any and all of it. But she was already going, then gone, toward the back door of the Tail.

I tried to get Jay's attention, to see if he knew her, but he was busy with a big group at the end of the bar. So I dropped my money on the wooden bar, slipped off my high vantage point and went rogue.

* * *

Nancy Drew is me, I thought as I headed out the back door into the parking lot.

Which should have been my first clue right there to turn around and go home.

The sapphire-headed woman wasn't visible at first, so I stepped through the cars, trying to look like I had a reason to be there. Other than the fact that I was following some poor woman through the darkly lit night. I was never so glad not to be a guy; it made me feel bad following someone as a woman. If I was male, and worried that I'd scare her, I never could have done it.

Not that I was doing a very good job of following her. There was nothing in front of me except the rest of the parking lot with its rows of cars, and the sudden shine of the street lamps on both sides. How could someone in such a shiny dress just disappear?

At the far end of the lot, I caught a glimpse of movement. There she was, threading her way through the cars, a lit cigarette bobbing in her hand. Despite how far ahead of me she was, she didn't seem to be in a hurry. Merely determined to get where she was going.

I followed her, asking myself why I was doing this. Was it the kiss she'd given me, the sweet taste of her open mouth, the way she'd tongued into me as though she knew exactly what my body craved? How she'd put one finger at the bottom of my chin, dragged the nail lightly over my skin?

Or was this me trying to right what I'd screwed up earlier? The fact that I didn't just call out to her, that I didn't flag her down and say something, or ask a question, made me even less certain about my intentions.

Either way, I went quietly along behind her, following her with the same methodical movements as her own. She stopped long enough to take a drag on her cigarette and look skyward. I wished I was close enough or it wasn't so dark; I wanted to see that tattoo again, to really make sure I knew it was the same. But that would risk everything, so I stayed behind, followed her down one block and then another. I kept hoping she wouldn't turn around, and then hoping she would.

She didn't. Every time I got close enough that I could smell the smoke of her cigarette, I dropped away a little. I kept thinking she'd see me in one of the million windows, a reflection of a shadow, a movement, something. If she did, she didn't notice.

Her dress shimmered lightly with her movements, showing off her curves. She should have looked utterly out of place here in her shiny dress and her high heels, and yet she didn't. She pulled it off with such absolute confidence that you almost wouldn't notice her if you walked by her.

Walking behind her, I noticed her, of course. Her stockings were also made of something that shimmered with every step, and I kept feeling my eyes drawn downwards, towards the muscles of her calves, and then up to that dark place between her thighs that you couldn't quite see but could almost imagine.

I'm a stalker, I thought. Not just a stalker, but a pervert. The thought almost made me laugh out loud.

Seriously, what was I doing here? Clearly she was just going to keep walking for ever. I needed to either talk to her or give up and stop stalking her.

What would Nancy Drew do? I thought. Well, clearly Miss Drew would never stalk a hot chick with an amazing voice just because she'd kissed her and had a keyhole tattooed in the hollow of her throat. Or would she?

Half a dozen blocks away from the bar she finally turned into a little alleyway. I gave her a couple of seconds and then followed her. The alley was tiny and unremarkable. Business garbage cans and compost bins sat on one side. A couple of fire escapes. Some white graffiti that was light enough and big enough to be seen in the dim light.

And her. Or the silhouette of her. Standing sideways, lifting her shadow hand to knock at a door. I could only guess it was a door. From where I was standing, it just looked like part of the wall. She knocked twice, two solid raps that I could feel in my teeth. She looked around, a gesture that sent my heart up into my throat – surely she would see me, surely she would scream or come running or something else. I waited, motionless, still as a scared rabbit. As if my stillness would give me an invisibility cloak.

Either she didn't see me, which seemed utterly impossible, or she saw me and didn't care.

One second she was there, looking around, and the next there was a beam of light that seemed to scan her face and neck.

Then she was gone. Not even her shadow form remained.

After waiting a couple of seconds, I stepped forward through the empty alley until I was in front of the place where she had knocked. From this viewpoint, it was clearly a door. There was no handle or hinges, but it was edged apart from the rest of the bricks by clear lines. I ran my fingers over it very lightly. The cracks felt warmer than the rest, as though whatever was inside was heated.

I pulled out my cell phone and turned on the flashlight feature, lighting up the door. It was nothing remarkable in any way. Except for a barely-there image in a black chalk that looked like it had been drawn a hundred years ago and rained away a hundred more times.

A keyhole. Just like the one on the woman's neck. Just like the one on Davian's paper.

This was the second confusing door I'd stood in front of in the past few hours.

I should call someone, I thought.

If I was going in here – and even as I considered it, I realised that I was, that I'd already made a decision – then I was dumb to do it alone. But I didn't know who to call.

I raised my hand and knocked twice on the brick door. A tiny hatch opened inside the door, and a thin stream of light shone out.

'Key,' a feminine voice said from the other side.

I caught a glimpse of two green eyes inside the door. The light scanned my face and neck. I realised it was looking for a tattoo. A tattoo that I didn't have.

* * *

After having two doors closed in my face on the same night, I was ready to call it quits. Everything had unravelled. Kyle and I were … somewhere. Kyle was somewhere. I'd botched my job, if you could call it that, of talking to Kitty. I hadn't found anything out about Davian's book. I'd gone rogue and hadn't learned anything new. Worse, I hadn't even gotten in the door.

At home, I did what I always do when I'm stressed and nervous. I slept, I cleaned the house – which needed it – I cleaned myself – which also needed it – and then I hunkered down on the couch with a pile of books and a handful of chips.

Sometimes thinking is like seeing things from the corner of your eye. If you think too hard about something, the solution escapes you. But if you think about other things, sometimes the thought police lighten up and let things slip through.

Unfortunately, my pile of to-read books at the moment was 90 per cent erotic, which meant that shutting off my brain, at least when it came to the dark and mysterious Davian Cavanaugh and what was happening with Kyle and me, and what had happened at the Cat House, was harder than it seemed. Every book I picked up reminded me of something Davian-ish or Kyle-ish. And yet I couldn't stop reading.

The man in the first novel threw the girl over his knees in her little skirt for a perfect spanking. Another had a whole scene about being bound by rope and leather that put the scent of saddle soap in my nose. Another told the tale of two women who had the hots for each other, but couldn't do anything about it other than lust from afar. Every single plot twist and turn reminded me of something from my own life. I couldn't put them down. The more I read, the more I saw Davian in everything. His hands. The way his eyes had flared to a golden cream right before he'd leaned in to kiss me. How much I wanted to run my hands over his hips, his thighs. To unzip him right there in my office and finally, finally introduce myself to his cock.

Masochist, I muttered at myself when I finally stopped reading. My clit was singing a maddening song of want, and I pushed both hands between my thighs, edging my thumbs along the tender nub. Despite all the sexuality in my life lately, the poor thing clearly felt neglected; as soon as I touched it, it responded with a pulse of pleasure that I could feel all the way down to my toes.

Maybe if I daydreamed like this for a while, an answer would come to me. I slipped my yoga pants down so I could spread my legs, then let my fingers slowly circle the pulsing bead of my clit. Heat rose in my pelvis and spread across the top of my chest.

Mind, go wander, I urged. Do something. Please.

Of course, what it wandered to was Davian. We'd only kissed once in real life and that wasn't much to build a fantasy on. But I'd seen enough of him dressed, I'd touched him enough to know that I wanted more. What if he came into Leather Bound and kissed me again? I'd let him. I'd beg him. I'd be the little slut that I was, that I wanted to be, for him. I wanted to undo those perfectly fitting jeans, unbutton his shirt one slow button at a time. I wanted that mouth on me, not just on my mouth, but other places too. The side of my neck, on my nipples, between my thighs.

I tweaked and tugged at a nipple, matching the rhythm of my fingers on my clit. I could already tell this orgasm was going to be fast and hard; if I didn't slow down, I was going to come before I could even give my brain some down time.

But my body was demanding. It wanted release and it wanted it now. Yesterday, even, if I could have made that happen.

I slid two fingers inside me, angling my thumb so its stroke was perfectly centred over my clit. I imagined my mouth full of Davian's cock, his length stroking slowly along the flat of my tongue while I fucked myself with my fingers. His fist in my hair, pulling me over him, faster, harder, nearly making me choke, making me groan around the hot pulse of him.

'Come for me,' he said in my head, and I did, arching up off the couch, my body convulsing and shuddering. Pleasure rolled through me, quick and hard, and then, suddenly, I was warm and glowy. And not more than a little tired. I collapsed back on the couch, my fingers soaked with my own pleasure, my stack of books tumbled around my feet.

'You are smart and driven,' I told myself. 'You will figure this out. Ideally without fucking your potential client, but you know what, if it comes down to that, I'm probably OK with it in the end.'

It wasn't the solution I'd been hoping for, not by a long shot. But at least I felt like I had a fuzzy plan. And my orgasm-happy body told me that was more than enough for now, so just shut up and enjoy the buzz. Which I did. I had a feeling it was going to be my last one for a long while.

CHAPTER 9

As it turned out, that wasn't true. I woke on Wednesday morning from a dream so hot and gripping that my body was still shaking when I tried to drag myself from bed.

I'd been up on stage at the Cat House, all by myself. But I could see Davian in the front row. And Kyle too. And Kitty. And the men who'd been on stage, who were somehow now entwined with the door guy. They were all waiting for me, watching me.

I was touching myself, as though hypnotised. I could hear a voice in my head, telling me what to do next, and it was as though I'd had to obey. I hadn't wanted to, or at least I didn't think that I did. But every time I followed instructions, my body rewarded me with a shot of pleasure. It was like Simon Says for sexy grownups. I hadn't come in the dream, I didn't think, but as soon as I'd woken, I'd touched the swollen, wet nub between my legs and had gotten off. Fast. Hard. Wet.

Now shaky. My legs refused to hold me, giving me grief until I was out of the shower, and rushing to get dressed.

There was a message on my cell from Kyle, saying that everything was fine, no need to call and he'd get in touch with me in a couple of days. That seemed odd, but he really did sound fine. Happy, in fact. I certainly wasn't going to call him when he'd all but asked me not to; no way was I going to rub salt in a wound that seemed like it was beginning to close.

I'd never been happier to head to work. I needed the comfort of books around me. I needed to see all of those stories that were told, and know that I was just one of many. My favourite heroines regularly screwed up their lives; in fact, wasn't it required that they do so? Maybe being surrounded by their stories would make me feel a little less stupid about my own.

I walked to Leather Bound, prepping myself for a day of setting things right.

Only to find Lily crying in my office.

Worse yet, she looked like me. By which I mean dishevelled. A simple dress, her red hair pulled back in a loose bun, hardly any make-up. I even thought I saw a chip in her orange-hued nails.

My first thought was that the rent situation had got worse.

'Lil?' I said. 'What's going on?'

'Nothing,' she sobbed.

'Even if you weren't crying, I wouldn't believe you,' I said. 'In all the years I've known you, never once have I seen you wear the same polish colour more than two days in a row, and I've certainly never seen it with a chip.'

I took her hand and flipped it around to show her the big missing chunk out of her thumbnail. 'So spill.'

'Just girl trouble,' she said. 'As usual.'

'Who do I need to beat up?' I asked. 'Is it the hot motorcycle chick?'

She brought a hand to her mouth and bit her thumbnail.

140

A second later, her face seemed to echo the shock that I felt. Quickly, she dropped her hand into her lap.

'Oy vey,' she said. 'I haven't bitten my nails since I was six.'

It was a funny little glimpse into Lily, into who she'd been long before we'd known each other. She was always so poised and polished that I'd assumed she was like that even as a child. But maybe that wasn't true after all.

'What's going on?' I said.

She shook her head. Tears glistened at the corners of her eyes, but her gaze was steady on mine, a kind of plea not to push her. Fair enough. I certainly wasn't going to make Lily cry, not if I could help it. Good gods, one pile of trouble onto another.

'You know I love you and I'm here for you, right?'

She nodded again, and this time a single tear did spill, rolling down the side of her nose in a perfect straight line.

'And how is it that you even cry perfectly?' I asked.

'I'm not crying,' she said, laughing a little, even as she wiped the trail of liquid from the side of her nose.

'Uh-huh,' I said.

She brought her hand to her mouth again, looked at it and then put it back down in her lap.

'Girls suck,' she said.

'Agreed,' I said. 'So how about I regale you with tales of my very crazy night with my ex-lover, never-going-to-be-fiancé, a woman named Kitty and the job I might have lost us?'

She perked, if only slightly. 'Yes, please.'

I told her everything.

'Kitty?' she said after I was done. Leave it to her to skip right over the secret club, the Smaug-like bouncer and the fact that Kyle was on stage licking a woman's clit, and focus on the woman's name.

141

'And that, Lily, is why I love you,' I said.

'I know, right? I mean, why don't women read books? Scarlett O'Hairy at the Taratopolis, for God's sake, is a perfect name for a sex show.'

'Hester Prim,' I said.

'And the Propers!' she added.

I groaned at that one but, as we kept going, I was appreciative of the banter, the kind we used to do a lot. I hadn't even realised I'd missed it, and the exchange left me feeling lighter and far less stressed. It was obviously making Lily feel better too, because she was smiling and laughing, coming up with names left and right.

Whatever was wrong with her hadn't been set right, that much was clear, but it was lessened a little. Sometimes it seems like the best thing we can do for our friends is alleviate their burdens if we can. I tried not to be a bad friend, but I knew that we'd grown distant of late. I wasn't going to let that happen again.

When a customer came in, Lily walked out with a little bounce in her step, which made me happy. And made me realise I'd totally forgotten to ask about the rent situation.

* * *

When I came back from a quick lunch, Davian was waiting for me at the store.

He was leaning against the big window, playing with Webster through the glass. Web would put one big paw wherever Davian's finger traced, following the movement. Dressed in a dark-grey pea coat with a chocolate-brown scarf wrapped around his neck, his dark curls lightly tousled by the wind, Davian was the most edible thing I'd seen in a long time.

He caught my arrival in the window reflection and watched me walk towards him, his fingers still tracing the glass for Webster's amusement.

'Could you stand out here and do that for a few hours every day?' I asked. 'He could stand to lose a little weight.'

'He seems like he's in fine shape to me,' he said. But his eyes were on me, rising from my black boots up my dark stockings and short skirt all the way to my face. 'We, however, are not. I heard that the Cat House was a disaster.'

I sighed. So much for just getting to stand here and drool over this chocolately man. I should have known it wouldn't be that easy.

'Come in and we'll talk about it?' I said.

He nodded, then watched me silently while I opened the front door.

'Make yourself at home,' I said. 'I just need to check in with Lily.'

I made sure Lily had everything under control, which she did and then some, and then I went and found Davian. He was draped over a chair in the velvet section, flipping through a copy of an erotic art book. The page was open at a collection of hand-carved stone dildos. Webster was curled up in his lap.

'Well, you do make yourself at home,' I said. 'The only thing missing is a naked woman resting at your feet.'

'I'm sure you could find a way to make that happen,' he said. His tone was light, but the way he was looking at me added far more meaning to his words. I was suddenly aware that I was in a tiny room with a gorgeously hot man and shelf upon shelf full of books about sex.

The sexual tension in the room was so strong it almost made me want to talk about how I'd screwed up at the Cat House. Almost.

'So, what do I need to do?' I asked.

'Well, first you strip naked,' he said.

'I mean about what happened at the Cat House. I'm really sorry for how that turned out. I'm also sorry for doubting you. I don't think I actually believed you about the sex club. I thought I knew everything about this part of town.'

Davian closed the book and set it on the table next to the chair. Webster shifted on his lap with a small meow of protest.

'I don't know that you can fix it,' Davian said. 'You didn't just fail the initiation, you made something of a ruckus. If anyone in that room didn't notice you, they were utterly blind.'

'I'm sorry,' I said. My cheeks went hot and pink, and I lowered my head, trying to hide my reaction. 'I didn't realise that she'd want me to go on stage. I have –'

'Stage fright?'

'No.' I fumbled for words. How to describe what was happening to me when I thought of being in front of people, especially in a sexual context? Sure, it was part fear, but it was something else as well. Something about my introverted self, about being seen. There was something about the danger that I both shied away from and, inexplicably, craved. I didn't have the words to explain it, so I just shook my head.

'Either way,' he said. 'It doesn't matter. What's done is done.'

He stroked Webster's head while he talked, the soft space between the cat's ears, and then under his chin, until Webster was purring so loudly the sound seemed to fill the whole room. I knew the feeling; I ached for Davian to touch me like that, to stroke me until I responded with audible sounds of pure pleasure.

'I can try again,' I said. 'I'll say yes next time.'

144

'There is no next time,' he said. 'Kitty chose you and you refused in front of everyone. That's the only way into the club.'

'I'll find another way,' I said. I was about to tell him about the blonde woman and the door, but realised I hadn't found a way into that either.

I wasn't sure why I was fighting so hard for this. Yes, we needed the money, but it was more than that. Something inside me needed this. And I was starting to think that something inside me needed Davian.

I knelt at his feet, realising too late that I was creating the picture that I'd had in my mind when I'd walked in. Minus the naked part. He clearly caught it too, tilting his head to watch me go down.

'Help me,' I said. 'Help me do this.'

He lifted his hand from Webster's chin, slipped it under my own. The pads of his fingers pushed upward, bringing my chin up so that our gazes met. The heat of his fingers made my insides warm and melty. I really was like chocolate in his warm hands.

'Why?' he asked.

'I ... don't know. It feels like something I should do.' There was no way to explain it more clearly than that.

The pause between us was long and filled with heat. Sexual, and something else. I could feel things trembling on the edge of whatever thin line was between us. If they went one way, this job, this opportunity, this man would be gone from my life, tumbling over a cliff too steep for me to follow. If they went the other way, I wouldn't be any less in danger, but at least we would all go over the edge together.

'There is an event coming up,' he said. 'We might be able

to get you in as a guest. But you'd have to practise. And really be willing to go all the way.'

I felt a million questions rise in me, but I didn't trust my tongue to work properly. It felt alive and bee-stung. My heart did a silly half-beat of joy and fear in my chest. I took a deep breath, the scent of him filling my nose. It was heady, the warm cinnamon and dark wood that rolled off his skin. Someday, when this was all over, I'd find a candle that smelled like him, and I'd hoard it the way that old single people hoarded cats. Or, well, the way that I already hoarded books.

In the meantime, I had to get over my fear. He knew it. I knew it. I flipped my mental rolodex for a female character to use as inspiration, but found myself coming up empty. Either I didn't read enough erotica or the heroines weren't particularly memorable. I'd have to do this on my own.

'We can practise here,' I said. 'After we close.'

'No,' he said. 'You can't practise getting naked and ...' He leaned in, trailing two fingers along the top of my thigh, right at the spot that made me shiver. His fingers lingered there, pressing softly, easing inward. My thighs parted instinctively to his touch. '... letting me do this in front of people if there aren't any people.'

'Yes,' I said, as much to his touch as to his words.

'So,' he said.

'So,' I said. He was waiting for something from me, but his fingers, promising, teasing, were edging under my short skirt, slipping slowly along the heat of my inner thigh. I didn't push myself into his touch, although part of me wanted to. I closed my eyes and stayed still, waiting to see if his fingers would deliver on their promise of pleasure.

They stopped just short of the laced edge of my stockings.

He tugged some of the fabric sideways, a minuscule movement, the slightest shift, but I felt it all the way to my teeth. My pussy tightened in want, and a groan – desire, a lament for what I didn't already have – slipped from my mouth.

'Janine,' he said. Firm but distant. Like his fingers.

'Hmm?'

'No more until we get public.'

'But ... but it feels so good.'

'Janine.' Firmer. His fingers leaving me. Another groan.

I opened my eyes at him. He had his mostly serious face on. Mouth set, his gaze firm on my face. Sometimes, I was learning, I could sway him my way. Distract him, tease him, get him to put his other plans aside to fuck me. But not this time. And, oh, how I wanted what he was offering. Yes, even if it meant something public. Even if the thought of the word made my heart hammer in my chest.

'Fine,' I said. 'Yes. But let's do it now.' Before I change my mind, I wanted to say. Now, while my clit was still beating its sweet little pulse of want.

'I know just the place,' he said. 'Get your coat.'

With my heart beating its song of want in my chest and my clit doing the same between my legs, what could I do but say yes?

* * *

'I can't,' I said. 'The store...'

'Lily has it under control,' he said. 'She's good like that.'

As if in a trance, I got my coat. As Davian and I walked out, I felt nothing but the presence of his body next to me and the wet heat between my thighs that seemed to intensify with every step.

I watched him walking next to me, that long confident stride, hands tucked loosely into the pockets of his wool coat. He cast his gaze sideways, caught my eye. His brow arched slightly, but he didn't say anything.

I stopped looking at him and started looking at where we were. The big black and purple building stood in front of us, its window displays filled with curvy mannequins in leather outfits, whips and toys in their moulded hands. Everything became real in that second.

'L&L?' I asked. 'Oh, no. No. No. No.'

His eyes narrowed just a little at my response, and then he started laughing.

'What's so damn funny?' I tried to inch backwards from the front of the building, as though he wouldn't notice when I suddenly broke into a frantic, fearful run in the other direction. Fight or flight, baby. I was a flighter all the way.

'Nothing at all,' he said. 'I should have known you'd know this place. Little voyeur like you.'

He caught the ends of my hair in his fist, held me captive. It wasn't just his grip in my hair that held me in place. It was the drop in his voice, that deep confidence that slid in, a timbre that seemed to vibrate at the same speed as my arousal. His golden eyes scanned my face, a quirk of a smile crossing his lips.

'I should have known you'd like to watch,' he murmured, his voice low. 'You like being all safe in the dark, while everybody undresses for you, sitting there touching yourself. You get off on that, don't you?'

Was that a question I was supposed to answer? It seemed so obvious that it didn't require a response. Not to mention that with him talking to me like that, I could barely think of what I was supposed to say, much less make my mouth do the thing it needed to do to form words.

He tugged my hair, pulling my head back to force a gasp from my lips.

'Well? Yes or no?'

'Yes,' I said, not even entirely sure what I was saying yes to.

'Yes, what?' he asked. 'What do you do to get off, Janine?'

I knew what he wanted me to say, and I remembered the thrill of saying it in my dream, of voicing my secret desires into his ear. It had been a revelation to me, how hot it was to say the words, and to watch Davian react to them.

But it wasn't a dream this time. We were in public, standing on the street, Davian looming over me, leaning in. He still had his fist tight in my hair, tilting my head back so that I could only look up at him, at his face. I had the sense that people were near, walking by us on their way to far less deviant things, but I couldn't see them. I could only see the dark spark in his gaze, the edges of his teeth, as he asked me again.

'I ...' I couldn't do this. I couldn't stand here in public and say what he wanted me to say. I couldn't get naked in front of strangers. No matter how much I wanted him – and oh, fuck, I didn't know that I'd ever wanted anything more – I couldn't bring myself to do it. 'I'm sorry. I can't.'

He didn't change his stance or his expression. His grip on my hair relaxed slightly, allowing me control of my head. I dropped my gaze to the ground, the prickled heat of my cheeks making me feel like I'd been crying.

'Janine.' I heard him say my name, but I didn't look up. Why was it always so easy for me to say no, even to the things I really wanted? Now I did feel tears threatening, their stinging arrival at the corners of my eyes. I blinked them back, refusing to give in.

When he leaned in this time, he came at me soft, as though he'd loosened his body to mould around mine. His mouth found the corner of my ear. As he brushed his lips along my skin, he talked to me.

'You can absolutely say no at any point. Now. Later. It doesn't change anything if you say no. Not. One. Thing.'

He paused, his lips trailing the edge of my ear, allowing me to think about that for a moment.

'But if you want to, we can do it together, you and me. I'll help you. I promise I will keep you safe. So you get to decide: do you want to do this?'

I tried to breathe, to hear something beyond the thumping of my pulse in my ears. Did I want to do this? Yes. And no.

Actually. Yes. Unequivocally. But I was scared. Of what, I couldn't say exactly.

I grew less afraid the longer we stood there, his breath on my skin, his quiet words bouncing around in my brain. I could say no. And all this fear would go away.

And on the heels of that thought: but so would the arousal. It wasn't just fear that made my pulse thrum under my skin, that tightened my breath at the thought of being in front of people. I did want to do this, and I wanted to do it with Davian. Oddly, I trusted him.

Surprising myself, I turned my head, pulling against his grip in my hair to find his mouth. His lips pressed chilled to mine, but the inside of his mouth was deliciously warm. His teeth caught my tongue, raked them gently. My shiver wasn't due to the cold.

He pulled back, licking my lips in the letting go.

'I guess that's a yes,' he said.

150

CHAPTER 10

I hadn't been to L&L since I'd thought I'd seen Davian here, cutting buttons off a woman's dress while I masturbated furtively in the dark. I wanted to ask if that really was him, or if I'd been imagining him, but I was afraid of the answer. If I was obsessed enough to accidentally fantasise his face onto another man's body, I didn't want him to know about it. The memory of it gave me the shivers, me in the dark, the way he'd bent towards her, dragging his hands along her neck, the weight of the scissors as they'd cut through the threads.

They hadn't fucked, but they hadn't needed to; watching them play had been enough, more than enough, to get me off. What did that mean for me now? Was he going to make me watch him again? Or did he have something else planned?

I couldn't read anything from his face as he led me towards the back, then up a small flight of stairs that I'd never noticed before. Through a red silk curtain, a woman in a black dress was reading behind a small desk. She gave us a courtesy smile, which deepened into something real when she saw Davian. She had the kind of smile that you can see from across the room, straight white teeth and dimples so deep you could sink your fingers into them.

'Well, hello, you,' she said.

They hugged, and I took the chance to check her out. It was a habit I'd got into, mostly keeping an eye open for Lily. I wasn't much of a matchmaker, but she'd been so damn unhappy lately. I kept hoping I'd accidentally run into her perfect woman. It could be at least one good side effect of this entire gig.

The woman hugging Davian – which was odd in itself, as I'd never seen him hug anyone, and was surprised at the relaxed ease with which he moved into her embrace – was almost exactly his height. Long straight black hair fell down her back, almost to her butt. But it was good long hair, the kind that's obviously had care taken of it, and because it matched her dress perfectly it gave her a sleek, otherworldly look.

Pulling back, she shifted her attention to me. Her gaze was a moss green that washed over me slowly before she nodded her approval.

'Want to go in?' she asked Davian. 'Ericka and Troy are just finishing. Should just be a couple of minutes for clean-up.'

Davian caught my eye, a brow lifted in question. Despite myself, I nodded.

'Perfect,' he said. 'That will give us a few minutes to get ready.'

'Room B is all yours.'

He nodded thanks, touching her shoulder softly as we walked by her, down the long hall. I wondered what their history was. Had he cut the buttons off her dress? More? I didn't feel jealous, thinking about him with her, but hot. All of these women, seemingly smart, together, sexual women, trusted him to take them places they couldn't go on their own. Why shouldn't I trust him too?

152

Room B was tiny, a loveseat, a couple of mirrors and a hanging closet full of outfits. One wall was covered with hanging floggers, leather cuffs and other toys. Beneath that, a table held a variety of disinfectants, lubes and condoms. I'd never thought about what happened behind the scenes here. I just assumed couples walked in and entered the centre space in much the same way as I walked in and entered a booth. Clearly, that wasn't the case at all. It was all very organised, and smelled faintly of disinfectant.

'This isn't very sexy, is it?' I asked. I picked up a bottle of toy cleaner and sniffed it.

'I guess not,' he said. 'I suppose we should just call it quits and forget about it.'

It wasn't until I glanced at the mirror that I saw his expression, how the low smoulder of his gaze belied his words. He came forwards, towards me in the mirror, until I could feel the full press of his body against the back of me. The touch was so light that I had to stay incredibly still in order to feel it, but it was there. Warmth and heat, and a firmness that made me tremble. His scent spilled over, erasing everything else. In the mirror, his reversed face was lifted, his caramel gaze so full of want and heat that I was afraid to turn around and look at him full on, afraid that I wouldn't see the same desire in his eyes.

'Point,' I said. The word stuck in my throat, the edges of it, and I tried to swallow away the want that rose and blocked my breath. He backed away, leaving the back of me cold.

'Do you want to change?' he asked.

Change? I hadn't thought about it. I was trying not to think about it at all.

I eyed my outfit in the mirror. 'Should I?'

He didn't even hesitate. 'No,' he said.

153

I heard the sound of a drawer sliding open and turned to look. He was pulling a pair of scissors, what looked like the same pair of scissors, from its depths.

'I have plans for that outfit of yours,' he said.

* * *

Stepping into a room without walls is harder than it seems. Walking into the centre room at L&L reminded me of the one time I'd walked across a transparent glass floor. While other people had been able to just step onto it, peering down at the people walking storeys below, I found myself stuck at the end, unable to take that first step. It was crowded, and I was holding people up, but none of that mattered. I knew in my rational brain that it wasn't any less safe than walking across something that I couldn't see through, but I still couldn't force myself to go forward. In the end, someone had jostled me, and I'd taken that first step by accident, swearing I was going to die even as I landed firmly on solid footing. I stood for a long time, breathing, my heart pounding, incredibly aware that I was still alive. After that, I thought it would get easier, that each step would be a movement towards less fear. That turned out not to be true. Every step was just as scary as the first; if I could have gone back, run to the edge, I would have. But the crowd was shuffling forward, carrying me along with it.

That's how I felt the second I stepped into L&L's centre room. I couldn't see the people on the other sides of the walls, but I knew they were there. Not seeing anything in this case was somehow the exact same as seeing too much had been with the glass floor. My pulse went boom inside my wrists. My head went light and fuzzy, and there were dark shadows at the edges of my vision.

'You're fine,' Davian said, his voice low. 'No one's in there right now. They close the viewings between shows.'

'They do not,' I said. My voice echoed in the mostly empty room, coming back to me with my denial.

He nodded. 'Yes. So they can clean. Take your time. Sit.'

In the middle of the room, a single chair. The same, or same enough, chair as the one I'd watched last time I was here. I ran my finger along the back of it, having a flash of remembrance. Davian in the pool of light. Surely it had been him. Now I was almost certain.

I sat in the chair, feeling its hard coolness against the heat of my body. I was facing the room where I'd sat last time, sat and watched and got off. The thought clenched my thighs, made me utter a single gasp of fear and want. But that was all I had time to do before he deftly slipped a gag into my mouth and tied it firmly at the back of my head.

'Good?' he asked.

Oh, my fuck. I was not good. None of this was good. My pulse was thumping my throat so hard it felt like someone's fingers playing a drumbeat on my neck.

Yet when he knelt in front of me, his hands on my knees, looking up at me, everything stopped. First it slowed and then it stopped completely. Everything went still. Except Davian's eyes. That heated caramel. The promise of his gaze. Safety and danger both. He lowered his face until it was just between my thighs. I could feel the heat of his palms through my stockings, heard him inhale softly as he closed his eyes and breathed me in.

I nodded and shook my head, both. All in one gesture. A totally incoherent response.

'Focus on me,' he said. 'On the sound of my voice. On the touch of my –' he turned his head and kissed the inside of my thigh '– mouth. Focus only on me. Can you do that?'

I nodded, this time a real nod. No denial in it this time. I wanted to do just that. Forget all the people who would be watching. Forget what this was truly about. Focus on his mouth, that beautiful mouth that was planting soft kisses along my skin.

'Good girl,' he said. 'Such a good …' Each time he said good, he followed it with a kiss that climbed higher up my thigh. 'Good.' The hem of my skirt. 'Good.' He pushed it up slightly with his cheek, letting his face rest against me. My body responded each time, a tiny shudder of want sliding through me. 'Good.' Catching a piece of stocking in his teeth, he gave a growled tug. 'Girl.'

My hips arched up involuntarily as he pulled away. If I could have talked, it would have sounded something like *pleasetouchme pleasetouchme pleasepleaseplease* but the refrain was only in my head. And I didn't think it would have mattered; he'd made it clear he was only going to touch me how and when he wanted.

'They're here,' he said.

As if his voice had brought them, I could suddenly imagine all of the people watching. Men, mostly. Couples. Maybe some women like me, women who liked to be in the dark. Hidden. I imagined them settling in, beginning to touch themselves, the lazy slow strokes of a body warming up for pleasure. A pleasure that was based on me, based on watching me sitting in a chair, gagged, about to be exposed. I closed my eyes.

'Open,' Davian said. 'Keep them open. On me.'

With a deep breath, I opened my eyes again. I found Davian in the room, tracked him. Moving slowly, he picked the scissors off the floor, then walked around me, twirling the blades lazily in his hand. In and out of my view, the soft sound of his footsteps marking the unseen orbit of his path. Every once in a while, he'd touch me in passing, an unexpected connection in the brush of fingertips to the back of my neck, the tug of his hand on my hair, his breath along my ear. The people outside faded away with each touch, became less real as my desire rose and blotted them out.

Davian talked as he circled me. 'I've been wanting to cut these stockings off you since I first saw them on you. I'm going to try to go slow. I'm going to try to be very, very patient, but I make no promises.'

I wanted to tell him that I didn't want him to go slow, that I wanted every piece of clothing off me so I could feel him against me, so my skin would stop aching with want, but the words wouldn't come out. I could only make a sound, somewhere between a whine and a groan, muffled and aching with need.

He stopped in front of me. I remembered him from before – clearly it had been him and not some figment of my imagination – the way he'd stayed hidden, out of the light. I thought it had been for show, for mood setting, but I realised that he probably hadn't even noticed how he'd appeared. He was so focused on what was happening between us that it was clear he didn't care about the audience. They were negligible to him. So why do it then? Why fuck in front of people if it didn't get you off? Maybe it was just the way he was able to interact with his partner, to bring her fears to light. I wanted to ask him what the appeal was.

'Stop that.' His hissed voice right at my ear, followed by a nip of his teeth.

My eyes widened involuntarily.

'Stop thinking. You're escaping into that pretty little head of yours. You're smart, Janine. Too smart. Stop using it as an escape. Be here. Now. Or I won't do this. I'll just leave you like this, alone in this room, and everybody out there on the other side of that wall can jack off to you sitting here by yourself.'

He waved the scissors at the walls around us to make his point. It was entirely possible that there was no one out there. But I wasn't willing to take that chance.

I shook my head at him. He wouldn't leave me here, would he? That was more than I could take. Way more.

'Going to stay here with me then?' he asked.

I nodded.

He stopped in front of me and pushed my thighs open so he could kneel between them. With the scissor blades still closed, he dragged them up the inside my thigh, catching my stockings, starting small runs like fires along their surface. Where the fabric broke, I could feel the cool metal of the blades against my skin. He pressed the closed blades against my pussy, pulsing them hard against me in time to my own flickering desire. I ached to push back, to feel their firmness against my clit, but somehow I knew I wasn't supposed to react. At least not externally. That was part of the game we were playing, wasn't it? All the heated want that threatened to spill over inside me, and trying to keep myself in check, trying so very hard to do as he asked.

'Sit very, very still,' he said.

The blades of the scissors slipped open, found their way into one of the holes he'd made in my stocking. The fabric cut so easily, as if it had been made for nothing more than this moment. I watched my leg begin to appear, the skin so pale beneath the black. When he'd cut all the way around the first one, he did the same to the second.

He took hold of the top of one stocking and slowly began to roll it down my leg.

'You have the hottest legs,' he said. 'Everyone out there watching, they've been thinking that since they walked in. They've been just waiting for me to cut these stockings off you, so they can catch a glimpse of your soft, pale skin.'

I shook my head, trying to deny what he was saying, even as I knew it was true. Even as I grew wet thinking about it.

'They think about being me,' he said, his gaze hard on mine as he rolled the second stocking down by feel. I thought he'd take my heels off, pull the stockings from my skin completely, but he left them on, pooled at my feet. Somehow that made me feel more exposed, more vulnerable. The pale length of my legs so naked between the two edges of black.

I tried to clamp my legs shut. Davian's hand was already between my thighs, keeping them apart.

'No,' he said.

He didn't have to say any more. He'd already said it. If I was going to do this, I had to do it fully. On my own. My choice.

I relaxed my thighs, forcing a soft breath between my lips. He ran a couple of fingers down my calf, stroked my ankle through the stocking fabric.

'I was going to bind you with these,' he said. 'Tie you to the chair. But I think that would be too easy. I think you'll just have to keep yourself still for me.'

He put his hands on either side of my skirt and slowly slid the fabric up. Past the black cut edge of my stockings, past the black line of lace that marked my thighs. Exposing me to the world. Or at least the world watching through L&L's one-way glass.

'Now this,' he said, 'is the important part. This is the part where they're going to pay such very close attention to your beautiful pussy.'

He pressed the very ends of the scissors to the seam of my pantyhose. I suppressed the hot shudder that rolled through me, but just barely. Even so, he must have felt it because he waited until it passed. When I was still again, he cut the crotch of the pantyhose in a long slit. I hadn't worn panties, and my pussy flared at the influx of cool air. I was hot where the air was cool, wet where the air was dry.

My gasp felt like it echoed inside the large room. But it was nothing compared to his intake of breath.

'Beautiful,' he said. His voice was gravel and lust. His eyes never left the cleft between my legs. 'Such a beautiful pussy, Janine.'

Suddenly, the roles switched. He was as enamoured of me as I was of him. I swelled with my own power for a moment. Watching his face, I opened my legs wider, exposed a little more of my pussy. I knew it was wet, pulsing, the lips plumping up the way they did when I was aroused.

His gaze rose to meet mine, a warm smoulder of want that forced me to grit my teeth to stay quiet. It was clear that he was working hard to hold himself in check. He had the look of a man who was trying very very hard to behave himself. It was a look that nearly threw me over the edge.

Slowly, I reached down and brought two fingers along the cleft of my pussy. I was wetter than I'd expected, my desire coating my skin so that my movements were slippery, my body spreading easily at my touch.

Davian watched me, that first slow stroke of my fingers up to the point of my clit, a half-circle around the tender bud.

Before I could make another move, his hand snaked out and grabbed my wrist, stilling me. He leaned down, the heat of him looming over me. His breath was tight and harsh, and when he exhaled it was with small groans of want.

I thought he was going to kiss me. I ached for it. That and more. If he let go of my wrist, moved his hand, his fingers would touch me. I wanted to feel them against me, to know what it felt like when he ran his thumb over my clit or slipped a finger into me.

He didn't do any of those things.

'I believe you're getting the hang of this,' he said. 'Do not get out of that chair until you come for everyone who's watching you. Do not close your eyes. Do not close your legs. I want to see you fuck yourself to orgasm so that all these men and women watching come from the sight of you.'

And then he let go of my wrist and walked out of the room.

* * *

Despite the fact that he'd given me specific instructions, I didn't know what I was supposed to do. I was sitting in a chair, exposed, by myself. I'd just touched myself in front of a bunch of strangers. Davian had walked out on me, telling me to keep going. By myself. That wasn't part of the deal. Was it?

I could just leave. Get up and walk out. Concede defeat.

But I'd asked for a second chance. Not only had Davian given me one, he'd offered to help me make it work.

If this was a test, I wasn't going to fail this one, damn it.

I closed my eyes. And then opened them. That was part of the test too, wasn't it? What had he said? Don't close your eyes. Don't close your legs.

I couldn't hide. Not even behind my own eyelids.

I wouldn't think of the people behind the windows.

161

Spreading my legs slightly wider, I swirled my finger around the point of my clit. It was still pulsing and greedy from Davian's work, taking as much pressure as I would give it and asking for more. I imagined that it was Davian touching me, finally, finally. That he was on his knees in front of me, spreading me with his fingers, dipping the point of his tongue between my folds.

In my mind, he slid a finger inside me, then another, his mouth suckling at my clit while his fingers curled into my g-spot. I wanted him to thrust into me like that, a perfect mimicking of what he'd be like with his cock inside me. Images of his cock – which I hadn't seen yet, but oh, God, I wanted to, so very much – made my mouth water.

And among those faces in my mind, pleasured, orgasmic, I saw Davian's. Could he see me too? Was he even now standing somewhere against a one-way window, breathing hard, watching intently? Was he stroking himself?

Fuck the other people watching. I'd give them a show if that's what they wanted. I'd give Davian a show, because that's what *I* wanted.

I needed both hands. I spread my legs to give myself more access. One set of fingers worked my clit, the other curled tight into my g-spot, thumbing the tender circle with a rhythm that pulled moans from low in my throat. I wanted Davian everywhere. His cock buried deep in my throat. His tongue in my pussy. His fingers nudging the tight circle of my ass.

My orgasm toyed around the edges of my pleasure, prom-ising, teasing. I shifted in the chair, straining for leverage, trying to find the movements that would get me off.

I groaned aloud as my fingers found that perfect rhythm, as I imagined all the things I wanted Davian to do to me. As I imagined all the people watching, stroking their cocks, sucking each other off, kissing and biting and grinding their bodies together. I pictured Davian watching me with that caramel gaze, stroking his cock, bringing himself to orgasm at the sight of me masturbating.

My orgasm hit me fast and fierce, hard enough that the chair scraped along the floor. I cried out, something that would have sounded like Davian's name if I hadn't bitten my lip at the last moment, turning it into a wordless cry of pleasure. A second orgasm, small but fierce, shuddered up my body, until I slumped on the chair, breathing hard.

My body felt limp and wracked, my stockings were pooled around my calves, who knew how many people had just watched me fuck myself to orgasm. But all I could think about was Davian, and whether he'd seen what I had done.

* * *

Somewhere in the back of my brain, I heard the sound of a door closing. A sound from the outside world.

Blinking, I came back to reality fast and hard.

Davian aside, I'd just masturbated myself to orgasm in front of all these people. Oh, my God. My face flushed hot. I touched my cheek, realised my hands were still wet with my own arousal and then rubbed my fingers over the fabric of my skirt to dry them.

How did one elegantly leave a room where one had just brought herself to orgasm and was now sitting with her pussy wide open and her stockings sliced off her and the man who'd turned her on nowhere to be found?

I had no idea but I certainly did not leave the room with any sort of elegance or decorum. I just ran.

I bumped smack into Davian, who was standing outside

the door, his arms crossed, looking both bemused and something that I couldn't quite read. I had no idea if he'd just seen my ... performance ... and I wasn't sure I cared. Now that my orgasm was over, I just felt freaked out. And a little dumb. And scared out of my mind. Don't forget scared out of my mind.

'Come with me,' he said.

He took my hand, first surprise, and then led me back to the dressing room where we'd started this whole venture. He shut the door and flipped the lock with one hand.

'Fuck,' he said. 'This isn't supposed to be happening.' He tugged a hand through his curls, and my clit did a little pitter-patter of want.

'Which part?' I said. 'The part where I'm getting off in front of a bunch of strangers or the part where you abandon me in the midst of it?'

I sounded angrier than I actually was. I was shaking, my teeth clacking together. Part post-orgasm, part panic, part that thing I always felt when I was around Davian. Some force greater than me, pushing me in a million directions.

He crossed the room in a movement that seemed to take less than a single stride, closing in on me. I stepped back to get out of his way, but he stopped me with his hands on my shoulders.

'The part where I'm falling in lust with you,' he said. 'That part is not supposed to happen. But fuck, Janine. You're just...'

He held me at arm's length, his gaze raking over me so hard I thought I could feel it. 'So fucking hot. All curvy and warm, and you smell like caramelised butter and I just fucking want to lick you all over.'

'Which is ...' He pulled away, stepped away, did the hair

thing again that always sent my insides flip-flopping. The lack of his touch so suddenly left me feeling dizzy, breathless.

'Which is not supposed to happen.'

I didn't know what to say. I wanted to tell him to stop talking, to get over here and shut up and kiss me, please, for the love of all things, kiss me, but whatever he was working out in his brain was his to work out. Why I was off limits to him I didn't know. But I understood the struggle. Hadn't I been having it myself, although for different reasons? How many times had I reminded myself that he was my client, that I needed to keep things professional?

'I'm going to need some clothes,' I said.

With a sudden growl, he turned and came at me, moving fast. His mouth opened on mine before I could get another word out, his tongue finding the heat of me. I met him before I could think, groaning against the press of his lips.

He kissed so well, the kind of play that forced my body to arch against him, seeking other points of heat. His teeth tugged at my bottom lip, sucking so hard I felt pain bloom, followed by a sharp pleasure.

I couldn't resist anything. I needed more, more, more. Ideally now. My hands slipped along the muscles of his hips, up the width of his lower back, urging him harder against me.

He complied, his body melding to mine, the hardening length of his cock pushing into me. I wiggled against him, my body doing everything it could to get as much of him as possible. A voiceless begging.

The kiss broke, leaving us both panting harshly. He dropped his mouth to the side of my neck, kissing along it, leaving little fires on my skin every place his lips touched.

'Janine,' he said, a near growl, his fingers digging into my hair to tilt my neck farther. His free hand reached back under my skirt and through my sliced panties to find the swollen and exposed pulse of my clit. His touch was light but perfect, a half-circle that dragged over the pleasure point in just the right rhythm. 'I want you,' he said.

I had words, but I couldn't find them in my brain, and my mouth was busy looking for new places to touch, to kiss, to nibble. My hands, however, did the work for me. I curved my fingers around the length of his cock, stroked him firmly through the fabric until I heard his low groan.

'Please,' I said. 'Please let me have this.'

He leaned his hips away from me, granting me access. I made fast work of his belt and jeans, pulling everything down just enough so that I could see the head of his cock. The sight of it made my clit pulse harder against his touch. The beautiful pale curve, the tiny slit that was already wet with arousal. I wanted him on my tongue. My body and brain were insistent that we do it *nownownow*.

I obliged my own desires, sliding the fabric down to release him entirely. A beautiful cock, long and lean, with a slight upward curve that made my g-spot give a silent cry of joy. Released, it bounced lightly, until I captured it with the curve of my hand and stroked its underside.

Davian groaned a couple of syllables that might have been my name, his kisses replaced by a ragged breath as I began a long slow stroke from his base to his tip, stopping just long enough to gather his moisture with my thumb.

'Mmm ...' The noises he was making were almost enough to throw me over the edge by themselves. Never mind that he was arching into my touch, leaning his hips in so his erection glided over the curve of my palm.

'God, Janine.' Every time he spoke, his voice seemed to be driven lower by his lust, and the sound of it made me want him all over again. 'If you keep doing that ... I can't ... I won't ... mmm...'

'Won't what?' I teased, feathering my touch down along the hang of his balls so that he groaned again. I liked having him in my hand, at my mercy, for once.

'I forget,' he said.

'If I do this –' I went down on my knees in front of him, looking up at him with his cock held snugly in one hand '– will you also forget your name?'

'I might,' he said.

I drew my tongue along the underside of his cock, long and slow, tasting as much of him as I could. He tasted clean and sweet, and I coiled my tongue around his head, suckling the moisture from his tip.

'Wait, I need to touch you,' he said. He stretched his hands out to me, but I was beyond his reach, already working to take the full length of him into my mouth. I liked having him this way, having him stuttering over his words, unable to help himself. It was a pleasure unlike any I'd known or expected. I toyed with him, licking and sucking, tugging softly at the soft skin of his balls, feeling every nuanced response, listening to every sound that come from him.

'Janine,' he groaned, his hands loose and soft in my hair. I released my grip on his hips, letting him set the pace, driving his hips forward. I loved the feel of him on my tongue, the way his body started to shake as he got close.

I pulled away, pumping the length of him slowly with my fist.

'I'm going to make you come for me,' I said. 'And there's nothing you can do about it.'

I took him fully into my mouth, savouring the taste and feel of him, letting him fill me. And then I grabbed his hips with both hands, pulling him tight to me, until my face was buried in the feel and scent of his arousal.

'Not like that,' he said.

He pulled away, a long slow tug that I resisted as much as I could. I didn't want him to leave me, I wanted to feel him come like that, to know his pleasure.

'Not like that.' He kept saying it even as he pulled me up from my knees, cupped my face in the curve of his palm.

'I want you,' he said. 'I want to be inside you.'

He nipped lightly at my lips, all of his questions for me tied up in his gaze.

'Yes,' I said. 'Yes, please.'

Dragging his fingers lightly between my labia, he sucked in his breath.

'You're so wet,' he said.

I returned the favour, closing my fist around his cock.

'And you're so hard,' I said. 'Please, please, fuck me. Please.'

My 'please's' were running together, my need for him moving beyond language into something far more feral. He reached for a condom out of the bowl on the table, and the sound of the wrapper opening was almost more than I could handle. As well trained as Pavlov's dogs, my body knew what that sound meant. A promise of reward.

He rolled the condom over his cock, gifting me with another glimpse of his beautiful curved erection, and then he lifted me up onto the table. My legs opened and went around him, pulling him towards me.

'Yes?' he asked. His question was growl and desire, and the sound was enough to send a slippery shudder up my spine.

By way of answer, I lined my body up with his, using my hand to draw the head of his cock along my folds. When his tip touched me, my clit gave a pulse of near-orgasmic pleasure.

Davian gripped my hips, holding me still, and then he shifted against me. My body was so slick with want that he slid into me faster than either of us expected and suddenly he was buried all the way in, filling me. It was like he pushed the air from me, taking my breath away, until all I could do was say 'oh' in a pleasured sigh.

His first thrust drove into my clit at just the right angle, and I felt the pre-orgasm pressure sweep through me. I'd just brought myself to two orgasms, and yet my body responded as if it had been days, weeks, since I'd come.

'I'm ... oh, God,' I said. I was trying to warn him, but the words were all tangled. 'So fast,' I added, already feeling a little sad at how good it felt and how fast I was going to tumble right over the edge.

Somehow Davian understood my nonsensical sex talk. He shifted, moving the pressure away from my clit, letting me feel the strokes of his cock inside my body, the long, leisurely in and out that both slowed down and heightened my pleasure. Moving forward against me, he captured my wrists in his hands, held me tight against the table.

None of me could move, not even my hips. I was caught in his grip, forced to take only what he would give me.

And oh, gods, he was teasing me. Pulling back as far as he could without actually leaving my body. Sliding in and up so that his tip bumped my g-spot with every stroke. I was begging, barely hearing myself uttering wild pleas of want.

'Faster, please,' I urged, trying to lift my hips and curl my legs, trying to force him to give me what I needed.

'If I go any faster, I'm going to come,' he said.

'Yes,' I said. 'Comecomecome.' My words smashing together like my own needs.

Davian slammed into me, his movements hard and fast, bringing a gasp from us both. My lust, finally getting what it wanted, zoomed into overdrive, sending out an orgasm so fast and sharp that it nearly clanked my teeth together. I felt my head going back and I was powerless to stop it, my pleasure pulling a near-howl of joy from me.

'Beautiful,' Davian said, and then I felt his body tighten in response. He came inside me with a broken groan, the end of it a whisper of my name.

Panting, we rested together for a moment, kissing, our bodies connected at hip and at mouth, his hands still tight around my wrists.

Then I started giggling. I couldn't help it; all that pent-up want and stress and panic and lust came tumbling through me, mixed up with the pleasure of having him inside me.

He didn't join me in laughter, but he grinned at me, his gaze full of pleasure. We slid apart, and I found my footing on the floor, still leaning against the table for support.

'You did good,' he said. 'Out there I mean.'

He paused. 'Well, in here too.'

I felt myself blushing at the jumbled compliment, my face, already warm from the sex, growing impossibly hot. My instinct was to say 'thank you', but that felt weird, so I just stumbled around, fussing with my clothes, trying to turn my stockings into thigh-highs, trying to put on something that was presentable to the outside world.

He dressed too, a movement that was both beautiful and sad. I watched his body disappear from my sight to be covered in cloth.

'Why does that woman know you?' I asked. 'The one who works here.' The sexiest man in the world had just fucked me, and now I was asking about his personal history?

I swear, sometimes I'm the human version of the cat that curiosity killed.

The look he gave me was of such intensity, such wickedness, that my mouth went dry even as the rest of me went wet. Again. I had to resist the urge to gloss my tongue over my lips.

'I work here,' he said.

Nice time for my mouth to stop working.

'I. You. What?' I said.

'Well, here and other places,' he said. His hands were on my shoulders. It felt like being attached to a jumper cable, the sparks that tumbled from him to me and then down through the rest of me. 'I'm a professional dom. No sex, just services.'

'I saw you,' I breathed.

He lifted that single brow in his customary quirk. Embarrassed, afraid he was going to ask for details, I shook my head.

'Never mind,' I said. 'I need to get back to the store.' And I needed to sit down and think about this. A professional dom. That explained so much. The mischievous smile when Lily had mentioned the sex toy store. Why I'd seen him there. Why he was helping me get over my fears of sex in public. It wasn't about me or even us. It wasn't about some super connection between us. It's just what he did for a living.

'I'll walk you,' he said.

We slipped out a side door of L&L that I'd never noticed before. Our walk back to the store was quiet, for the most part. It was chilly out, but I barely paid attention; my insides were all warm and fluttery. Not just from the great sex. And not just from the way Davian being a professional dom turned me on in weird, unexplored ways. But also because

171

I'd bested my demon. When Davian and I went to the next event, I would be all over this. I had this under control. Fuck literary heroines. I was the hero of my own story now.

I said as much when we turned the corner towards Leather Bound.

'I've got this,' I said.

'You do,' he agreed. He kissed me again, a softer, sweeter kiss, seeming to seek something different now that our needs were temporarily sated. When he pulled away he said, 'I'll call my friend and see if she'll take you as her guest.'

'Wait,' I said. A coldness worked its way through me that had nothing to do with the wind that was picking up. 'You're not coming with me?'

He shook his head. 'No, of course not. I thought you understood. You have to do this all on your own.'

On my own. Not with Davian.

'You can do this, Janine.'

He kissed me again, so hard and perfect that my nipples went all tingly.

I kissed him back, meeting his ferocity with my own sudden, insatiable need.

'Yes,' I said, when he pulled back. 'I can do this.'

That was starting to be the story of my life, at least around Davian. Promising things without an inkling of whether I could actually deliver.

CHAPTER 11

My lips were sore for days after. Every time I touched them, and I am not ashamed to admit that I touched them a lot in the days that followed, they bloomed with tiny sensations of bruised pain. I liked it. My body liked it too. The pain was a reminder of Davian, of the things I'd wanted him to do to me, of the way he'd looked when he'd finally pulled away. A ferocity in his eyes as he struggled to get a hold of himself. A look of want that nearly seemed to burn my skin everywhere it landed. The way his voice was husked with desire, even deeper and dark than usual. All of that came back to me every time I touched my lips to anything. A glass. My pillow. My own fingers.

I'd be walking down the street, accidentally bump my hand against my mouth, and it would all come flooding back, making me shudder. I was supposed to be thinking about Leather Bound and money and the book and Kyle, but all I could think about was fucking Davian. How his mouth had felt on my body. How his body had felt on my body. The heft of his cock in my fist, how it had fit so perfectly into my mouth. He'd tasted sweet and spicy all at the same time. I'd wanted to eat him up for ever.

And then when he'd slid inside me, the perfect fit of a lock to a key.

I tried not to think about the upcoming event, or my fear of it.

Everything else was underwater, washed out and hard to hear. Customers had to ask for help twice. Even Lily struggled to get my attention.

'You,' she said finally. I looked up from the book I'd been shelving. The same book I'd been shelving for who knew how long, even though it was still in my hand. 'Into your office,' she said.

I put the book in its spot and followed her.

'What's wrong with you?' she said.

'Wrong?' I said. My hand, as it often did lately, reached up to my mouth, my fingers playing over my lips.

'You're barely here,' she said. 'Is this about Kyle?'

'Kyle? No.' The underwater sensation was leaving, slipping away as Lily held me by the shoulders. I realised I hadn't thought about Kyle in days.

'We have a lot of shit going on here, in case you haven't noticed,' she said. 'In fact, I'm pretty sure you haven't noticed, but I could really use some help.'

'I'm sorry,' I said. 'I just …' I just what? What was wrong with me? I'd never felt like this in lust before. Lust was good and awesome and hot, but it never made me feel like this, as though nothing else really mattered in the grand scheme of things.

'You're falling for Davian, aren't you?' Lily asked.

'No. I've hardly spent any – I mean, we've only – No,' I said finally, but it wasn't with very much conviction. Love wasn't something I had a lot of experience with, but I knew you couldn't fall in love with someone when you'd just met them. Or just had sex with them. Whatever it was that Davian and I were doing.

'Uh-huh,' Lily said.

I shook myself back into focusing. Lily stood in front of me in a green sweater dress that made her skin turn peaches and cream and brought out the notes of emerald in her blue eyes. While I was pretty much a shambles, she was back to her usual put-together self. Clearly, whatever girl trouble had plagued her was in the past.

'You're right,' I said. 'I've had a lot on my mind. Let's powwow while it's slow. Tell me all your news. Life first, then work.'

She hesitated a moment, which was unlike her, and reached down to stroke Webster as he went by. The front window was growing colder as fall moved on, and more and more I found him curled up in the chair behind the velvet curtain or snuggled up in my office chair.

'I met someone new,' she said.

'Really?' My heart did a little leap for her, even though it never ended well when she said things like that. 'Tell me all.'

She grinned at me. Her lipstick was the colour of rich wine and it showed off her eyes. 'Not yet,' she said. 'I don't want to jinx it. And this one is … different.'

'Mmm, I'm intrigued.' I really was. Maybe this one *was* different, if she wasn't telling me all about it. I really hoped so.

'What about you and Kyle?' she asked. 'And Davian? I know I was teasing you, but I'm genuinely curious.'

'I have no idea about either,' I said. 'Kyle's fine. Moving on, I get the impression. Or trying to. Which is, you know, exactly what I want for him.'

So why then was I tearing up a little just saying that? I did want the best for him, and clearly the best for him wasn't

me. Still, it stung a little. I liked his company. I liked him.
But like wasn't enough. He knew that. And now I did too.

'And Mister Caramel Eyes?'

'He does have those eyes, doesn't he? Really, like melty
caramel. I could just –' I shut myself up when I realised I
was gushing. 'You did that on purpose, didn't you?'

'Who, me? Use super secret and totally obvious tactics
to get you to open up to me and spill your guts? Of course
not.' She blew on her apricot nails, rolling her eyes in
self-congratulation.

'Hmph,' I said. 'Jerk.'

'Well, you obviously like him,' she said. 'So please please
tell me you fucked h– Oh, my God, you totally did!'

'How do you always fucking know?' I groused. My stupid
cheeks did their heat thing and I put a hand on one to try
and cool it down.

'I don't, until you give it away,' she said. 'Well, usually
I don't, but this time your eyes did this funny thing. They
got lighter or something as soon as I asked you if you were
fucking him. See? There, they did it again!'

'That's not true,' I said.

'Don't make me get out my mirror so you can witness the
transformation,' she teased.

'No, not the mirror!' I shook my head, still laughing. 'OK,
onto business. Thanks to, as you call him, Mister Caramel
Eyes –,' I couldn't stop grinning as I said that, even though
I tried to keep it in check '– we have enough money to
pay all of Leather Bound's bills this month. If I succeed in
finding this book, we'll have enough to keep us afloat for
some of next month as well. Which brings me to our lovely
landlord and his attempt to drive us out of here. Did you
get a chance to –'

The front door chimed, and Lily grinned at me.

'Let's hope that's some money,' she said.

'Or some good news,' I said.

* * *

It was neither. As if summoned by our conversation, our newest walk-in was our landlord.

I'd only ever seen him once or twice before, and only to deal with Conrad's passing and our lease changing hands. He'd introduced himself to me as Mister Montgomery, which was probably why it took me a while to remember his first name, Wes.

From what little I knew about him, he seemed the strong, silent type, the kind who didn't feel the need to say a damn thing because his presence said it all. But, like lots of guys like that, he was so fucking sexy and over-the-top in his attitude that you were never sure if he was an asshole or a complete sex machine that you needed to have right now. Mostly, I got the impression that he was the former.

It was part presence, the way he held a room and a gaze. It was also part physical. Wide shoulders and chest that snugged perfectly inside his long-sleeved button-down. Stormy eyes that went green or pewter depending on the light. Short brown hair swept back off his sharp cheekbones. A little dusting of a goatee. Hot and mean, all rolled up in a little ball of attitude.

Personally, I was torn between wanting to suck on the muscles at the side of his neck and punching him in his pouty mouth.

Which is probably why Lily took the lead.

'Mister Montgomery,' she cooed. Lily can really turn on

the charm when she's up against the wall. Sometimes it makes me laugh, but mostly I'm grateful for her people skills. 'We weren't expecting you. I thought you and I were meeting tomorrow.'

Wes was looking around the place like he owned it – which I guess, if you wanted to get technical, he did. Disdain in the curl of his lip. His fingers dragging over the spines of the books. Funny how two people can make the exact same gesture and one makes you dream of his running his fingers over part of you, while the other makes you want to slap his hands off your possessions.

'Lily, no one ever expects me,' he said, in utter seriousness.

I concentrated very hard on biting my cheek so that I wouldn't break out in laughter. Clearly, he thought he was a superhero. Wes Montgomery, Superman's nemesis. Imagining him in a pair of black and silver underoos and a yellow cloak actually made him so much easier to bear.

I glanced at Lily with my what-the-fuck gaze, but she was focused fully on Wes. If I didn't know her better, I'd say she was eating him up. God, she was good.

He was walking through the aisles, Lily trailing him. I stayed where I was; I could see them clearly and being this far away meant I wasn't going to try and clock him in the face with a book. I didn't want to do that. Not only would it bode poorly for Leather Bound's future, I liked my books too much.

'Those picture windows are too gorgeous to be wasted with something like books,' he said, clearly raising his voice to be heard by us both.

OK, now I *was* going to punch him. I took a step forward, but Lily caught my eye and shook her head, once. I stopped where I was, listening. My feet itched, trying to behave.

Lily went up to him and trailed one hand along the shelf near him, eyeing him carefully. To most people, her expression was coy and fully interested, maybe even a little flirty. But I knew her well enough to know she was listening carefully, trying to dissect the situation. 'Were you hoping to talk about the rent situation now instead of tomorrow, Mister Montgomery?'

Without answering her, Wes continued to walk around the store, sizing everything up. My office door was closed and, from his lack of interest in that area, I guessed he didn't know it existed. Which made me happy for reasons I couldn't explain.

He did duck his head behind the velvet curtain, but it seemed perfunctory compared to the rest of his inspection. It was as though he was looking for something, but I didn't know what. A reason to shut us down, maybe, so he could lease the place to someone who would pay more.

The only time he talked was when Lily tried to go off and do something else, and then he would call her back, acting like he needed something, when of course he just wanted her at his side, following him like a puppy dog.

After a while, he ended up back at the front of the store, in front of the register, where I'd been not so coyly watching the two of them.

'It's never about the money,' he said as though he was picking up a conversation that had happened just seconds ago, instead of nearly an hour. He turned towards Lily. With hardly a pause, he reached out and put one hand lightly on the back of her neck. It was an intimate gesture, far too much so for their posture. I saw Lily's spine straighten as she worked hard not to react. Then her hand came up slowly to take his wrist and move his palm away from her neck.

'What *is* it about, Mister Montgomery?' she asked. Her voice was lightly clipped, sharp, but not so sharp that it was offensive.

'Power,' he said. For the first time he looked past Lily and caught my eye. His expression was sharp, his lids narrowed as he watched me through them. I worked hard to keep my face impassive, trying to prepare myself for whatever he might say next.

Of course, with someone like Wes, it's impossible to predict what's going to come out of his mouth.

'I'll have this store, and everything in it,' he said.

Then he turned on his heel, a gesture so full of grandeur and self-importance that I would have fallen over laughing if I didn't feel so shell-shocked. When he walked out of the store, the chime gave a single short ding of good riddance.

'What the hell was that?' Lily asked.

I was still staring out the window, watching him walk away.

'I don't know,' I said. 'But I think it's time to skip the talk with our landlord and talk with our lawyer instead.'

'Done,' Lily said. 'That man is just so over the top.'

'If he was a villain in a novel, he'd be one of those ones who stood around telling everyone how he was going to rule the world,' I said. 'And then I'd send a book flying at his head and it would hit him right in the nose, and he'd get a concussion and when he woke up he'd be the nicest guy and he'd go around righting all his wrongs.'

Lily looked at me. 'And I thought I read too much,' she said.

'Seriously.'

CHAPTER 12

I hadn't heard from Davian since our rendezvous at L&L. It was odd how much time I spent thinking about him, a man I barely knew. Not just his body, although the image of him naked, my hands running over his chest, his mouth against mine, was never far from my mind.

But also the mystery of him; he kept so much hidden inside, and there was part of me that wanted to keep it like that for ever and part of me that wanted to see if I could crack him open, get a glimpse of what shone inside his tough shell exterior.

Trying not to think too much about him meant I filled my time by researching the hell out of the Keyhole Club.

Not surprisingly, I found very little. A few archaic references to a Freemason-type club way back in the '30s, where the men and women met in the basements of local businesses to conduct sexy parties and have orgies. It sounded a little like what I knew of the Keyhole Club, but there was nothing else to tie the two clubs together. Clearly, whoever wanted the club kept secret had done a good job it, although I had no idea how that was even possible in this day and age.

I needed to know more. I was no closer to finding this

book than I'd been when Davian walked in the door on that first day. But I had an idea. A dumb idea, but an idea nonetheless. I was going to get inside that door if it killed me.

Lily said she was staying late at the store to organise some books – something she did once a month or so. I think it was her way of blowing off steam. So when Leather Bound closed for the night, I left her to her book sorting and headed to the one place I really didn't want to go: Kyle's tattoo shop. If I was going to get into the club, then clearly I needed the right tattoo.

Stupidly, I'd worn little more than a wool dress, and it was pouring. As if even the world was trying to tell me this was the stupidest idea. Which maybe it was. But that had never stopped me before. I supposed I wouldn't let it stop me now.

By the time I stepped into kInked, I was steaming and soaked, rain dripping off me onto the tiled floor.

I'd only been here once or twice, but enough to know that kInked wasn't the kind of place where you got sailor tats or pictures of Marilyn Monroe. It was the kind of place where they hired someone with expensive taste and equally expensive rates to do their décor. The tiles were alternating shades of cream and black, the matching couches and chairs carefully positioned to seem both inviting and private. There were no magazines on the tables, but rather stacks of beautifully bound art and tattoo books. The walls were lined with a velvety fabric in burgundy. It was the swankiest tattoo place I'd ever been in.

kInked was also the kind of place where they had a red oak welcome desk that came with a drop-dead receptionist, a buxom blonde with a '50s polka-dot dress and perfectly waved hair. Tats in bright colours decorated her arms and legs, an intricate painting that covered the majority of her pale skin. A beautiful green leather collar graced her neck, highlighting the green in her eyes and tattoos.

As if I didn't already feel like the world's most drowned rat. Or sheep, in this case. Now I had to face pin-up-girl perfection while wearing wet wool. Great.

The receptionist flashed me a ruby and pearl smile and pulled a giant towel from somewhere in the desk and brought it around to me without missing a beat. Apparently they either ended up with a lot of drowned rat-sheep-girls or, more likely, she was very well trained in customer service. I thanked her and then attempted to dry myself off, but somehow ended up with a still wet me and an equally wet towel.

'Welcome to kInked,' she said when I'd stopped swabbing myself with the damp towel. 'Do you have an appointment with one of our ink masters?'

Ink masters? I almost giggled at the pretentiousness of it. Nothing like taking yourself a little too seriously. Suddenly I felt better about dripping on their pretty tiles. I prevented myself from laughing at the last second, realising it was my own nervousness that was making me giggle-prone, and handed the towel back to her with a nod of thanks.

'I was hoping to see Kyle,' I said. 'I don't have an appointment.' After a second, I added, 'Yet.'

'You mean Master K.' It wasn't a question. More of a sweet-as-sour-cherry reprimand.

I almost died right then and there. Kyle, sweet, adorable, laugh-a-second Kyle was now Master K? I wondered if my mouth was open, and if it would look stupider if I left it like that or if I just reached up and shut it with one hand.

'I'm afraid you'll need an appointment.' Pin-up girl's customer-service training was either failing her or else it was really kicking in. Her disdain for my lack of an appointment and my disregard for proper address was clearly evident in her voice. And in the whip-snap folds she was making of my wet towel. 'Among other things.'

'Other things?'

Her shiny black heels echoed on the tiles as she retreated to the safety of her desk. Now she did look me up and down, her ruby lips pursed. Whatever thoughts I might have had about her being sexy were quickly erased by her puckered expression.

'I'm terribly sorry, but I don't believe kInked is quite right for you, Miss...?' This was a question but, before I could answer, she continued. 'Perhaps you'd be more comfortable at another tattoo establishment. I'd be happy to offer you some suggestions should you need them.'

I so did not need this. No, no, no. I wiped my wet palms on my dress, which made them even wetter. And kind of fuzzy.

'Listen,' I said. 'I've had a terrible, horrible, no good, very bad day.'

From her blank expression, neither the quoted book title nor my own anguish stirred anything in her. 'Please just let me see Ky–' I cleared my throat and managed to get the moniker out without a hit of hysterical laughter. 'Master K. Five minutes. I'll be fast.'

Part of me wanted to pull the pity-party thing on her, tell her just how bad my day had been and see if it helped me gain access. The other part of me, that new part of me that I'd just discovered and still didn't know quite what to do with, that part of me wanted to try pushing her a little, see if I could discover a hidden submissive inside that snotty exterior. Either one was a crapshoot, likely to get me thrown out.

I was trying to decide in which direction to swing, or whether to just try climbing out through one of the large storefront windows instead, when one of the burgundy wall coverings shifted. It slid sideways to reveal what looked like a small room. Kyle stepped into the reception area and the fabric wall closed behind him.

Kyle took one look at me, and I literally saw his expression change from placid calm cool artist to *what the fuck*.

'Janine?' he said. As though he couldn't quite place me. I wanted to punch him for that. It hadn't been *that* long.

Except that he looked, oh, my God, so fucking hot. Hot like a guy always looks hot after you uncertainly break things off with him and aren't really sure you did the right thing. But also hot as in wearing dark-blue jeans that fitted him perfectly and a teal shirt that made his eyes look like big, pure oceans. I wanted to suck the salt from him, lick the pale beaches of his skin.

What few parts of me had managed to stay dry in the torrent were now as wet as the rest of me. Which was exactly what I did not want. Not now. I needed to focus. I needed to figure this out and get it done and get out of here. I needed to not be in a wet wool dress, smelling like a rain-blasted sheep and getting hot and bothered about my ex-lover.

Kyle had a tattoo gun in one hand, the machinery looking so out of place among all the elegance that I fully expected Miss Pin-Up to yell at him for dirtying her space.

Instead she went all demure on him, even lowering her head a notch to acknowledge his arrival. 'Master K,' she purred. 'I was just letting Janine know that she needed to make an appointment.' So she was quicker on the draw than I'd thought. Having plucked from his stuttered question both my name and the understanding that Kyle and I had some kind of history, she was quickly changing her tone.

'I'm on my way home,' he said.

'I just need five minutes,' I said. God, it killed me to plead like that, not just in front of Miss Pucker-Face, but in front of Kyle too. I needed to know if he'd help me, though, and I didn't want to give him too much time to think about it.

'Two,' he countered.

I nodded.

'Thanks, Cece. I've got this.'

He flashed her a smile. I wondered, briefly, if they'd slept together, and felt a pang of something in my stomach at the thought. It wasn't jealousy so much as a hope that, if he was sleeping with anyone, it was someone I could warm up to a little more easily. Miss Pin-Up was cute, but she hadn't exactly charmed me so far.

Cece nodded once, glancing at me over her shoulder, as if to remind me that I was still in way over my head and might be better off at one of those other establishments. I resisted the urge to flip her off.

'In my office,' Kyle said. He was looking in my general direction, but he wasn't looking at me. His gaze kept sliding off to the side as though he couldn't bear to keep it on me. Oh, this was going to be fun. What had started out as a clearly bad idea was now moving into the realm of ridiculously stupider idea. Times twelve.

He slid the wall panel and ushered me inside. The room behind the door didn't look like an office so much as someone's favourite reading room. It was surprisingly small after the spacious entryway and equally surprisingly cosy and private. A mocha-coloured leather recliner held centre stage, while tattoo equipment, books and art rested on either side on long cream-coloured shelves. Candles flickered around the room, filling it with the scent of cloves and oranges. Under that, the barest hint of sanitisers and, of course, my

186

own lovely wet-wool scent. The walls were lined with tattoo images, most of them mounted and hung with simple black wires. Everything about the room said money and elegance. It was like no tattoo place I'd ever seen or even dreamed about. Kyle's old shop was a rag-and-bone kind of place, build with a love of art and not very much in the way of funds. What had brought him *here*?

Kyle slid the door shut behind us. It locked into place with a heavy click. I wondered if it was soundproof. After all, in a lobby like Miss Pin-Up's, it wouldn't do to have the sounds of distressed clients flowing out.

'Thanks for rescuing me,' I said, once he'd turned to face me. I tried to keep my voice light. 'I thought she was going to eat me.'

'Who, Cece?' He set the tattoo gun on the shelf without looking at it. He wasn't looking at me either, though. He mostly stared at the floor. 'Don't mind her. She's just a little … overzealous.'

'Overzealous?' The bite in my voice was more obvious than I'd meant it to be. Calling her overzealous was like calling a mother bear a little protective.

He lowered his voice. Maybe those doors weren't sound-proof after all. 'Why are you here, Jae?'

No one called me Jae except Kyle. It hadn't been that long since I'd heard him say it, and still the sound made a lump in my throat. I had to swallow around it in order to speak.

I swallowed. And then realised I had no idea what I wanted to say. I hadn't made a plan beyond step one, which was to find Kyle and ask him some questions. I just didn't know what questions to ask.

'I miss –' I clamped my teeth down on my tongue, hard. That was not what I'd meant to say. It certainly wasn't why

I'd come here. Not even in the most hidden recesses of my brain had that been my purpose in coming here. And it wasn't fair. He was moving on. I was too. Yes, I missed him, but I needed to say something, anything, else.

'I'm serious, Kyle.' My instinct was to reach and touch his arm, to connect with him, but I forced my hands to stay at my side. He looked at me finally, straight at me, those green eyes intense. I'd always liked them, how they darkened slightly when he was aroused, how they looked almost white in the sunlight.

'I need you,' I said. Headsmack.

'You need me?' He took a step back, as though I was less ex-girlfriend and more poisonous viper material. 'I don't want to be an ass. But you kind of dumped me, Jae. Right after I asked you to marry me.'

'Not right after,' I said. 'And I think it was kind of a mutual dumping.'

He made a movement with his head, the kind that asked if I was really going to argue semantics. I supposed I wasn't.

'I'm sorry about that,' I said.

He sighed. 'I know you are. We already talked about this. If I sound angry, I'm sorry. It's just been a long day. And you were the last thing I expected to see. Seeing you out there, dripping all over Cece's perfect floor in that form-fitting dress, made me realise how much I miss you.'

His body this close made me ache and clamp my teeth tight. I wanted him with the same urgency I'd always wanted him, but I refused to pull him into something. I refused to beat him up again with promises I couldn't keep.

'And how much my cock misses you,' he said.

The low cadence of his admission, combined with the fact that my mind had not forgotten, at all, what his cock looked like, sent my lust another notch higher. I should not do this, I thought. I should not.

And then he kissed me, and I had no more thoughts that made any sense. Fuck, he kissed like a dream, an urgent hot dream from which there was no waking.

I pushed back, gasping like I'd been drowning, catching his gaze.

'I can't give you my love,' I said.

'I'll take your lust right now,' he countered, nipping at my chin, at the lobe of my ear. 'Please let me take your lust right now.'

I dragged my hands across his flat stomach, over his hips. It was all so familiar and yet so strange. I knew where and how to touch him, but I also didn't.

Thankfully, he was kind enough to help me.

'Lower,' he urged, pushing against me.

I undid his jeans and slid my fingers under the fabric. The tip of his cock was already wet, and I dipped my finger into the fluid and drew it lightly over his head until he shuddered. I wanted the length of him inside me. I wanted to feel the push of his hips as he slid into me. I wanted. I wanted. I wanted.

'Please take this damn dress off me,' I said. 'It's wet and cold.'

In a single move, he tugged the dress over my head, and then brought his heat to mine. The contact made me shiver, my teeth clanking together.

His fingers spread my legs, tugged my labia apart. I was wet already, coating his fingers when he dipped them into me. He brought his hand to his mouth, licked my juice from his fingers while I watched him.

'Sweet,' he said. 'So sweet.'

'Please, Kyle,' I said. 'Please, if you're going to fuck me, please do it.'

He pushed himself against me, his cock nudging my hip, one arm wrapping around my back. He opened one of the drawers and pulled out a foil wrapper. I wanted to be the one who slipped it over his cock, who felt the pulse of his erection as he wrapped it, but he did it so quickly, I didn't even have time to reach for him.

We fell back into the tattoo chair, me wiggling around the arm that threatened to poke me in the back. I spread my legs as best I could. He teased me with the tip of his cock until I was gasping and arching, nearly begging.

'You're beautiful, Jae,' he said, looking down at me.

When he entered me, it was slow and sweet, a connection that carried our past with it. It made me want to cry and come all at the same time. Kyle's eyes fluttered, but his gaze stayed on mine. I knew he was feeling the same thing I was. That this was goodbye.

I closed my eyes so I wouldn't cry and focused on the feel of him against me and inside me. We moved together, slow and sweet, until we could no longer stand it. And then we fucked. Hard, fast, with an urgency that wouldn't be curtailed or tamed.

His thrusts shoved us both half off the chair, until we were giggling and fucking, the pleasure increased by the contractions of my body from laughing. When he leaned down and kissed me, the pressure changed, the base of his cock snugging up against my clit with every thrust. I stayed still, riding the pleasure, feeling orgasm sneaking up on me.

'Come for me, Kyle,' I begged. 'Please, I want to feel you.'

'You first,' he said. 'You. First.'

With one hand, he snagged the hair at the very back

of my neck and tugged lightly. The unexpected roughness, combined with that pitch-perfect stroke against my clit, was just enough. I came with a shuddering groan. Kyle followed a second after, giving me a second baby orgasm that felt like little tickly feet through my stomach.

Silent except for our heavy panting, we snuggled as best we could in the chair. No easy feat, but we managed. I wasn't ready to leave him, because I knew that, when I did, it would be for the last time. We would move into that space that all ex-lovers moved into, unless one of them died early. A space of distance that was never quite closed by shared moments and memories, a space that was so very small and yet impossible to cross.

'Kyle, what happened that night at the Cat House?'

He shrugged and shifted against me. 'Nothing, really. Kitty and I danced on stage, and then I went off to some party. There was a lot of leather, and more than a little sex.'

'And?' I said.

'And nothing. I went there, I made out with a cute woman and then I went home.'

'What about the club?'

'What club?'

'Listen,' I said. 'I know you're not supposed to talk about the club, but it's me.'

He opened his hands in my direction. 'I really don't know. It was fun, but they were all a little too out there for my taste. I like my sex pretty vanilla, I guess.'

'I never thought we were vanilla,' I said. But looking back, I realised that wasn't entirely true. As fun as our sex had been, it was pretty straightforward. Not that there was anything wrong with that, but I was discovering that I wanted, maybe needed, something more.

'It's OK, Jae,' he said. He said it with the kind of smile that made me wonder if he'd found someone who matched his taste exactly. I grinned back at him, feeling my heart loosen a little in its constraints. If that was true, I was glad.

'Have you ever done a keyhole tattoo?' I changed the subject.

He shifted away from me, pulling himself up to stand without taking his eyes off me. 'You know I have.'

I watched Kyle watch me. I could ask him again, beg him for the tattoo that I wanted, that I needed, but I knew he would say no. He always could stand up to me, when push came to shove. It was one of the things I'd always adored about him.

But I needed this. I had a plan, and I had no other way to get it.

'Please, Kyle,' I said. 'I need one.'

'For that job?' he asked.

'Yes.' And for something more. But I wasn't sure what.

'Sorry, Jae. I'd give you the world. But I'm not tattooing you for some wild-goose chase you're on. Especially not your first tattoo. You know me better than that.'

It was true. I did. I also knew Kyle well enough to know that once he'd said no to something that he believed in, there was little chance of changing his mind.

'Just a little one?' I said.

He eyed me.

I nodded. He was right, of course. Getting a tattoo was stupid. And I'd regret it as soon as it was done.

'Have Lily draw you one,' he said.

Which is something I should have thought of easily enough, but hadn't. Stupid lust-addled brain.

'Thanks, Kyle,' I said.

'Just be careful, Jae,' he said.

'Promise,' I said.

All these promises. Not a single one of which I'd been able to keep so far.

* * *

I practically ran back to Leather Bound. If nothing else, I was getting my exercise this week.

The store was mostly dark; only the little lights at the back – what Lily called reading lights, even though they weren't – were shining. I imagined her among the rows of books, coffee and cat by her side while she worked.

I slipped my key in the lock, still loving the ritual of it, even in the rush, and opened the door.

There were noises coming from my office. Not noises like 'Hi, I'm Lily and I'm working' noises. Noises like two people arguing, although I couldn't make out any words. I tried to see if one sounded like Lily, but it was muffled. What were people doing in Leather Bound, much less in my office? We'd never had a break-in, but they weren't unheard of in the area.

I looked around for some kind of weapon. Which then felt dumb. What was I going to do, take down an intruder with a bookmark? An ancient copy of *Ulysses*? Webster's claws?

Don't be a hero this time, I thought. There are no women heroines who follow a trail of noises in the darkness of a closed book store and have it end well. When you read books with those women in them, you yell at them, Janine. Just call the cops.

I slipped behind the counter, crouched down and pulled out my cell phone. I had my finger on the 9 when Webster brushed against my ankles, making me shriek. I dropped the phone and it clattered to the ground.

The voices from my office went silent.

I tried not to breathe in case they heard me. When the noises resumed, I exhaled hugely and patted around the floor, trying to find my phone in the dark.

From the enclosure of my office, I heard Lily's laugh.

That loud, obnoxious, overly boisterous guffaw was the best possible thing I could have heard at that moment.

Lily's voice came again, muffled with laughter, not in pain or fear. She said something that I couldn't hear – the acoustics always did suck in here – and then laughed again. Low and breathy.

I grabbed the cracked-open office door, about to say something, when I saw Lily. Really saw her.

Bent over my desk, in a next-to-nothing black skirt. A skirt that was now even less than next to nothing because it was pushed up over her ass. She was clad in stockings of just light enough a grey that I could see her tattoos through them.

Behind her stood a woman in a three-piece suit. The woman had short black hair that tucked behind her ears and a pair of feather earrings as big as my hands. I couldn't see her face, but she fitted into that suit like it was custom-made to swirl over her curves. Tight, but not too tight. So you could see everything and nothing at all.

Her fingers slid over Lily's dark grey stockings with a shushing sound, toying with her. Lily moaned softly, a sound I'd never heard her make before, a quiet sound of pleasure.

As I watched, the woman pulled her hand away, cupped it, then brought it down hard on the fleshy curve of Lily's ass. Lil's response was quick and loud: a cry rose from her lips, a mingling of pleasure and pain that I knew all too well as of late. In a single swift move, the woman tugged Lily's stockings down over her ass, baring the pink skin to the world. She brought the curve of her palm down again and again, hitting the line of Lily's ass where the fabric ended, where her flesh was bare and turning a darker shade of scarlet with every spank.

I shouldn't have stayed, shouldn't have kept watching, but it was too hot not to look. Even without touching my clit, I could feel it blooming between my legs, practically begging for attention. I ached to finger myself, to rub myself against something hard and firm. But I stood still and held my breath, unwilling to spoil the moment by so much as moving.

The woman was saying something to her between hits, but I couldn't make it out. As she spoke, her free hand returned to the spot between Lily's thighs, curling her fingers in, giving her something to squirm against. Lily did so, whining low as she wiggled against the clutch of her fingers.

'Please,' Lily murmured.

'Please, what?' the woman said.

'You know what,' she said. 'Please don't make me say it. Don't make me ask.'

'I want to hear you,' she said. 'I want to hear you ask.'

'Please fuck me,' Lily said.

'Spread your arms.'

Lily spread her arms across my desk, across the wide oak expanse, her breasts mashing into the wood. She looked like a beautiful bird about to take flight.

Until the woman behind her drew her hand back in a long, lazy arc and brought it down in a flash on Lily's ass. Lily cried out, loud, every part of her that could come off the desk doing just that, taking off.

I gripped the edge of the door, arousal making my breath tight.

'Please take me,' Lily said.

Not missing a beat, the woman ceased the spankings, dug her hand into the back of Lily's red hair and pulled the wrapped curls out of their updo with a single tug, so they cascaded down her back. Using Lily's hair as leverage, she pulled her head up, forcing her to turn her neck and look over her shoulder at the woman.

I could see Lily's face clearly now. Her red lipstick was smeared, the usual perfect black lines around her eyes smudged and streaked. And yet her eyes were dancing, alive with a smouldering desire that should have burned her.

The woman clearly caught the look too, because she leaned down and kissed her, nipping at Lily's lips with such ferocity that I expected blood. She tangled back, their mouths meeting, so hard I thought I heard the clash of teeth. There was their captured breath between them, the woman's low groans, and then Lily's voice, still begging incessantly to be fucked.

I was panting hard, just watching the two of them, my own pulse creating an echoing drum in my throat. It was sexy as hell. Part of my brain was telling me to go, to give them their privacy. The other part was telling me to hike up my wool dress and stick my hand between my thighs.

As I stood there, a war of lust raging inside me, the two stood, kissing fiercely, breast to breast, their hands between each other's thighs. Lily's nipples peaked hard as they rubbed against the fabric of the woman's outfit. The woman lifted Lily's ass all the way up on my desk, forced herself between her stocking-clad thighs. With one hand, she opened Lily, stroking into her until Lily was again begging, pleading, crying out.

Unzipping her fly, the woman pulled out a beautiful latex cock, long and firm. She pumped it slowly, leisurely with her fist, the movement so tantalising my pussy began to ache with emptiness.

'Is this what you want?' she asked.

Lily nodded, nearly frantic, her hands reaching for the dildo, her legs opening wider as she sought to angle herself closer to the woman.

'Greedy little slut,' the woman said. My clit pulsed as if she'd said those very words to me.

The woman slid both hands under Lily's ass and nearly lifted her off the desk. She settled Lily at the very head of her cock.

'You want?' she asked.

'I want,' Lily said, more growl than speech.

She entered Lily in a smooth slow stroke that made all three of us groan. I clamped a hand over my mouth, forcing myself quiet. Jesus fuck, this was so hot I felt lightheaded. I thought of my shoes, imagined their bottoms painted with stop words – *stay, don't move, stand still* – so that I wouldn't go in there and beg them to let me join in.

They moved together, thrusting hard, bodies in unison. So much so that my desk rocked beneath the movement, the short leg banging down hard on its supporting book as they fucked.

Lily's movements became greedy, restless, shifting herself hard onto the woman's cock and finally reaching a hand between her own legs, fingering her clit as she murmured *pleasepleaseplease*, nonsense syllables that got louder and louder until she came with a fast hard clench that shook her for a moment and then sent her into peals of loud laughter.

'I love it when you come for me,' the woman said. 'I love the way you laugh.'

Lily laughed again

She moved her body forward, reverse thrusting with the cock inside her.

'My turn,' Lily said.

Lily worked to angle her movements until she got the response she wanted – a bit-lip cry from the woman.

'That's the spot,' Lily said. She moved again and again, a hip-rolling stroke that brought visible shudders to her partner. 'Touch yourself, come for me,' she chanted.

The woman reached down with a shaky hand and tucked it into her waistband. She gasped, and I echoed her. I knew that sensation, when you're so wet and wanting that the faintest touch nearly sends you over the edge. She came a second later, nearly silent, her eyelids fluttering with pleasure.

'Fuck,' Lily breathed. 'I adore you.'

This time the kiss between them was soft and sweet, a gentle touch of lips and then noses and then foreheads as they rested together. I could hear them breathing in unison, catching up with their bodies.

I bit my lip, my head spinning. I hadn't come, but I ached with the need to do so.

There was something else too. I tried to tell myself it was lust, wanting, desire. But Lily's face had been so beautiful when she'd come, and when the woman had leaned down and kissed her, there was something more there. Not just lust, but something deeper. It made my heart glad to see Lily here, clearly falling in love with someone who adored her equally. It also made me a little heartsick, after Kyle. I'd told myself that wasn't something I wanted, and here I was, aching for it almost as much as I was aching for the sex I'd just witnessed.

Quickly and quietly, I stepped back through the stacks until my hand found the front door. I slipped outside, panting slightly. By the end, I'd been holding my breath without even realising it.

I wasn't going to get a tattoo from Lily either, it looked like. Which pretty much left me entirely to my own devices. If I had any devices left after watching that display of lust.

CHAPTER 13

Outside the door where I'd been turned away last time, I dug a black pen out of my bag and drew the worst-ever keyhole on the palm of my hand. There was no way in hell this was going to work. But I had to try.

This time the door opened partway when I knocked. I was so taken aback that I stood there for a moment with my mouth open.

'Yes?' It was Smaug. Oh, dear gods. Why did this always happen to me?

He squinted at me. 'I know you,' he said.

I nodded. I clearly couldn't disagree with him.

'This isn't a public event,' he said.

'I know,' I said. 'I just need to get in to find a friend. To help a friend.'

'I know you're lying,' he said.

I sighed. Everyone always knew.

'Please,' I said. I knew I wasn't supposed to talk, but I couldn't help myself. I blather when I'm nervous. 'I'm trying find this book and I promised Davian and –'

'Davian?' he said. 'Oh. You're the one.'

Suddenly the door opened all the way. 'Not a word of

201

this,' he said. 'Between you and me, I like Davian.'

At first I didn't move. I had no idea what was happening.

'In,' he urged, tugging me forward.

He shut the door and everything went black.

'Straight down the hallway,' he said. I got the impression he was pointing, just from the sound of his movement, but I couldn't see a damn thing. Why was I always getting myself into this stuff anyway? I was pretty sure that if I was willing to sit still long enough for some kind of therapy, a shrink would tell me it was because I was easily bored. Or craved a challenge. Or had some kind of sexual issue.

Which was probably why I'd never sprung for a therapist.

I put my hand out, feeling for a wall. I had to lean a little to find it. If anyone could see me, they'd be watching the back of a very confused, wobbly woman trying to make her way down a very dark hall as though she were blind.

I expected to come out of the dark hallway into the light of a larger room. But the hallway, and the dark, just seemed to go on. I got the impression, oddly, that I was travelling not downwards, to a cellar, as I might have expected, but upwards, towards an upper floor of a building.

The wall abruptly ended, and my hand stretched into black air.

Someone took it. I bit back a quiet yelp of surprise. The hand in mine was soft and supple as fine leather. It took me a moment to realise it *was* leather. A glove, calfskin by the feel of it.

I wanted to bend down and rub the fabric against my cheek. Even in the dark, I controlled myself. Or rather, the fear that was at war with the lust within me kept me from doing anything stupid.

Stupider. I was already standing in the dark I-didn't-know-where holding hands with some gloved stranger. How much stupider could I possibly be in a single evening?

Not stupid. Daring. Doing my job.

Right. Keep telling yourself that. I couldn't even conjure up Nancy Drew any more. That was how far gone I was.

Silently, the hand began to guide me forwards. I resisted, holding my free hand out, trying to touch the air, trying to make sure I didn't run into anything. There was a sense of murmuring, of people around me, but mostly it was very quiet, and pitch-black. I couldn't get a sense at all of the number of people in the space or how big the space was. I also couldn't tell how much of what I was hearing and sensing was real and how much was some kind of audio recording. It was like trying to tell if faraway music was coming from a great sound system or being played live.

After a while I came to trust the hand that was guiding me. Even if I couldn't see, they either could, which seemed impossible, or they knew the room and the space well enough that they were taking care with me. I didn't walk into anything. The noises around me ebbed and flowed. Sometimes we passed places where I actually heard snatches of conversation. Other times, it got quiet.

It felt like we walked for ever, but in truth I think we were just walking slowly, taking our time. In the dark, it seemed twice as long in both time and space as it actually was. Maybe he or she or whatever was holding my hand was just making sure that I was safe each moment.

The hand holding mine tightened just slightly and then we both stopped.

'Your chair, madame,' a voice said. So it was a man after all. From his voice I had a sudden vision of a tall, thin blond man dressed in a tux and black gloves. I wished I could glimpse him, just to see how far off my perception was. My experience has been that, from their voices alone, people never look like you think they will.

He took both of my hands, this time from a slightly different angle, and set them on something. After a little exploration I realised this was the back of a chair. I hesitated a moment. Sitting down meant I was going to stay, no matter what.

But I'd come this far.

Not to mention: I really didn't know how to get out. I had a general impression that if I just turned fully around and walked in a straight line, I'd find that door. But I didn't think that general impression was at all correct – we'd taken at least a few turns between here and the door, and we'd moved so slowly that I sometimes couldn't tell if we were turning or walking in a straight line.

So I did the only thing that seemed reasonable. I whispered 'Thank you' to a man that I couldn't see, pulled out the chair in front of me and sat down in the pitch black.

I was at a table, covered in cloth. There were at least a few people at the table with me. I could hear shuffling and the occasional ting of plates and cups. From time to time someone whispered something.

Putting my hands on the table, I felt a plate, another plate, a cup, silverware, a napkin folded into a shape that I couldn't work out. It was a dinner table. A formal dinner table, if the fork above the plate was any indication. I wondered if I'd stolen someone's invitation by working my way in. How could they even keep track in the dark of where people sat? I had no idea.

I wanted to ask someone what was going on, but I was

afraid my voice would be overly loud. Not like anyone could turn and look at me, but since I couldn't exactly find my way out, I didn't want to be the centre of attention. Plus, leave it to me to shout out something like that at the very moment when they turned the lights on. Floodlights, knowing my luck.

But they didn't turn the lights on, and no one said anything that gave me any indication of what was going on. The longer I sat there, the less solid the darkness got. At first I thought they were turning up the lights, very gradually, allowing us to see small things. But I realised it was just my eyes adjusting. It wasn't that I could actually see anything. But shapes began to show up, small movements. If I stared really hard, it seemed that I could see the white of the plates in front of me, just slightly.

Soft music started up somewhere in the room. I turned my head, trying to figure out where it was coming from, but it was nearly impossible. Unlike earlier, when I'd been uncertain if the noise was real or recorded, this music was clearly being played somewhere in the room. A slow, soft classical piece with a lot of violin.

Beneath it, a quiet voice on a microphone wove through the sounds. It took me a moment to realise she was speaking, not singing. It was the blue-haired woman from the club.

'Good evening,' she said. Her speaking voice was as beautiful as her singing voice, huskier and with a slight accent I couldn't place. 'Welcome to the Blind Café. You know the rules, of course, but I'd like to reiterate them if I may. First, no lights of any kind. Not even a phone. The Blind Café is designed to provide you with a sensory culinary experience unlike any other. Second, if you are a designated lock, your keyholder sits on your right. This is your dining partner. Please treat them accordingly. Lastly, you may not excuse yourself from the table prior to dessert. Other than that, the servers will be glad to provide you with anything you need. *Bon appétit.*'

My heart hammered in my chest. I wasn't supposed to be here. I had no idea what was going on. Locks? Keyholders? I wiped my hands on my skirt, even though no one could see the way my palms were sweating. Maybe I could just walk out. Maybe I could make it to the door before anyone turned on the lights. What did it matter if I ran into things? I'd just make a break for it.

I felt a movement on my right. A soft voice said in my ear, 'Hello, I'm your keyholder.'

Davian? It was the first thing my mind dredged up. Of course it was.

It wasn't him. This man sounded like him, sure. But only in the way that some men in the dark sound alike. Mostly, it was just my lustful brain wishing for him.

This man's voice was a little lower, more gravelly. I was grateful for the dark because of the way I started blushing, the heat in my cheeks making me reach for my water glass. It took me two tries to actually find it, and I lifted it with both hands, feeling suddenly that I wouldn't be able to hold it well since I couldn't see it. I brought it to my face and pressed first one cheek to its coolness and then the other.

'I guess that makes me your lock,' I said.

He laughed, quiet, closer to my ear than I expected him to be. A second later, I felt the air move around me, and then his hand was on my arm, a firm and exploratory touch.

'Do you come here often?' he asked, his voice a soft sigh in the darkness. It seemed we were supposed to be whispering, and so I kept my voice equally low.

'Never,' I said.

'Me neither,' he said, but I got the impression from the laughter in his voice that that wasn't entirely true.

At my side, the sound of a voice from above me and off to my left. 'I'll be bringing a plate around your left shoulder,' a woman said. 'This is your appetiser. You'll be fed by your keyholder.'

Fed by. Oh, gods, this was just getting better and better. Not only was I sitting totally in the dark, I was going to be fed something I couldn't see by some stranger?

I felt a hand slide up my jawline, begin to explore my cheekbones, the corner of my mouth. It was exploratory, tentative, blind, the same way I'd explored the table earlier.

'Ready?' the stranger asked. His thumb was still at the corner of my mouth as if marking the place where it sat. I didn't dare open my mouth and dislodge his thumb, or send it into the heat of my mouth, so I just nodded my assent.

A piece of something pressed against the centre of my lips. I realised he was using the other hand as a marker.

'Open,' he said.

I opened my lips just enough to realise it was a piece of fruit. Peach, sprinkled with cinnamon and sugar. I closed my teeth around a piece of it, let it fill my mouth with flavour and texture.

Oh, my gods. It was so good. I'd heard people describe food as orgasmic before and I'd always thought it was rather over the top. But this was just that. The perfect textures and flavours melding in my mouth, making me never want to swallow.

Suddenly, I was all sex. It was the realisation that there was this way to focus, to lose all of the outside world and focus on just the thing in front of me. I wanted to fuck that way, in a slowed-down world where I only noticed the smallest of things. The very taste. Lick of a cock, the scent of someone's skin. The way the tip of their cock felt against the slow curl of my tongue. I wanted to slip under the table and listen to every single slide of the stranger's zipper. I wanted to lay my head in this stranger's lap and smell his scent through his clothing. I wanted to explore his cock the same way he'd explored my face.

I knew that if I reached down and put my fingers between my thighs, I'd find myself already wet. For probably the fourth time tonight. I was insatiable lately. Everyone, and apparently everything, turned me on.

It suddenly occurred to me that I could do just that. Who would know? It was dark, completely and utterly dark. There was soft music playing. The sound of people murmuring and feeding each other around me sounded surprisingly like sex.

I slipped one hand between my legs.

'Fuck,' the man next to me said.

Actually he said 'fork', but my sex-addled brain heard something entirely different. Still, my mouth opened of its own accord as it had been doing every time he said something to me. This time, it was something light and fluffy, a buttery crust that seemed to fall apart on my tongue. Savoury and sweet.

While he fed me, I shifted in my seat to open my legs slightly. I reached down with one hand and tugged my skirt up a little. And then farther. No one could see me. No one could see that I'd just brought the hem of my fabric up way past my hips to expose the curve of my lace thong. No one could tell that I was slipping my hand under the lace, bringing two fingers to touch my already wet cleft while a strange man fed me sensual and wonderful food.

I curled my fingers into the heat of my body, let myself

focus and feel. I didn't want to move fast, I didn't even particularly want to come. I just wanted to feel and focus and see what every sensation felt like. It was the slowest, most leisurely masturbation session I'd ever had.

By the time he got to the sweet and salty caramel cream that he was spooning onto my tongue, an orgasm was building itself up inside me, a sweet and salty thing of its own. It rose in me, slow and fierce, a swirl of pleasure that ran up my spine and met with the pleasure in my mouth. I tried to stay quiet, to keep the sound of pleasure from leaving my lips. It came out as a sort of mmmm, only louder and more forceful than the ones at the tables around me.

'You're beautiful,' he said, just as I came.

'What?' I asked, breathless, confused. I was sure I hadn't heard him right. I was too busy tasting sweet and feeling sweet and breathing deep into my chest with the soft pleasure of the orgasm that had run through me.

'I said you're beautiful,' he repeated. 'Especially when you come.'

He reached out and found my wrist, the one that was still buried under the table, the one that was attached to the hand that I had been masturbating with. He did it directly, without feeling around, without trying to find his way. And he curled his fingers around my wrist and brought my hand up to his face.

I curled my fingers into a fist, to keep the lust scent and dampness of my fingers from his face. A flush of embarrassment ran through me as he brought his hands to his mouth and ran his tongue around and around the soaked edges of my fingers before sucking them into the heat of his mouth. My already sensitive pussy gave a twinge every time he sucked. Jesus.

Around me, I heard other murmurs of appreciation, the sound of fingers getting sucked in mouths. Was everyone around us fucking themselves as I'd been? I would have thought I could hear that, would have noticed that, but apparently I was so busy fucking my own self that I hadn't even noticed.

He sucked my fingers, murmuring low sighs of appreciation. Licking them round and round, then dipping between them to clean the space between.

It was so good, but I couldn't stop thinking about what he'd said.

'What did you mean, beautiful when I come?' I asked, trying to keep my voice super low. Trying to whisper a thing that I really wanted to shout out. 'How did you know?'

He brought my hand up to his face for the first time. I explored the edges of him. Sharp jaw, a little stubble. Nice full lips, still wet from my juices. Nose, cheekbones. The bottom edge of a pair of glasses. I was careful not to put my fingers on the lenses. Not that it would really matter here.

I realised that they weren't actually glasses. Not reading glasses, at least.

I used both hands this time, touched the edges and the lenses.

Binoculars? No. Goggles. And not just any goggles. Night-vision goggles.

I had an image of myself, getting off while we were eating. Hitching up my skirt. Fucking myself. Of him down on his knees in front of me, exploring every part of me.

And then, worse, I had an image of all of the tables around us. Did everyone have night-vision goggles on?

Oh, fuck.

'Don't worry,' he whispered. His voice tickled the edge

of my ear. 'I'm the only one who can see you right now.'

I let out a stupid sigh of relief.

'But I can see you well enough to know you don't belong here.'

I was sure the thump-thump of my heat was giving me away. I squirmed in my seat. Around us, others still made low noises of appreciation, murmurs and sighs.

'I'm new,' I whispered.

'No,' he said. 'I know who you are. Why are you here?'

I shook my head. 'I can't say,' I muttered.

'Good girl,' he said. 'We're all rooting for you.'

What? I leaned in to ask what he meant, but he covered my mouth with the front of his hand. Someone walked past us, steady footsteps, a pattern of breath that seemed familiar somehow. I stayed quiet.

'Let me help you out,' he said. Without waiting for a response, he took hold of my hand and pulled me out of my chair.

When we got to a hallway, he sent me out on my own, turning away and leaving me in the dark before I could ask any questions. I found my way outside, blinking in the shine of the streetlights.

Rooting for me? What did that even mean? Clearly he'd confused me with someone else. Which was bad. What was worse was that I'd discovered nothing – nothing – about either the sex club or Davian's book.

CHAPTER 14

'Coffee?' Davian's voice, even through my cell phone, did that thing it always did to me, sending little shivers along the edges of my stomach.

'Coffee?' I fumbled. I was at my desk, trying to find a first edition of *Pride and Prejudice* that was in good condition. I would have said it was a near-impossible task, but I had a new perspective on such things. This was nothing compared to what Davian's book was putting me through.

His laugh was deep and warm. I liked the way it washed over me like a blanket.

'Yes,' he said. 'Would you like some?'

'Are you asking me out for coffee?'

My heart did its silly little pitter-patter. I was already calculating in my head whether I could sneak away some time today. It was tempting, oh so tempting, but I already knew the answer to my own question. It was no. Lily was off talking to our lawyer, and then she was going out with the new girl of hers that I still knew nothing about. Well, the new girl I might know *something* about, if the lemongrass scent still lingering in my office was a leftover from her. But I couldn't leave the store empty, as much as Davian's offer might tempt me.

'Actually, I'm asking you *in* for coffee,' he said.

'I don't know what that means.'

'It means I'm standing outside your picture window watching Webster chase mice in his dreams and hoping you'll let me into your nice warm bookstore.'

I leaned my head out the office door and looked toward the street. There he was, coffee in each hand, his phone tucked between his shoulder and his ear.

'Is the door locked?' I asked. I knew it wasn't – we didn't close for another ten minutes – but I wanted to look at him a moment longer. He looked so perfect standing there, a dark-blue scarf wrapped around his neck. I didn't mind him in clothes. Not at all. In fact, he looked even better in them now that I knew what was underneath.

'I haven't tried it,' he said. 'My hands are a little full.'

'How did you dial my number, then?' I asked, unable to resist teasing him.

'I had some little old lady on the street do it for me. Now can you please let me in?'

'You did not,' I said.

He spied me through the window, narrowing his eyes. 'Clearly, you do not want coffee,' he said. 'Therefore I shall take it to someone more deserving –'

'There is no one more deserving of coffee than me,' I said. 'Do. Not. Move.'

When I let him in, he brought the scent of fall fires and mochas with him.

'You smell yummy,' I said.

He kissed me before he even put the coffees down, a fierce hard kiss that bruised my lips all over again. He'd already dipped into the coffee; he tasted like caramel and cream. I licked his lips, nibbling at the sweet meat of them. The heat

214

of my body was cooled by the press of his chilly frame. I could already feel his hips push to meet mine, and my own hips answering with a hard, fast pulse of their own.

'I'm sorry,' he said, pulling away suddenly. 'I don't know what's gotten into me. I came here to give you the information about tonight –'

'And bring me coffee,' I said.

'And bring you coffee,' he said. 'And then I saw you watching me through the window with your hair up and your glasses on, like some prim little librarian, and I thought about you naked and I just had to kiss you.'

'I'm complaining, clearly,' I said, as I ground my hips lightly against his. He still had a coffee in each hand, his arms open wide. Grinning wickedly, I backed him against the counter, forcing myself to not care, just for three seconds, who might see.

'Besides,' I said. 'You could have called. You could have just called me with the information. But you came instead. I wonder why.'

I didn't actually need to ask. The heat in his eyes told me everything. He'd come because he wanted to see me, because he'd been thinking about me, even as I'd been thinking about him.

Rising on tiptoe, I leaned hard on his body, letting my hips meet his right at the point where I could feel his cock hardening beneath his jeans. I circled against him while I brought my mouth to his, tasting him anew. Each time it was the same and yet slightly different. He uttered a low groan against my mouth, raising his hips hard against mine. I could practically feel his cock lengthening with every stroke of our hips and the movement left me struggling for breath.

'You have too many clothes on,' I said. 'Take them off.'

'It's cold out,' he said, then laughed low against my neck. 'And my, aren't you the demanding little hussy today.'

'Yes,' I said. 'Yes, I am.'

'You do remember –' he drew his mouth up the curve of my neck, the heat of his breath rising up my pulseline '– that you're at work, right?'

'Work, schmerk,' I said, incoherently. I'd kind of forgotten. 'Wait one moment, please.'

I practically ran to the front door to lock it and flip the sign. It was a few minutes early, but I couldn't be bothered to look. My heartbeat had slipped down between my thighs and it was demanding every bit of my attention.

I kissed Davian again. This time I was the urgent one, dipping one hand into his dark curls to bring him hard against me.

'My office,' I said.

'Yes, Miss Librarian,' he countered, his gaze running lazily and greedily up my body to rest on my glasses.

I took his hand and led him back to my office, watching him duck his head to fit under the doorway. He kissed me again, this time taking my ass in his hands and pulling me up against him.

'What were you saying about too many clothes?' I asked.

'That was you,' he said.

'Oh, right. You have too many clothes on.'

'What are you going to do about it?' he asked.

One naked man, no waiting. The coat and scarf were first to go, then I started on his jeans. His zipper hated me, and he rescued me, opening his fly with an adept move.

I reached for his cock out of some kind of instinct and wrapped my palm around his length.

'I've missed this,' I said.

'It's only been a few –' When he started, his voice was teasing, but then I tugged my fist along his length and he hissed a sigh. 'I've missed this too,' he said.

He undressed me as best he could around my movements, never forcing me to let go of his cock, which I was exploring with both hands. I ran a couple of fingers testingly over the curved hang of his balls and he inhaled with a sharp shudder.

When I was down to my bra and underwear, he caught my wrist hard and fast. 'My turn,' he said.

Then he backed me against my desk until I was forced to sit.

I'd never fucked here, nor in any part of Leather Bound, but it had always been a fantasy. Hot man running his hands through my hair, the smell of old books in my nose. Even my desk, which I knew I'd chosen not just for its gorgeous wood but for the hope that somebody would do just what Davian was doing, laying me down on its big top. He stood over me, grinning down at me, wicked and wanting.

He tucked two fingers into one side of my panties and tugged them down to my knees. Cold air licked my flesh and a moment later the heat of his tongue did the same. If I lifted my head, I could see his expression, his gaze wolfish as he caught me watching.

Slowly, so slowly, he ran the flat of his tongue up my cleft, opening me, and then he clamped his mouth down on my clit.

The suckle was fierce and yet soft, a fiery velvet tug and release that made me groan. He explored me with his fingers, dipping them into me so deeply I heard the wet sounds of my body sucking him in.

He ran his mouth up the front of my thigh, biting lightly at my hipbone. Kisses crossed my stomach, worked their way up to my breasts. He pushed my bra down over my breasts with his free hand and coiled his tongue around first one nipple and then the other. All the while, he worked his fingers inside me, turning them just so, gauging my reactions. I wasn't sure I'd ever slept with anyone who paid such attention to my responses, who fine-tuned his every action to get a louder groan, a bigger shudder. He found my g-spot, and when I staggered a breath, he laughed, low and dark.

'I'm going to make you come for me,' he said.

He tightened his mouth around one of my nipples at the same time as he slammed into me. I felt his teeth scrape across my sensitive flesh, a sensation of pleasure and pain that flashed red across my vision.

The suck of his mouth and the pound of his fingers were the perfect combination. My rational mind shut down, leaving only my little lizard brain clamouring for more pleasure. I planted my feet on the desk, giving myself leverage, pushing my hips up so that I met the thrusts of his hand. He twisted his fingers inside me, moving his hand so that my clit bumped against some part of it every time I rose.

My orgasm danced around my pleasure centres, and I willed it to stay away just a little longer, to let me revel in the almost there, in the impending arrival that it promised.

But Davian caught my gaze, my nipple still in the pull and suck of his mouth, his fingers twisting inside me, and the heat I caught there, the unleashed want in his eyes, sent me tumbling, falling, moaning down into my orgasm.

* * *

'You're going to be late,' Davian said.

'Mmm,' was as articulate as my brain could go. 'Don't care. Lizard brain happy.'

He laughed. 'I'm glad to hear that. But you're going to have to get up at some point. You have work to do.'

'No, thank you.' Now that my body was coming back to make a connection with my brain, I realised that I was still stretched out on my desk, still mostly naked, with Davian sitting, still mostly dressed, beside me.

'Besides, I didn't even get to touch you hardly,' I said. My tongue felt too big for my mouth, my words slurred with post-pleasure goodness.

He laughed, then leaned down to kiss me. He tasted like me and like coffee. 'Something tells me you will get another chance.'

I dressed while he watched, his gaze a combination of approval and desire. When I stood before him fully clothed, he shook his head.

'Jesus, Janine,' he said. 'The things you do to me. This isn't supposed to be happening.'

'Why?' I said, my teeth nipping at his jawline. 'Because we're working together? I think we bypassed that when you fucked me in a dressing room.'

'No,' he said. 'Not that.'

I stepped back, giving him a little space. He had that same look he'd had the first day I'd met him. A fierce sadness that rested in his gaze.

'I know you do this for a living,' I said. 'I'm not expecting anything of you.' I was surprised to feel a little ping of 'ouch' in the centre of my chest when I said it.

His eyes had narrowed at me. 'I don't do this for a living. I don't do you for a living. Dominance. Submission. Never sex.'

'And *I'm* expecting things of me. Things I just don't know if I can deliver.'

Wow, did I know that feeling. I wasn't sure if it made me feel better or worse to know that we were in the same predicament.

I ran my hand over his chest, loving the heat of it beneath his shirt.

'I went to the Blind Café,' I said. 'But I didn't find anything out. I'm sorry.'

'You got into the Blind Café without being part of the club? How did you manage that?' he asked.

'I'm not entirely sure. But some guy there said he was on my side. What does that mean, exactly?'

Davian shrugged, but it wasn't the movement of a man who didn't know the answer. It was the movement of a man who didn't want to talk about something. I let it go. I trusted him. Which was bizarre, considering that not that long ago I would have bet money that he was crazy.

Grinning, he changed the subject, and I let him. 'Come on,' he said. 'Get your ass dressed. You're going to be late.'

* * *

'Where am I going?' I asked. Davian had offered to walk me to the address and introduce me to his friend. We were both hunched in our coats against the cold, our now lukewarm coffees tucked in our palms.

'Do you really want to know?' he asked. 'You seem like the kind of person who, if given too much information, starts panicking about it.'

'That might be true,' I said. 'But I still like to have a heads-up. For example, if we're going to L&L again –'

'Nope,' he said. 'This is entirely different. I mean, entirely. I think it's best if you wait and see.'

'You're enjoying this, aren't you?' I asked. 'All this mystery and intrigue.'

He stopped and put one cold hand on the side of my face. I leaned into the strength of it, surprising even myself. 'Only because I know you can handle it.'

We'd walked to the very far end of the Sweet Spot, where the apartments and tiny houses gave way to half-mansions. The place he stopped in front of was one of those.

'We'll go in the back way,' he said.

The back way was nicer than most people's front ways. Stone walkway, perfect late-fall foliage, a dark-red door with a brass doorknocker.

Inside was even nicer. The door opened into a room that was small and intimate, but was really gorgeous and plush. I wanted to sink into the couch, which looked like red velvet and for some reason seemed to smell like strawberries and cream.

A short woman with a great big smile crossed the room in just a few steps. Her dark hair was pulled back in a long, low ponytail. She'd clearly embraced the steampunk look, wearing a button-up white shirt under a grey top and dark pants. Black leather gloves rested loosely in the hand she wasn't shaking with. Oddly, the look suited her.

'You're here,' she said. She wasn't talking to me, but to Davian. While she made sure to include me in her smile, most of it was reserved for the man at my side.

They hugged tight, and she pecked his cheek. 'I've missed you,' she said.

'And you. This is Janine. Janine, this is Estrata.'

'Janine.' Her gaze flowed over me. 'Yes, you're going to be perfect, I think. You chose well, Davian.'

'Perfect for what?' I asked, to whoever would answer me.

Clearly that was no one.

Estrata was already busying herself with taking off my coat and laying it across the back of the couch. Davian, who had occupied the corner of the red velvet couch with a grin, was clearly going to be no help.

'Now, stand quietly please,' she said.

I stood, suddenly focusing on my breath, on every little waver of my body. She began to walk around me in slow circles. I could feel her gaze on me, appraising. She clicked her tongue against the roof of her mouth, suddenly making me wish I'd worn something more form-fitting instead, a dress that showed off my figure. I didn't know this woman, but already I didn't want to be found wanting by her. Or by Davian, who was watching her assess me.

She kept circling, tapping her gloves against her fingers.

'I believe we'll have to make adjustments on the ropes,' she said. Her voice should have seemed affected somehow, with its soft lilt and an accent that I couldn't place, but it seemed to fit her. 'But she'll do.'

Now I wanted to kick her. And Davian too. I'd do? I raised a brow at Davian, an absolute look of what-the-fuck?

Davian gave me a wicked grin, but didn't answer my unasked question. Typical. I tried to breathe through my nose. I was nervous suddenly, being the only one in the room who clearly didn't know what was going on.

'You'll need to strip, please,' Estrata said.

I glanced at Davian, who was reclining on the couch, one arm across its back. He was clearly enjoying this. His gaze – full of heat and expectation and something else I couldn't name – gave me the strength I needed to start taking my clothes off in front of yet another perfect stranger.

Estrata watched me without comment, then pulled two

lengths of rope out of a basket near the couch. One was a shadowy red that seemed like it shimmered when it moved. The other was black as night, thicker around. She focused on uncurling the ropes, running them through her hands with a soft whispering sound.

I unbuttoned the front of my dress, waiting to see if she would look up. She didn't, but Davian was watching every gesture with a quiet smile.

He held out his arm when I pulled the dress away from my body and I dropped it in his hand.

'All the way,' Estrata said, still not looking at me.

I unhooked my bra and let that loop over Davian's arm as well. Slipping out of my panties, I cast a final look at him. I stuffed the black lace thong into his hand and he fisted his fingers around it without missing a beat. His grin went from slightly wolfish to complete and utter predator.

I grinned back. I could get used to this. I liked it when he looked at me like that. I liked it a lot.

'And now I just need you to stand there and be very still,' Estrata said.

With those words, she began.

Being tied up the ways she was tying me up was not like anything I'd experienced before. I'd played around with bondage in the past. Leather cuffs around my ankles, silk around my wrists, trussed to a bed in a variety of ways. I liked it, having something else anchor me to something.

But this was entirely different. Her ropes weren't holding me to anything. They were ... well, holding me together was the best way I could put it. Even that didn't quite make sense.

This tying up was about being free. I could feel it as soon as the first loop of rope slipped around my waist. Soft as silk, the red rope curling about my stomach on the first loop. She wrapped and knotted, humming as she worked, back and forth, in and out of my vision, occasionally saying something like 'Breathe out. Good.' And 'How does that feel? Not too tight?'

I stood for a long time, but it didn't feel overly long. I focused on her soft breathing as she wrapped me, on the contrast between the velvety rope and the rough rasp of her fingers. She hadn't touched my hands or my feet; most of her work was focused on my waist and chest, some on my shoulders, across my back. I was facing away from Davian, so I couldn't see him, but I could feel his gaze on me, watching as she worked.

It was as close to a standing massage as I'd ever had and, when she said she was done, I felt a twinge of sadness.

'How do you feel?' she asked.

'Great,' I said. It was true. The ropes corseted my waist, making my posture high and tight. My breasts tingled slightly, the nipples hard and aching from not being touched, the rest slightly constricted from the circled ropes.

'Turn,' she said.

I did so, expecting Davian to be still stretched out on the couch. But he was standing almost in touching distance, the firmness of his gaze drawing over me as truly as any hand.

'You look –' he started, and then shook his head. 'Fuck. I wish I could go in with you.'

'Me too,' I said. It wasn't just the heat I saw in his eyes. It was his presence beside me, the way he made me feel like I could do anything, as long as he was there.

Of course, his presence wasn't coming with me. I had to do this alone.

'I –' I started, and then closed my mouth hard. I'd been about to say I wasn't sure I could do this, but I was tired of listening to myself say that.

'I'll be there in spirit,' he said. He leaned in and kissed the very corner of my mouth, one hand snaking over the ropes that wrapped my waist.

'It's time to go,' Estrata said.

I took a deep breath – well, as deep as the ropes around my waist would let me, which was more than I expected, but not as much as I needed – and then I stepped through the door, into the cool expanse of the empty hall.

* * *

Last door on the right, Estrata had said.

I wasn't sure if I was supposed to knock, so I stood in front of it for a long time instead, waiting to see if someone would come. No one did. I knocked and still there was no answer. Finally, I lifted the metal latch and stepped inside.

The room was circular, the walls covered with shelves higher than my head. Most of them held books, turned so their pages were out. It made for a disconcerting experience. I liked my book spines, loved to run my hand across them or even just look at them, all of the titles lined up like invitations to other worlds.

Yet this was beautiful in its simplicity. Pages all looked the same lined up like that, somehow, and yet different. I wondered how anyone could tell them apart like that. How would you ever choose the book you wanted? Or maybe that was the point. A random pull of a random book was like a new adventure every time.

I let my gaze slide from the backwards books to the far end of the room. A red tile fireplace was set into the far wall.

Near it, a lone woman sat curled in a chair. She seemed

to be watching the flames, not turning as I entered. Her profile was backlit by the fire, a long nose and sharp chin. Short blonde hair was cropped close to her head, accentuating her dark brows and dark red lips. A long cigarette sat, unlit, between her lips as if waiting for someone to bring it to life. In fact, she looked much the same way, almost doll-like in her still, quiet pose. She wore a black jacket with a ruffled white shirt beneath it, a short black skirt, her long white legs crossed at the knees. A pair of black boots laced up almost to her knees.

At her feet, on a plush brown area rug, a long grey dog was stretched out, paws crossed over each other. His brown-eyed gaze rested on me, one eyebrow lifting as though he was inquiring as to my purpose there. Other than that, he was as motionless as his mistress. Not even his sides moved in breath, and his tail didn't lift from its curl around his hindquarters.

I stopped just past the doorway, uncertain what I was doing there, unsure where to go next.

She moved with a kind of fluid grace that seemed other-worldly, plucking the cigarette from her mouth.

'Come a little closer, won't you?' she said.

The woman's voice was like silk over my skin, soft and fleeting. I wanted her to say more so that I could grab at it and hold it tight in my fists. I stepped closer, my bare feet making hardly any noise on the softwood floor. The wood was warmer than I expected, obviously heated from underneath, and for some reason that made me feel more calm.

The woman still hadn't turned to look at me. And I wasn't sure how much closer was closer. I stepped forward again, softly, and again. Waiting for her to tell me when I was close enough. The dog had closed his eyes, and wasn't moving at all.

She didn't. Even with my slow steps, which slowed even more the closer I got to her, I was at the end of the couch, nearly in touching distance, before she spoke again. And when she did, it was to beckon me even closer.

'Here,' she said, gesturing with her cigarette hand toward the place right in front of her. I stepped around the dog, who still didn't move, and onto the small area rug, the deep brown pile welcoming my feet and letting me sink in.

I stood there for a long moment, listening to the fire crackle, listening to the rise and fall of my own breath. Somehow I seemed to be the only one in the room who was breathing. Or perhaps I was simply more aware of my own breath, caught as it was inside the grasp of the rope corset.

I explored her profile with my gaze. It was impossible to tell how old she was. Her skin was alabaster, clearly sun-protected, and, with her face turned away and immobile, she didn't have a single wrinkle or laugh line or even dimple.

I waited what felt like for ever. I was pretty sure it was for ever. I didn't know what I was supposed to do. The dog didn't seem to care or notice that I was even there. If she hadn't already talked to me, I might have thought the same of her. I had a sudden urge to see the rest of her, to see what she wore under that buttoned-up shirt, to explore that alabaster skin beneath my hands. I imagined she was warm under her clothes, like the softwood floor had been warm, heated from the inside by some unknown and unseen force.

I looked away, toward the circular walls covered in books, their pages beckoning me in much the same way she did. With a silent, white draw of promise.

She moved, turning her face fully towards me for the first

time, and my breath caught hard in the cavity of my chest. I tried to quiet it, sure she would hear me, sure I would offend her somehow, sure that she would take my being caught off-guard as a comment that I didn't mean.

It wasn't that she was beautiful, although she was. High cheekbones that seemed carved out of her alabaster skin, the pout of her red-lipped mouth, the tiny stone that sparkled in the flicker of the flames.

It was her eyes. They were so light that they were almost silvered, and I wondered if they had any colour at all when she was outside or if it was just the fire that lent them their shadowed gleam. They were speckled with dark-brown flares along the edges. It made her look both beautiful and haunting.

It also made me realise that she couldn't see me.

'You can breathe again,' she said, her silken voice made even more delicious by the laughter that coated her words. 'If I didn't like dramatic reactions, I wouldn't have set you up like that.'

I relaxed, letting out the breath I'd barely realised I was holding.

'I'm sorry,' I said. I felt the need to gush about how beautiful she was, but I closed my mouth. Would I have done that if she hadn't turned out to be blind? No. I probably would have just kept quiet and thought about how beautiful she was. So that's what I did.

She said a gentle word that I didn't understand. It wasn't until the dog stretched, yawned, then pulled himself up and sauntered toward the fireplace, nails clicking, that I realised the word wasn't for me at all.

'You're Davian's girl,' she said.

I started, not sure what to say.

'Never mind, don't answer that. I can smell him on you.'

Then, 'Spread your legs,' she said.

I did, wondering why she asked for something that she couldn't see. Would she know if I spread my legs, how far, could she tell by the sound? There were so many things I wanted to ask her, so many things I wanted to know, but I felt nervous and shy, not wanting to offend or sound stupid. Also, there was a purpose in my being here, which had nothing to do with that. Even if I still wasn't sure what my purpose was, I didn't want to botch everything by being overly curious about the wrong things.

She lifted her head, exposing the hollow of her throat, and opened her mouth slightly. It was the gesture of a woman perfectly poised, a woman who knew what she was doing, even if I had no idea.

'You're wet,' she said.

She hadn't touched me, but what she said was true. As I'd stood there, imagining her body, feeling naked and exposed and uncertain, my body had been reacting.

Still I had no idea how she knew.

'I can smell that on you too,' she said, as though I'd asked. The phrase echoed something Lily had said, what felt like for ever ago, in another world. I had a sudden image of Leather Bound, of Lily, of Kyle who'd asked me to marry him. Had that just been a few weeks ago? Had that really been me? It seemed so far away.

I started to step backwards, suddenly feeling over-whelmed by it all, sure that somewhere along the line I'd made a mistake. Why was I chasing this book so earnestly? Why did I trust Davian so implicitly? In truth, I barely knew him.

My foot lifted from the rug, found its place a step back. The woman reached out with one hand, her movement as sure as if she could actually see me, her fingers falling perfectly against the wet hollow between my thighs. I couldn't help it; as soon as she touched me, her fingers much cooler than I expected and somehow so very right, so like living granite that they were both powerful and soft, I groaned low in my throat. It was a shuddered, animalistic sound, more like a dog's noise than one of my own, and I found myself fighting it, trying to stay quiet.

'I quite like Davian,' she said, as if she was talking to herself. 'You, however. Well, it remains to be seen.'

She toyed with me, just the very tips of her fingers, pushing me open a little, then receding. Somehow I knew to be still, not to move, as if by staying silent and quiet she might not be able to sense me, might not be able to press all of my buttons. I didn't want to beg. I didn't want to weep. And I certainly didn't want her to do the things she was doing now, stretching me softly with her fingertips, leaning in as she canted her head, smelling me.

'Lovely,' she said.

Gripping the rope corset with her free hand, she slid a couple of fingers all the way inside me, spooning them together and then spreading them once she was in me. My legs shook, my head snapping back as I tried to open my body to make room for her sudden intrusion. That transition happened so fast; suddenly I was wet and open and wanted more from her, aching to have more inside me.

I didn't know what it was, but if I thought my libido was wild before, Davian's presence had certainly made it more so. Everything turned me on. Everything made me wet. It was as though my body had fine-tuned itself to a state of constant arousal.

She twisted her fingers, a soft scraping that heightened the pleasure. She was sure and true in her actions, a confidence that wasn't lost in my libido as she tugged and twisted along the inner edges of my body. Without stopping the motion of her fingers, she bent over and touched the very tip of her tongue to my clit. Her movements were swift and strong, almost too much, but my body gave in fast, unwilling to miss out on the pleasure that came along with the sensation. I was surprised at how quickly it moved from not-quite-ready to oh-my-fuck-yes-please.

In seconds, I was the one pushing against her mouth, bucking over her fingers. She caught my clit with her teeth, giving it a couple of sharp nips that nearly brought me to orgasm.

I knew we were on a time crunch, on our way to some-where, but I didn't want to rush it. It didn't matter; she wasn't waiting around for me. Reaching up with the hand that wasn't already inside me, she tugged on my nipple while she finger- and mouth-fucked me. The triad was too much, too fast. My whole was sliding into nothing but a single red spot of pleasure.

The ropes were stiff about me, pulling tight as I writhed. No matter what I did, I was going to come. I couldn't hold it back. My body arched into her fingertips at my nipple, pulling a sharp barking cry from me.

When she dug her fingernail into one nipple, I came with a hard buck that caught the edges of her teeth. Her fingers danced inside me a little more, her mouth a firm suckle over my clit, and I came again before the first was finished, a joyful little aftershock that nearly made me giggle.

She let go of my nipple and my clit and aimed her face up at me, her smile wide, showing her perfect teeth for the first time. I panted, broken, as small ripples of pleasure went slip-sliding through me, my nipples twanging in painful pangs of desire.

'Very good,' she said. 'So very good.'

I grinned too, panting. Exhausted, but happy. It was over. I was done. I'd passed the test.

'I think we're ready to go,' she said. And told me her name: Cherise.

* * *

Crap. I'd forgotten there was more. We hadn't even left the house yet.

Moving deftly, Cherise opened a black box that sat at one side of the couch and pulled out a leather contraption. It didn't take me long to realise it was a wide, flat handle like the ones that guide dogs wore.

She snapped it to the back of my rope corset. No, not a corset. I realised it was a harness.

'Just stay low, stay quiet and listen,' she said. 'You can walk upright for now. But during the party I'll expect you to be down on all fours.'

'What?' It was, oddly, a barky sound. As if I'd already made some kind of surreal transition from human to dog.

'And while we're there, you won't speak. Or stand. The only way this is going to work is if you are almost unnoticeable as human.'

'What if I have to, I don't know, pee or something?'

'If, at any point, you need to break the arrangement, you just need to lick my hand.'

'What?' I said again, feeling stupid. My tongue and brain swollen things in my mouth.

She put her fingers on either side of my chin, tilting my

head towards her as though she was looking right at me. As though she could see every ripple of trepidation and arousal that coursed through me. 'Do you understand?'

Her fingers weren't uncomfortable, but they were strong. The same strength they'd had when I felt them moving inside me. I spoke through her grip.

'Yes,' I said.

She nodded, as if there was no other response she'd expected.

'Davian said you were smart,' she said. Her fingers left my face, but she didn't let go of the leash with her other hand. Her smile was somewhere between sweet and wicked. I had a feeling that whatever I was agreeing to was not what I thought I was agreeing to. I was almost getting used to that topsy-turvy feeling.

'Come,' she said.

The car was in an attached garage, but I was still shivering by the time we were sitting in the backseat. A curvy dark-haired minx clad in a barely-there drape of a red chauffeur's uniform slipped behind the wheel. She gave me a smile in the rearview mirror, and then cranked the heat.

I tried to watch the streets, to see where we were and where we were going, but it was impossible in the dark. What was I doing here? Was this worth it? I still felt like I was wandering, uncertain and unsure, and yet I couldn't stop. Maybe Lil was right. Maybe I was losing it, spiralling down into something that I didn't understand, something that was way beyond me. I didn't feel like I was in danger, at least not in the physical sense, but sometimes in the emotional sense, in the way of being wholly and truly me.

From the seat next to me, Cherise put her hand on my leg. She was impossibly warm, her palm soft. As she moved,

I caught the scent of her, a soft peach interwoven with the scent of my own desire. Somehow her touch calmed me. And that was even more odd: that the touch of a near-stranger would be enough to make me feel less nervous. A stranger who'd just stripped me naked and put her fingers inside me, nonetheless.

The city slipped by, lights and streets and the woman in the front turning on something soft and melodious. If it hadn't been for the soft touch of Cherise's hand on my leg, I might have fallen asleep. But, every time she shifted, her nails scraped lightly across my skin and I was jolted awake, my pulse thumping.

'Where are we going?' I asked. I felt like we'd been driving for ever, but it might have just been the way I was trying to pay attention.

'We're here,' the red-clad driver said. She turned, sliding one arm over the seat, and glanced at me. It was the kind of glance that said a lot more than 'We've arrived'. It also said, 'I adore this woman who's holding your leash. If you so much as make her take a single faltering step, I will come after you and hunt you down.'

I wondered if Cherise knew; after all, she'd never seen that look. Did they have a relationship or was the woman staring me down just hoping that some day they would, just serving in silence, wishing that one day her employer would notice her? I hoped it was the former. I wanted everyone to have the love they wanted, even if I didn't always know what *I* wanted.

'The Harlion House,' the woman said.

'Thank you, Galin,' Cherise said.

I took a moment to glance through the window at the house. It was the kind of place you see in movies, when they want to show that someone's rich and slightly eccentric. Big old brick house with lots of gables and details. High walls around the yard, lots of soft lights that you knew were probably plugged into some high-end security system. Big circular drive with a couple of very expensive cars idling near the door.

The place was either saved from being a total cliché or turned into an even bigger cliché by the statuary along the driveway: tall green shrubs perfectly groomed into naked men, women and mythical creatures. A mermaid statue spat water from her mouth into a fountain filled with granite people fucking under the spray.

'You may walk until we're inside, and then I fully expect you to be in proper position,' Cherise said. Her voice wasn't unkind, but it was the voice of power, of authority. Clearly she was used to people obeying her. I wondered what would happen if someone gave her a hard time or rejected her orders. I had a feeling she knew just how to handle that.

We walked to the front door, Cherise's hand on my elbow. The instinct to guide her properly just rose in me, and I made sure she knew where the flagstones were and the steps and anything else that would trip her up. She walked beside and a little behind me, her touch light. She had far more confidence than my bumbling attempts would seem to give her, and I wondered if she'd been here a thousand times. Maybe she was just holding my arm to give me the impression that I was helping her, when in truth she didn't need me at all.

I rang the front-door bell, and someone opened it before I even took my hand away from the pearl buzzer.

'Please,' the young man at the door said. He wore a black suit, with a black shirt and a black tie. The combination was sharp and sexy and slightly unsettling against his pale skin and blond hair. 'Come in.'

He was in a small foyer-like space that was empty except for coats and outerwear. When we entered, he closed the front door behind us, sealing us into the small room. It was warm in the space, and cozy for a foyer. More like an inner room in a house than an entrance way. I wondered how someone accomplished that.

'You may prepare for the party here,' he said. 'Anything you leave will be quite safe.'

'Thank you,' Cherise said.

She reached out and found the buttons of the wrap she'd covered me with. Sometimes she moved with such authority, such confidence in my own movements, that I forgot she couldn't see me. How did she know exactly where I stood, or where the buttons fell? Had she memorised my body the first time she'd touched me? Was that what she'd been doing when she'd run her hands all over me and I'd just been swooning in lust at her touch?

The coat fell away and I didn't think about it any more. Suddenly and fiercely, I was exposed. And afraid. I hadn't thought very much about this moment, not really. And now it was here.

The man in the black-on-black-on-black took the coat from Cherise and then eyed me slowly, up and down. It wasn't leering, but appraising and appreciative.

'Lovely choice,' he said.

'Isn't she?' Cherise touched my cheek with her fingertips, a soft stroke of appreciation.

'Are you ready for this?' she asked. 'Last chance to turn back.'

'I'm ready,' I said. I had no idea if that was true. My

knees were shaking, and this time I knew it wasn't from cold. Cherise took hold of the leash and looped it loosely over her wrist.

Then she leaned in and kissed me, that kind of kiss that leaves you breathless and panting even as it's happening. Her lips were soft as velvet, cherry and peaches, her tongue a soft invitation to go deeper, to lean in and lose myself in the depths of her. I shivered slightly when she pulled away, her pale eyes unseeing, and yet, I knew, seeing some part of me, something that I wasn't entirely sure I'd seen myself.

'Down, girl,' Cherise said.

I stood for a few moments, uncertain. Part of me – the aroused part, the turned-on part, the excited part – wanted to do as she said. To just get down on my hands and knees, to be her dog, to lead her around, to be naked in front of everyone. The rest of me, all of the rest of me, oh my fuck the entire rest of me, wanted to run screaming back to somewhere, anywhere else.

I'd left Leather Bound so far behind, hadn't I? It felt like it. It felt like all of those miles between there and here were far longer than they seemed, and we'd entered another galaxy, another dimension, a Twilight Zone place where nothing was as it appeared to be and I would never be able to go back. And if I could go back, if I returned to my old life, would they remember me there? Would they look at me and say, 'Who are you? I'm sorry, I've never seen you before in my life'? All pictures of me would have disappeared; even Davian would be shaking his head, giving me that 'I'm sorry, but I don't know you' smile. Like some kind of bizarre Twilight Zone.

'Janine?' It was the first time I'd heard Cherise say my name in a while, and it brought me back into the moment. My real life was far away, yes, but it wasn't gone. It was just waiting, on hold, until I figured this out. And that was OK, wasn't it? This was me, standing there, in a foyer, wearing nothing but leather and rope, under the control of a blind woman, a stranger who'd finger-fucked me in her living room and was now getting ready to parade me around like a show dog in a room full of people I'd never met. All so I could find a book for a man that I was, what? Falling for? Maybe.

Was I really and truly OK with this? Yes.

Not only that, I was aroused by the idea. I knew I was already wet. I could feel myself dampening the ropes between my legs, could feel the heated lust rolling off my body, already beginning to take over the anxiety. This was no different than what I'd done before. With Davian.

OK, it was entirely different. But I could do it. I could.

Slowly, I lowered myself to my knees and then to all fours. The perfectly pressed pants of the man who'd let us in. The shoes of the others who'd come in and left them behind. Cherise's tall heels. It was different down here, but somehow exciting.

Cherise moved to kneel in front of me. Her hands caressed the collar at my neck and I heard the jingle of metal, something I couldn't see.

'You'll need a name while you're here,' Cherise said. My collar shifted and then I heard the sound of a click as she attached something to it. 'So everyone knows what to call you.'

I expected her to tell me what it said, but she didn't. Instead she stood and gave the leash a soft tug. 'Let's go,' she said.

The man in black opened the door for us, and I led us through. The carpet was soft pile, plush and thick, cushioning my way. I had never thought of being glad of a carpet until that very moment.

Inside, the main room was filled with people. Some were on their hands and knees, or sitting patiently on their haunches, clearly waiting for their master's command. Some of them even wore collars attached to leather or chain leashes. But it was clear from first glance that I was the only one in the room who was playing at being a dog. So much for being discreet.

Those who weren't waiting were already tangled in piles, kissing and licking at each other. Soft grunts and groans were mixed with murmured pleas, and everywhere the sound of skin meeting skin whetted my senses.

As we walked in, a number of guests turned to look at us. Men and women fully dressed, and clearly seeing me. Some eyed me for a long time, not leering but definitely appraising. Smiling at me as though they clearly approved of the view.

I balked, pulling back behind Cherise, suddenly trying to hide. Why had I stupidly assumed that everyone would be blind here, that no one would be able to see me in this getup? I'd even assumed that everyone else would be a dog. I bonked hard against Cherise's leg, felt her wobbling slightly in her heels. Her fingers tightened on the leash, not in anger but in an attempt to right herself from my jostling.

Damn it. I could do this. I could.

I closed my eyes and inhaled deeply, forcing myself to come back to centre. If I needed to be on display to get what I wanted, then I would do that. Let them look. Let them think I was crazy or awful, let them remark on my body, let them think what they would. The one thing I wouldn't let them think was that I was scared, that I was ashamed, that I wanted to roll up in a ball and die of my own cowardice. Which, of course, was what I really wanted to do.

Instead, I opened my eyes and lifted my head. I shifted

myself away from my hiding place against Cherise's leg and lifted my butt into the air. I could feel Cherise grow steadier as I did, and when I craned my neck to glance up at her – dear God, how did dogs do this all the time? They must have far more flexible necks than I did – I saw that she was smiling, the corners of her red mouth curled up as she lifted her own head. OK, I could do this. For me. For her. For Davian.

A pair of legs approached, clad in perfectly pressed dark jeans and a pair of well-shined leather shoes. Funny the things you noticed about people at this level.

'Cherise, how lovely to see you. And who's this new girl? She's delightful.' A hand reached down and gently touched my hair. I leaned into the soft touch almost instinctively. Everything felt good. My body was alive with electricity, with arousal, with the newness of it all. If I was going to do this, then I was going to do it all the way. No half-assed job for me, dammit.

Cherise murmured something I didn't quite hear, and then a face appeared in front of me. Dark hair, pale-blue eyes, the kind of smile that is disarming and wicked all at once. 'Well, hello there, little one,' the face said. 'Let me see what to call you...'

He plucked the tag on my collar between his fingers and read it to himself. His laugh was strong and beautiful, a cry of delight.

'Hussy,' he murmured. My face flushed, my cheeks going hot and prickly. Was that really what my tag said? Hussy? 'That seems apropos,' he said. He looked up at Cherise, one hand stroking me gently under my chin. 'Are you planning to share your lovely pup with the rest of use, Cheri, or is she just for you this time?'

Again, Cherise murmured something that I couldn't make

out. If I had had real dog ears I would have perked them just to try and hear better. As it was, all I could do was turn my head sideways, but that didn't help much.

The man responded with another laugh, and then his face lifted out of my view, leaving only his jeans and shoes again.

On one of the couches a man lounged, his arm along the back of the cushions. At his feet rested a woman wearing nothing but a purple leather collar and a matching pair of wrist cuffs. Her lips were pinkish-red, the colour of a tongue. Or of a pussy. I couldn't stop looking at them, their wet plumpness, their dark contrast against her white skin. She caught my eye and flicked her tongue out, a gesture that was part playful and all sex. I felt my own mouth moisten in response. She leaned in towards the man, not touching him, but making him respond nonetheless.

He turned from the woman he'd been talking to – a fully clothed upright woman dressed in a long, simple black dress – and brought his hand to the pale woman's shoulder. As he turned, I caught a glimpse of the man's jaw, of his mouth, and then his face.

Wes?

I squinted, narrowing my eyes to see clearly.

Yes, it was Wes. A hundred per cent. What the hell was he doing here?

I ducked my face towards the floor, trying to hide my profile behind my hair.

If Cherise noticed my discomfort, she didn't say anything. She was busy talking to a black miniskirt in knee-high boots whose submissive was leering at me from the end of his too-long leash.

I lay down on the floor the best that I could, trying to make myself small and forgotten. *Look. Listen. Hear. Keep hidden.*

That's what Cherise had said. So that's what I would do.

The leering submissive moved in on me. Damn. He was all tongue and face, and I backed away from him. As though it wasn't bad enough for my asshole landlord to see me while I had this guy trying to hump my leg … This was just getting worse and worse.

I started to say something, but then I remembered I wasn't supposed to speak.

Sighing, I realised I was going to have to take matters into my own hands. Or paws, as it were. How did I get myself into shit like this?

The next time he came towards me, I snarled at him. A low sound in my throat, gravelly and totally inhuman. It was my first time trying it, so of course, it was way louder and much meaner than I meant it to be. The guy gave a yip like I'd actually bitten him or something, and backed off. Suddenly, Cherise was there, with a hand on my head. Black boots pulled her sub's leash in tighter. The room was quiet. Everyone, and I do mean everyone, was looking right at me.

Even Wes.

Fuck. Fuck. Fuck.

'Don't draw attention.' Isn't that what Cherise had said. 'Be unnoticeable.' That too.

So clearly the first thing I should do when I arrived at a place was draw every eye to me by getting into a fight. I wanted to stand up and say, 'And this, ladies and gentleman, is why I stay home and read books.'

Wes sauntered our way. God, why did assholes get to be hot? It just wasn't fair.

He came close enough that he was all shoes and pant legs.

'That's quite a little fighter you have there, Cher,' he said.

'In need of some training, if you ask me,' Cherise said. Her voice had been sharp before, but now it was nearly bitter. Cutting. If it was fake, it was a good fake. If it was at all real, I felt like the world's largest asshole.

'What's she called?' Wes asked.

Cherise's response was a murmur, but this time I could hear her clearly. The room was still silent, although the soft sound of talking was beginning to return.

All I could think about was what I must look like. Wes was standing directly in front of me, so close I could smell him, that dark musk of his skin. I didn't dare look up. Maybe he couldn't see my face, couldn't tell that I was one of his tenants. I kept my eyes on the perfectly stitched seams of his dark jeans, on the leather of his shoes.

I caught another snatch of the conversation taking place above me, and cocked my head sideways to listen.

'I'd be happy to take her in hand for you, see if I can't teach her a thing or two,' Wes said.

'That would be absolutely lovely,' Cherise said. 'If you think you can work some magic on her, I'd be in your debt.'

'I do believe I can do just that,' Wes said.

He had my leash in his hand, and he snapped the end of it lightly against my thigh. It stung, just barely enough to make me yelp. Wes laughed above me, then squatted down in front of me. He caught my collar in his fingers and tugged it, forcing my head up.

'I know you,' he said. 'You are –'

A voice cut him off, a voice I knew. 'Why don't you let me have a go at her instead? So that you can attend to your party, Wes.'

I couldn't hear Wes's answer, but I could hear Davian's voice say, 'Please, don't worry about it. It's my job.' I was never so happy to hear that man's voice.

The next face in front of me was Davian's.

'Come along, Hussy,' he said. The sound of my puppy name on his tongue sent a shiver of want through me, a shameful desire, a feeling so sharp and strong that it made my pussy flare.

Jesus, I really was a hussy, wasn't I? Everything turned me on these days. But especially, especially, this man who was taking my harness in both hands, who was urging me towards the back of the room.

I cast a glance at Cherise, who nodded as though she could actually see me. Her ability to sense what I was feeling was uncanny, and I wondered if that was part of what made her such a great lover. Without her sight, she was intuitive in her understanding of what those around her wanted and needed. So intuitive, so aware, in fact, that I wondered if her ignorance of the sub harassing me had been feigned.

Davian had said he wouldn't be here. So what was he doing, leading me on my hands and knees towards the door?

* * *

'I should like to see your form of discipline, Davian.'

Wes's voice followed us. Ahead of me, Davian stopped so abruptly that I nearly ran into the back of his legs.

'It is, after all, my party,' he said. 'And you've brought an uninvited guest.'

I wanted to say that he hadn't brought me, but I wasn't sure if I was still bound by the rules of dog-ness. Besides, I'd already got myself in more than enough trouble.

Wes continued. 'So, I'd like to watch you do your work. I've heard you're quite good. And this –' I heard Wes approach and lowered my head yet again, but he caught my chin in his fingers, forcing my head up again '– is quite a lovely specimen. Aren't you, Janine?'

I've never wanted so badly in my life to bite someone's fingers.

Instead, I stayed quiet and brought my gaze up to Wes's. I'm not a hater, usually, but I hoped he could see my intense dislike of him in my narrowed eyes.

Davian turned, catching my gaze with an unspoken question. I nodded at him as best I could while still being held by Wes's tight grip.

'I'll need a table,' Davian said. 'Something knee-height.'

Wes snapped his fingers at one of the naked men holding silver trays. In moments, a long low table appeared next to me.

'Return to your conversations,' Davian said, opening his arms to the entire crowd. 'I need a few minutes to prepare.'

'Up,' he said, popping his hand on top of the empty table. I hesitated, uncertain. I was pretty sure I could crawl up there on all fours. Most of the eyes in the room were on Davian, but I knew that, if I followed Davian's command, those eyes would be on me sooner rather than later.

But I'd promised. And I'd come this far.

So I slowly shifted my weight and climbed up onto the table.

While fussing over my harness, Davian leaned in close to my ear.

'How does Wes know you?' he asked.

'What are you doing here?' I asked in return. 'I thought you weren't supposed to.'

'Listen to me,' he said. His face was so close to mine I couldn't believe our lips weren't touching. But there was none of the heat that had been in his eyes. It had been replaced by anger or confusion, or maybe both. 'How does Wes know you?'

'He's our landlord,' I said. 'Lily's and mine. At Leather Bound.'

'Fuck,' he said. He dropped his head for a moment, sighing. 'You really are a pain in the ass,' he said. 'And so fucking irresistible I can't keep my hands off you. You make me insatiable, always, but roped up like that, on your hands and knees, with your leash in my hands? I can barely think. And right now I need to think.

'We're going to have to get out of here,' he said.

'But I didn't find the book yet.'

He shook his head, telling me that it didn't matter.

Someone brought him a tray full of toys and, watching me, he chose one, a thin black crop. It had been a long time since I'd played like that, but I remembered it well, the whistle and slice through the air, then the crack and sting of the leather hitting my ass. I didn't think I could get any wetter, but my body certainly seemed to be trying. I clamped my thighs tight together, aware that there were eyes on my exposed ass, on my naked and pulsing pussy.

Davian cocked a brow at me, a question in its own right, and I nodded. I wanted to tell him the whole story, how long it had been and how much I wanted that, maybe needed that, from him. But I couldn't. So I merely did what Cherise had recommended. I leaned forward and licked the hand that held the crop.

Grinning, he caught my collar in one hand and ran the crop lightly over my curves with the other. The leather teased in its soft touch, almost tickled. He trailed it between my thighs, smacking the insides lightly.

He pulled it back and a moment later, brought the end of

the leash down against my ass, the leather cutting into my curves, causing a yelp to come tumbling out of my mouth. The pain was unexpected but delicious, a single sear of fire that ran down my skin and then faded to nothing.

A crowd was gathering around the table. I could feel the weight of their gazes as Davian began to move around me, reaching out to tweak a nipple with one hand, his other moving my thighs farther apart. The harness kept snagging against my labia as I moved, a pain that eased into pleasure, and then seesawed between the two until all of my senses were focused on the hollow space between my thighs. A space that Davian quickly filled by inserting two fingers.

I groaned in pleasure as he scissored his fingers inside me, then remembered that I was supposed to be a dog and let the sound turn into some kind of growly noise that felt right. Especially when his thumb began to circle the tight tenderness of my ass. I clenched, pushing back into his touch, aching for that, barely noticing how quickly I'd stopped noticing or caring about the gathering crowd. All I cared about was Davian touching me and where and for how long and why he wasn't doing more of it.

'She's delicious.' An orange minidress and thigh-high boots came to stand in front of me, running her hands lightly through my hair. 'Are you going to share her?'

'She's hardly mine,' Davian said. 'I found her being unruly with her master.' He pinched and tugged a nipple as he spoke, sending little spasms through me so that I gasped. 'If she likes you, you're welcome to her.'

The woman knelt down in front of me and leaned in to kiss me. She had short dark hair and light green eyes. But I recognised the mouth, those perfect lips. Kitty, without her wig and contacts. Her smile was cherry red and full of lust, and I met the press of her lips with a fierceness that surprised me.

'Mmm,' she said. 'You taste as good as your partner.'

Kyle? Davian? I didn't know who she was talking about. I wanted to ask, but a moment later, she held a red ball gag in front of me. It was clear from her expression that she was waiting for me to accept it. I opened my mouth, and a second later I was nearly gagging, the red orb keeping my mouth wide and full.

'Gorgeous,' she breathed. She kissed me around the gag, licking my lips with her warm pink tongue.

If I kept my head down, I couldn't see Wes, standing there, his arms crossed over his chest. If I kept breathing, my gasps ragged and harsh around the rubber, I could almost pretend that I wasn't in front of an entire room of people who were watching me. Davian brought his crop down on my ass again and again, until my flesh was pink and sore, his fingers working my clit with a fierceness that made an orgasm hover just out of my vision. The woman in front of me had a hold of my nipples, every tug of her fingers causing little mewling noises to come through the gag.

'Come for me, hussy,' Davian hissed. 'Come for me, you little bitch.'

I couldn't help it. I came for him, my pussy clenching hard and fast, my head snapping back with the pleasure of it. If I hadn't had a gag in, I swear I would have been howling at the moon.

Instead, I let a second orgasm roll through me, a sweet surrender that had me shuddering and breathless.

It wasn't until I felt Davian's hands softly caress my burning ass, felt him touch the top of my head and heard him whisper, 'Good girl,' into my ear, that I could breathe again.

CHAPTER 15

Once my orgasm receded and my lust was sated, at least temporarily, I wanted answers.

I didn't think I was going to get them tonight.

Davian barely got me through my front door before I felt exhaustion come over me. I yawned, my jaw cracking. He'd unwrapped me after the party, peeling the layers of rope off of me until I'd stood before him, naked and tingly. Then he'd run his fingertips over every indentation left by the ropes before he'd wrapped me in a coat and taken me home.

'Tell me everything,' I said, as I peeled my coat off, not even caring that I was entirely naked in front of him. 'I need to know everything.'

'After you sleep,' he said.

He said something after that but I lost it in another yawn.

'To bed with you,' he said.

I had a moment to realise he was leading me into my bedroom, and another moment to think about how surprisingly comfortable I was with that. He'd never been here, but he moved like he knew the place. I was OK with that too.

Sleep kept threatening me, especially once Davian got into

bed with me, still clothed, his body radiating heat next to me. But there were a few things I needed to know.

'Why was my landlord there?' I asked as I snuggled up next to him, fully aware it was an action that would speed sleep towards me but unwilling to resist. 'And why were you there? I thought you weren't supposed to be there. Or something.'

When I get sleepy, my words catch on themselves. I fought it.

'I didn't know he was your landlord,' he said. He kissed me on the corner of my mouth, and I turned into it, unable to resist feeling the press of his lips against mine. 'You were so hot, all roped up, that I couldn't stand not to come. I thought I'd just stand in the corner and watch, but when I saw Wes coming toward you, I wanted to save you. He's kind of a dick.'

I laughed at that.

'You rescued me?' I had no idea why that made me feel all warm and fuzzy, but I was going to blame it on the blanket that he threw over me.

'Yeah,' he said. 'But I blew it. You didn't need rescuing, and I made everything worse. Now he knows that we're together.'

Together. I felt him pause when he said that, as though he hadn't expected to say it any more than I'd expected to hear him say it.

'Which means we're going to have to find the book another way,' Davian said. 'If Wes knows you're looking for the book, he'll try to stop you.'

'Why?' I asked. The pieces were finally coming together, but they were still shadowy and dark, and sleep was threatening to overtake me.

Davian moved closer to me, throwing one arm around me and tugging me towards him.

'Because whoever has the book runs the club,' Davian said. 'And Wes wants, more than anything, to have that power. The trouble is, no one else wants him to have it, but they're too scared of him to say so.'

'Who runs the club now?' I said.

'Wes thinks he does,' he said.

He was kind of talking nonsense. I tried to process everything, to work my head around it, but one thing kept eluding me. The trouble was that I couldn't even figure out what the thing was, so it wasn't like I could ask about it.

'Where's your tattoo?' I asked. 'You must have a tattoo.'

'I'll show you tomorrow,' he said.

Which ended up being fine because about a second and a half later, I was out, lost to the world of dreams and sex.

* * *

I woke in the half-light, Davian spooned around my body, breathing lightly in my ear. Sometime in the night, he'd stripped himself of his clothes. My bed smelled like the two of us, and the heat of his half-hard cock was a beautiful thing against the curve of my ass.

I was starving and achy all over. But there was no way I was going to get up right away. This moment was too perfect.

He snugged his body to mine, murmuring half-sleepy things in my ear.

'Yes,' I said back to him, assuming he would never hear, assuming that my words would be little more than dream fodder.

'Good,' he said. He was awake with a suddenness that surprised me. He leaned over me and caught my mouth in a rough kiss, his stubble raking my face. How fast he brought me to desire, with little more than a touch, a word. Barely awake, and still I wanted every part of him inside me, wanted to feel the lust of his body against my own.

I rolled onto my back, loving the look of him looming over me, his gaze both sleepy and wanting. I reached for his cock and stroked the underside softly. He rewarded me with a shuddering groan, his cock growing harder with every touch.

'Spread your legs,' he whispered, and watched while I did so. His gaze on me as I dipped two fingers into my wetness almost undid me. Never before had I wanted to be watched this way. I never wanted him to stop looking. I rolled my clit between my fingers, listening to his sharp intake of breath that nearly matched my own.

'Condoms?' he asked. And then he found them on his own anyway. He didn't take his gaze from mine as he rolled the condom over his erection. That gaze was filled with so damn much. Want. Greed. Lust. Something else. Something that I knew was echoed in my own expression.

Slowly, he lowered himself between my thighs, sliding his hips forward so that his cock nudged against my opening. Kissing me, he shifted forward. Giving me just a little. Teasing me.

'Stay still,' he said.

He kissed me again and moved into me, slightly deeper. A small stroke of pleasure. A promise.

I couldn't stand it. I wiggled against him, urging him deeper.

He pulled away, laughing.

'What did I say?' he said.

'I don't know?' I countered. 'Forgive me?'

'Against my better judgment, you are irresistible,' he said.

He gave another tiny movement forward, pushing deeper. I ached to stay still. I wanted all of him, every single bit, as deep as he would go.

'You should know,' he said. 'Before we get any deeper into this...'

'Mmm, yes, deeper, please...'

'I'm serious, Janine.'

'If you're so serious, you shouldn't be talking with my pussy full.'

'It isn't full yet,' he said. He entered me, fully, his hips pushing to mine. Every part of me came alive, starting with my pussy and echoing upwards and outwards. My toes curled. Meaningless words came out of my mouth.

'Now it's full,' he said. He didn't make it to the end of the sentence before his voice dropped off, growing guttural and snarly. It was hot as hell.

Little shivers worked their way up and down my spine, tiny promises of what was to come as he leaned down to kiss me, still stroking inside me. My hips slid up to meet him, greedy for, well, everything. I wanted it harder, faster, fuller. And yet I also wanted it slower, sweeter, the lingering almost-there of orgasm that I loved so much.

He gave me both, bringing me to the edge and easing me back down again until we were both panting, grinning, our desire sliding into that euphoria of sustained pleasure.

'No. More,' he said. Sliding himself upright, he brought me with him, until I was nearly on his lap. He lifted me again and again, bringing me down hard over his cock. I leaned in to kiss him, and it was all teeth and snarl and ohfuck. I touched my clit with a finger. More little sparks, the kind that went straight to my head, sang light and sweet songs of pleasure.

'I'm going to come,' I whispered against his mouth.

'Me too,' he said. He stroked into me, hard, his beautiful eyes half-closing even as he struggled to keep watching me.

I stroked my clit, once, twice, and then I was over, moaning his name, good, strong pleasure filling my body and brain. I felt him come before I heard him, a long shuddering stroke, and then he was kissing my face, my cheeks, the corners of my mouth.

'Janine,' he whispered.

And somehow that was everything.

* * *

'What were you saying before?' I asked. 'When you wanted to get all important-talky and I just wanted to fuck you?'

He laughed low against the side of my neck.

'I just wanted you to know that I wouldn't always be so nice,' he said.

'That was nice?'

'I mean –' he said, his voice serious '– that I'm a professional dom for a reason. I like my kink. Bondage and leather and a gorgeous girl with tousled hair and glasses down on her knees sucking my cock.'

Even if he hadn't been touching me while he talked, his words alone would have made my nipples ping the way they were, would have made my pussy constrict the way it did.

'I like my kink too,' I admitted. 'Don't get me wrong. I dream of you fucking me sweet and slow, but mostly I imagine you cuffing my wrists, bending me over, tying me down or up. Using those big hands on some tender part of my body.'

He growled softly and tightened his body against mine.

'Good,' he said. 'Very very good.'

A moment later, he draped his arm over me. 'Also, here,' he said. He turned his arm to show me the inside of his wrist, the one where he usually wore his watch.

A small tattoo. A keyhole and, next to it, a skeleton key.

'Both?' I asked.

'Keyhole first,' he said. 'Then key.'

Keyholder, I thought, remembering the man who'd fed me in the Blind Café.

'Thank you,' I said.

He murmured something unintelligible against my neck and in seconds, he was asleep. My body threatened to follow suit if I didn't get up. I wanted nothing more than to stay in bed all day, curled up with Davian, drifting to sleep together, but that wasn't an option. Leather Bound, the current mistress of my life, called her siren call. I'd left too much of my work in Lily's hands lately. I needed to get back to my real life.

Leaving the bed and Davian's sexy, warm body was one of the hardest things I'd done in a long time.

I wanted to kiss Davian more, to feel his lips against mine, but he was already conked out again. I guessed he needed the sleep just as much as I did, and I didn't want to wake him. Looking down at him before I left, I had a slippery moment of déjà vu, of time moving ahead and still leaving you in the same place as before. I fully expected Davian to wake up and say something life-changing when I walked out the door, but he was silent except for the soft sound of his breathing.

Walking to the bookstore, I realised I desperately needed three things: food, coffee and something that resembled a normal day.

* * *

I was surprised to find the front door of Leather Bound unlocked when I got there. Lily must have beaten me here and forgotten to lock it behind her.

I shut the door behind me and turned.

'Hey Lil, I –' My voice died away as I saw the store. Leather Bound was trashed. Shelves sat almost empty. Books littered the floor in haphazard piles and jumbles, most of them opened, as though some ADD-addled child had riffled through all of their pages, found nothing of interest and thrown them back down.

Oddly, nothing else was touched. Lily's hand-drawn signs were still intact. The ladder leaned, haphazard as always, looking as if it had been used, but unharmed. The register still squatted its frog squat on the front counter. Even the window displays were pristine. Someone had ransacked the velvet room, but no more than they had anywhere else. My office appeared to be still locked, which was one small joy in the midst of a thousand sadnesses.

As I stood there, confused and miserable, something else ripped through my gut. An anger that made me clench my fists. Assholes. It was one thing to ruin someone's store, to try to destroy their livelihood. And entirely another to destroy the thing they loved most. To destroy someone else's story. What right did anyone have to do that?

I forced myself to breathe, pushing air in and out of my lungs with a fierceness that left my light-headed and huffing. But at least I felt like I was in a little more control. I still wanted to punch whoever had done this, but I didn't want to punch them with a crowbar any more.

'Lily?' I called.

'Back here,' she said. Her voice was wobbly and broken.

I found her kneeling on the floor, already trying to piece things back together. She looked up at me as I approached, her fingers moving still on the page she'd been flattening. She wasn't crying, but it was clear she'd done so before I got there; her usual perfectly done eyes were smeared, her nose a soft pink. Her lips trembled as she pinched them tight. Webster was curling around her legs, mewling at her, clearly confused but unharmed.

'What happened?' I asked. 'Did you call the police?'

She shook her head, tried to speak, then closed her mouth when tears welled up again.

'I'll call them,' I said.

If I was speaking, it was only because my mouth was still going, as though it was trying to finish the sentence it had started when I'd walked in. But clearly Lily's wasn't doing at all what she wanted it to.

I couldn't look in her eyes or I would have joined her in the tear club and then we'd both be blubbering. And I didn't dare touch her; I was afraid we'd both lose it for real.

I kneeled down to help her, choosing a book at random, lamenting the creases at the corners of the pages. I started to ask what happened, but that wouldn't come out, stuck in the tight close of my throat.

Our dream seemed like it was falling apart, bit by bit, like the seams of your favourite sweater unravelling while you weren't looking. Pretty soon I felt like I would wake up naked, with nothing but a pile of yarn next to me, having no idea what had just happened.

First Wes and his stupid rent hike. Then losing the book trail. Now a break-in. If someone was sending me a message, it was coming through loud and clear.

Lily and I worked in silence for a while, I don't know how long. Smoothing out creases the best we could, putting books back in their rightful places. Some of the books didn't even belong to this section of the store; it was like someone had flung them as hard as they could across the store just to see where they'd land. We started making piles of those, and as they rose higher and higher, all I could think about was how much work we had cut out for us.

When my fingers felt like they'd taken all of the paper cuts they could, I plopped myself on the floor with a sigh.

Lily tucked a few more books back into their proper places. The shelves near us were almost full again. Lily looked stronger too, more together; putting things in their proper place always made her feel that way, I think. I felt like I was the last one to join the party; my gut was still too tight, my legs shaky, my throat like a tiny straw that was impossible to breathe through.

Lily dropped down beside me and we looked at the incomplete shelves for a long time. Our dreams were still messed up, and getting worse. But at least I wasn't alone.

'I'll go call the police,' I said.

I reached over and took her hand, and she let me, even tightening her fingers around mine.

'We'll get through this,' I said. 'Us, and Leather Bound. We'll all survive this. I promise.'

'I know,' she said. 'I just thought it would be easier than this.'

My laugh was sharper than I meant it to be, harsh. It came out of my chest in a sharp push. 'Yeah, I think that about a lot of things lately.'

Lily leaned into my shoulder, and I put my arm around her. Her sobs were fierce, shaking her whole body as she cried.

'I'm sorry,' she said.

I had no idea what she meant.

* * *

I called the police while Lily went and, in her words, 'fixed her face.'

When she came back, her make-up was perfectly put together. You could barely tell she'd been crying, except for the tiny patches of pink at the corners of her eyes. I envied her for a moment, but I also didn't. In the midst of pain, the last thing I wanted to add to my plate was worrying about how I looked.

'What'd they say?' she asked.

'They said they'd be right over, and asked if we touched anything.'

'Um,' Lily looked at the books we'd already put away. 'Whoops.'

'Yeah, I'm sure it will be fine. They said not to touch anything else. Besides, it's not like they're actually going to find out who did this.'

'You don't think?' She started to pick a couple more books off the floor and then realised what she was doing and put them back down.

'Janine,' she started. 'This might be my fault.'

'What do you mean?'

'I mean, I came here last night and I might have forgotten to lock the door.'

She clearly had more to say. She was rubbing her tattooed ear, blinking at the floor.

I waited.

'I told you I met someone,' she said finally. 'And she, she likes to have sex here, in the bookstore. I might have forgotten to lock the door.'

A vision of Lily on my desk filled my mind. Did I tell her I'd seen her? Would it make her feel better or worse?

I didn't say anything. I just gathered her in my arms,

saying, 'It's OK. It's not your fault,' until the police arrived.

They showed up quickly, two men, all dressed to the nines despite the early hour.

They asked a ton of questions and took a ton of photos. They were polite and thorough, but didn't give us much hope of catching the people who'd ransacked the store.

'It is odd that the door wasn't jimmied or broken,' said one of the officers, a tall thin man with short graying hair, who'd said to call him Jim.

I didn't say anything. I wanted them to find out who did this, but not at the expense of Lily's guilt.

'Who else has your keys?' he asked.

Lily and I looked at each other.

'No one, as far as I know,' I said. 'We had them made special when we renovated.'

'Where do you keep them?' he asked.

I sheepishly pulled mine from around my neck to show him. He raised a brow, but didn't say anything. Not even when Lily, less sheepishly, but with exaggerated ease, pulled hers from a secret pocket inside her skirt band. I almost cracked up at that; I knew she wore hers on her at all times, like I did, but I assumed she wore it around her neck as well, or maybe in her cleavage. I hadn't expected the skirt.

'So just two keys then?' he asked.

'Yes,' I said. 'Wait. Actually no. We had three keys made. But one of them was for our original landlord, Conrad. He liked to come here and read books sometimes when we were closed.'

'Where is this Conrad now?'

'He ...' Was this the first time I'd tried to say this out loud? My heart did a funny little stutter step, like it wanted to run away in fear but banged itself against the wall of my ribcage and couldn't go any farther. Lily reached out and took my hand in hers. For the second time that day, I felt the fluttery pulse in her thumb as our fingers entwined.

'He passed away a few months ago.'

'I'm sorry for your loss,' Jim said. It was such a common phrase, one you heard all the time, but he actually sounded sincere. I liked him for that. 'Do you know where that key might have gone?'

'I don't, actually.'

A moment later, I said. 'You know what? I might. Our new landlord might have a copy.'

I gave him Wes's name and address, which he wrote down in a little book. 'You should consider getting your locks changed,' he said. 'I can recommend someone if you'd like.'

'That would be great, thank you,' I said.

He pulled out another small notebook and wrote down a name and number. 'I'd recommend not waiting,' he said. 'Locks like these are easy to pick.'

'How do you know so much about locks?' I asked.

He smiled, and I saw that some of those laugh lines were smile lines. They were a nice frame to his eyes. 'My early days on the force were mostly breaking-and-entering. There was a lot more of that kind of crime then. These days, it's mostly shootings and meth heads and ...' He waved a hand through the air as if he didn't want to go on and on with such a list. 'Awful stuff,' he said finally. 'I kind of miss those days.'

'Not to devalue what's happened to you and your store,' he added quickly. 'It's devastating, to be sure. But no one's bleeding, and that's a real positive in my book.'

Bleeding. I hadn't even thought of that. In all the worry about the books and the store, it hadn't even occurred to me that something far worse could have happened. What if

Lily had gotten there just a little earlier, what if she'd walked in on whoever had done this while they were doing it? If something had happened to her...

This time, it was my turn to wave the thought away. I didn't want to think about it.

'Thank you for your help,' I said because I didn't know what else to say.

'It's my job,' he said.

Which was true.

'Besides, I love books.' That soft smile again, and I wondered yet again what his home life was like, who he was when he wasn't in uniform. I imagined him in a big easy chair in front of a fire, a dog stretched out at his feet, a book in his hands. Somewhere in another part of the house, someone was humming or singing or talking. It was a good image, out of a good story. Lately, I felt like I needed more good stories in my life. More happy-ever-afters and fewer hungry wolves in the woods.

'Well,' I said, 'consider Leather Bound your book version of a coffee shop. Come in any time. I can't afford to give you free books, but I can promise to take really, really good care of you.'

'Will do,' he said.

His colleague joined him, and he tipped his hand at me, in that old-fashioned kind of way that I loved. I watched them walk away, basking just for a moment in the way that everything felt right with the world. And then I went back inside to face the reality of the disaster that was my life.

* * *

Lily looked as exhausted and dirty as I felt. We'd cleaned up a lot already, but we were still so far from done that it made me want to cry. Books still littered the floors. Shelves gaped half-empty. The SHUT sign hadn't been turned. Nothing was where it was supposed to be. Except, thankfully, my office, which looked like it hadn't been touched.

'I think we're going to have to stay closed for a couple of days,' I said.

'Can we afford that?' Lily asked.

'No,' I said. 'But I don't know what else to do. We can't open like this and ...' I had to stop. I wasn't going to fall apart. I refuse.

'Maybe we can just miss today,' Lily said. 'It's only ...' She leaned around the shelf and looked at the clock over the counter. 'Crap. It's later than I thought.'

'I know.' The inertia, the lack of ability to actually accomplish what we needed to do, seemed to stop us both in our tracks. We stood for a moment, surrounded by homeless books, panting as though we'd been running a marathon instead of reshelving.

'I need coffee,' I said. 'If I have coffee, I can do this.'

She perked. 'Think we can get them to deliver us some?'

I didn't even wait to answer. I called Cream.

'Cream. How can we sugar you, sugar?' It was the same woman who'd waited on me last time.

'Hey, is Stefan there?' I hated calling in a favour. Well, it wasn't even a favour. Stefan didn't owe me anything. It was more like calling in a friendship. I could only hope that Stefan wouldn't mind.

'I'm so sorry,' she said. 'He's gone for the day. Actually –' she dropped her voice low, as though sharing a secret with me '– they're all gone for the day. They left me here all by myself. I tell you, if I didn't love this job ...' Then she brightened. 'But I can take a message for you.'

'It's OK.' I said. The phone was too heavy for me to hold any more. Such a simple thing, a way to save us from ourselves, a cup of coffee delivered. And we couldn't even have that. It was silly, but it felt like the last straw, the thing that was going to make all of this impossible.

Lily was behind me when I turned, her face expectant. That changed as soon as she saw my expression.

'Well, crap,' she said.

'Yeah.' We looked at the mess, at the clock.

'Let's make the best of it,' I said. 'No one got hurt, nothing is broken.' I was nowhere close to convincing myself, and it was clear that I wasn't convincing Lily either.

* * *

It wasn't twenty minutes later that there was a knock on the front window.

Stefan waved at us through the glass, then lifted the coffees in his fists as offerings. Behind him stood half a dozen people. A couple of baristas I recognised from Cream. Jay, looking half-asleep. I was sure Stefan had roused him from bed long before his bar-nightowl self would have liked. The blue-haired singer from the bar. It was a motley crew, but one I was incredibly glad to see.

I opened the door and ushered them in. They smelled like cold air and lots and lots of coffee.

'Coffee delivery, sugar?' Stefan asked.

'I have never been so happy to see someone in my whole life,' I said. Just saying that made me want to cry. I could hear Lily laughing behind me in delight as the others laid down fixings: coffee, bagels and a bunch of spreads.

'You girls eat and caffeine up for when the store opens,' Stefan said. 'We've got this.'

I didn't even recognise Kitty until she hugged Lily with a low murmur. Then I recognised her twice: first as Kitty and then as the woman who'd fucked Lily so lovingly in my office. Despite everything that had happened so far today, watching the two of them together made me smile.

Stefan ran the team as efficiently as he ran Cream, putting everyone into an aisle and telling them what they needed to do. Soon, the sound of books being reshelved was all around us. Lily and I stuffed our faces, then got to work beside everyone. Less than an hour later, nearly everything was put back in its proper place.

'I think we can open now,' Lily said.

'Turn that sign, Miss Lily,' Stefan said, laughing.

Lily turned it. When everyone cheered, I did cry. Tears came hot and fast. Jay put his arms around me, squeezing me so hard I wasn't sure I could breathe.

'All right, crew, prepare to move out,' Stefan said.

Once they were outside, Stefan leaned in and kissed Lily's cheek, and then mine.

'Thank you, Stefan,' I said. I had to ask the question that had been bugging me. 'But how did you know?'

'Hello, sugar. Coffee shop. Cops. I know everything that goes on our lovely little neighbourhood. But next time, if you need help, you call and ask me, yes?'

'Promise,' I said.

'Good,' he said. 'Now go sell some books. And, you still owe me a very sexy tale, do you not?'

I nodded.

'Don't make me wait,' he said.

* * *

A few books hadn't made the reshelving process for one reason or another. Too damaged. Or someone didn't know where they belonged. They were piled on the end of the counter, and I flipped through them. Maybe we could put them all on sale, a special discount.

I picked up a book of black and white photos and flipped through it. Something fluttered out from the back. A photo, from the looks of it, with something written on the back. I leaned down and picked it up.

Davian and C.K., it read.

I took a deep breath and turned the photo over.

It was a black and white photo, the kind of artsy shot that can sometimes change someone's features, make you wonder if it's really who you think it is. But I'd fucked the man. I would recognise Davian anywhere.

He was standing, profile to the camera, dressed in a '40s-style outfit. Those perfect-fit pants, a white button-up, a jacket that showed off his wide shoulders and thin waist. A hat cocked in a perfect jaunt on his head, and his hair pulled back. He had grown a small goatee, and it darkened his features just a little, brought the sexy out.

It wasn't Davian's image that surprised me the most. Next to him, his arm slung over Davian's shoulders, was a slightly older man, his dark hair clearly silver-tipped even in the photo. He was looking at Davian and his smile was a beautiful thing, full of love.

Something clicked about that smile. I'd seen it before, aimed at me. I took the photo over closer to the light from the picture windows and tilted it until I could see the man's face clearly.

The man in the photo was Conrad.

* * *

'Lily,' I said. 'Look what I found.'

I handed her the photo and heard her sharp intake of breath. 'I knew I recognised him from somewhere,' she said.

'You've seen this photo?'

She shook her head. 'Not that one, but one like it. I just can't remember where.'

Her eyes scanned the shelves, her mouth musing. Moments later she came back with another book, one I didn't recognise.

'I found this when I went through Conrad's books,' she said. 'I left the photo in because people like their ephemera. Of course, I didn't realise who it was at the time.'

She flipped to the back and there was another photo. In this one, the two men were harder to distinguish. They were kissing, their mouths pressed tight together, their bodies equally close. They were clearly intimate, and just as clearly in love.

'That's incredibly hot,' I said.

'I know, right?' she said.

'That also explains how Davian had one of our disaster cards,' I said.

I sat down on the nearby chair with a whoomp. Things were starting to come to light, finally.

'So Davian's friend C.K. is our friend Conrad,' I said. I had to say the stuff out loud so that my brain would start to clear out. 'That means, Conrad is the man who sent Davian here to find a sex club book that he lost.'

'Conrad would never lose a book,' Lily said. 'He took better care of his books than anyone I've ever known. And I'd say they were more than friends.'

'Yes,' I said, musing. 'That's what I don't get.'

Add Wes to the mix and things got really complicated.

It was an odd triad, with me somewhere in the middle. I wondered how much Davian actually knew about all this. He'd seemed genuinely surprised to realise that Wes was my landlord, which meant he probably didn't know that Conrad was my former landlord. And Wes had obviously been surprised to see me at his party.

Which meant that there was only one person who actually seemed to know what was going on.

And he'd been dead for months.

* * *

I needed to think, and clear my head. I thought about going to L&L, but I didn't think this was the kind of clarity that could be achieved through sex. For once, I needed something else. Something simple. Like a walk around the block.

Which I took, despite the cold. My mind kept spinning the questions over and over, but it was like being stuck in a rut. If Davian and Conrad knew each other, why hadn't Conrad ever mentioned Davian to me? I got why he'd never mentioned that he was head of the Keyhole Club. Vow of silence and all that. And was there even a book? If so, why had Conrad set Davian on the task of finding it, when he could have just come to me?

Here were the answers I found on that walk: not a single one.

When I got back to the store, Lily was manning the front counter. She gestured toward my office with her thumb. Davian was there, looking at the photos we'd found. I watched him from the door for a moment, revelling in his forearms, in the way his long legs tilted as he leaned against the counter. I wanted to run my hands through his dark curls.

Tug off his glasses. Kiss him until he begged me to fuck him. Instead, I cleared my throat.

Davian wrapped me in a bear hug that smelled so strongly of cinnamon and sugar that it nearly made me cry with desire and sadness. 'I'm so sorry this happened to the store,' he said.

'Me too,' I said.

Davian released me and then picked one of the photos off my desk. 'He was an amazing man, wasn't he?' he said.

'He was.'

'I loved him fiercely,' Davian said. 'But we were better friends than lovers. I think he was always sad to see me alone.'

'Why didn't you tell me?' I asked.

Davian shook his head. 'I didn't actually figure it all out until the morning. Well, actually, as soon as I heard the place was ransacked, I knew it was Wes, looking for the book. And then I put it all together.'

'Wes realised that raising our rent wasn't an option, so he came looking for the book on his own,' I said. Because, of course, if Conrad was going to lose a book – or in this case, hide it from someone – why not right in the midst of a million other books? 'Oh, God. What if he found it?'

Davian shook his head. 'I don't think he did. We should have heard about it already. He's not the type to keep his bragging to a minimum.'

'OK, so Conrad hid the book here. Maybe. But why? Why not just give it to you?'

Davian sat in the theatre chair, and I thought of the day he'd first come here, asking for help, and how I'd turned him down. Oddly, if it hadn't been for Wes and his stupid scheme to raise our rent, I never would have called Davian back. In some ways, I had Wes to thank for that.

'I never wanted to run the club,' Davian said. 'Conrad

knew that, if he asked me, I'd only say yes because I loved him and because he was dying. And he wasn't the kind of man to guilt someone into something. He gave me a sealed letter, and asked me to open it on a certain date and follow the instructions.'

'The day you came here,' I said. 'He wanted to give you time. And to make the book seem at risk.'

Conrad. How I loved him even more for taking care of someone that I was in love with.

Oh. That. I hadn't expected that thought.

'What was that look for?' Davian asked.

'Nothing,' I said.

'Liar.'

'I just, um …' I didn't know how to say it. I tried to dredge up a literary heroine, but all I could see was myself. 'I just realised I might be falling in love with you.'

'Really?' Davian asked, all grin, all wicked, wicked grin. He leaned back against my desk and pulled me against him. 'That's good to know.'

'It is?'

'Yes,' he said. 'I don't want to be the only one.'

It was like the first kiss all over again. Only better. Fuller. It carried our lust and this whole new thing, this swirl of emotions that made every part of me fluttery and warm. Forget seesaws. This was gravity-defying. Even the world seemed to shift off its axis.

And then I realised it wasn't the world. It was my desk, tilting on its bad leg.

I fell against Davian, laughing.

'Sorry,' I said. I almost said, 'Lily must have knocked it loose while she was getting fucked on it,' but instead I said, 'There used to be a book under there. I've been meaning to fix that.'

I got down on my hands and knees and felt around for the book. It was still under the short leg, but just barely. I pulled it out.

'Can you lift the desk, and I'll slide it back – um. OK. Wow.'

'What?' Davian said.

I held the book out. It wasn't the ancient, beat-up book I'd watched Conrad tuck under there so long ago. It was beautiful. Mahogany leather, so soft it felt like it was melting against the heat of my skin. Probably stretched and softened and cured by hand. Cream stitching up the spine. The front was hand-stamped THE KEYHOLE CLUB. And beneath that a keyhole shape was cut out of the leather, showing creamy paper inside.

There was a tiny indentation on the cover from the desk leg, but other than that it was unmarred.

'It's been here all along?' I said. 'Right here?'

My mind was moving faster than my mouth. Or maybe it was the other way around. Whatever was happening, I was pretty sure I didn't understand a second of it. The book I'd been, we'd been, looking for had been here, in Leather Bound, right under our noses.

My heart did that tight thing it does when it doesn't know what else to do, and I felt the prickle of tears.

'Open it,' Davian said, lifting his chin in my direction.

I ran a finger along the cover, over the indented title letters, across the clear-cut keyhole so I could feel the paper underneath. When I opened it, I caught a whiff of cured leather and paper, of the blue ink that covered the book's pages.

The front page had a single handwritten quote.

'Keyholes are the occasions of more sin and wickedness, than all other holes in this world put together.'
– Laurence Sterne

A piece of thin paper, newer and whiter than the other,
was stuck between the pages, near the middle, and I opened
the book there. It was folded in thirds.

I held the book out to Davian and he took the paper from
between the pages and opened it carefully.

'It's a letter from Conrad,' he said.

He started reading out loud.

Davian,

*If you are reading this, then I hope you're standing
in a bookstore next to an absolutely gorgeous
raven-haired woman. You can yell at me later for
attempting to set you up, but if you're where I hope
you are, then you already know that she's smart and
funny and absolutely perfect for you.*

I pulled back, startled. Did he mean me? Was that what
this had been about? An elaborate set-up? I didn't think that
seemed possible, not with everything else that had happened.

Davian kept reading.

*But of course, there's a more serious reason for this
note as well. I know you don't want to lead the club.
And that's why you're the right choice. And God
knows, the only other option is Wes, who's been
sniffing around since I got sick. God, he's such an
utterly self-centred pompous prick.*

The keeper of the book is the keeper of the key.
I write this, I dream of you at the helm of the
Keyhole, with that luscious woman at your side.

Yours (unless you stupidly refused either that amazing
woman or the book, neither of which I will ever
forgive you for),

Conrad

That was it. Davian folded the note again and tucked it back into the book. He looked as stunned as I felt. Neither of us said anything.

Lily's approach was accentuated by the tap of her heels.

'What's happening?' she said. 'Someone fill me in. I'm losing my mind.'

I passed her the book and let her read the note.

'Holy fuck,' she said.

Davian and I didn't say anything, but holy fuck was about as perfect an expression as I could think of. The pieces were falling into place, click click click, like a Rube Goldberg machine. You see something that doesn't make any sense, but as soon as you drop in the first marble, everything becomes clear at lightning speed, until you're just left standing there, in the middle of a glorious event.

'Are you going to take it?' Lily asked Davian. 'The position, I mean. Not the girl. I think we all know you're going to take the girl.'

My stomach looped.

'I don't know,' he said.

I watched his face, the emotions warring in the depths of his

273

eyes. He wanted to honour Conrad, of course. And to make sure the club that he cared about was protected, that it was kept safe from the likes of Wes. But I also knew he didn't want to be in control, didn't want to be at the helm of anything.

Although his desires manifested differently from mine and were for different reasons, he wanted to be anonymous, wanted to be away from centre stage, as much as I did. We were the same in that way. And yet he'd taught me to face that fear, to stare it down and say yes to it. It was easier with him at my side, of course. Easier knowing he was protecting me. I couldn't tell him what to do, but I could show him that I'd be there.

I stepped forward and put my hand over his.

'Whatever you choose,' I said. The rest was implied. *I will support you. I will stay by your side. I will share this new adventure with you.*

'If you mean that,' he said, and he paused, looking at me until I nodded, 'then we both sign it. We do it together.'

He pulled a fountain pen from his pocket and held it out. It was warm from his pocket, but his hand was warmer as he settled the pen into my palm. He opened the book at the back, where there was a long list of names. Two pages' worth, with Conrad's flourishy signature at the very bottom. Davian flipped to the next page.

'A new page,' he said. 'For a new way of doing things.'

Turning the book so that it was right side up for me, he held it out, his palms under it to steady it.

'I think you should go first,' I said. 'Conrad passed it to you.'

'I'm pretty sure he passed it to both of us,' he said. 'He's rather sneaky like that.'

'He is, isn't he?' I couldn't help but use the present tense; I knew he was gone, but it was like he was here with us, this man that we'd both known and loved, the man who'd changed our lives in so many good ways.

'Sign it, Janine,' Davian said.

I signed it, my full name, in a flourish, leaving room next to it for Davian's signature. He took the pen from me and added his name after mine. Smaller, more tightly curled. Together, they occupied exactly the width of the page.

We stood in silence, letting the ink dry. Then he closed the book.

'Not too late to change your mind,' he said to me. 'We can just rip that page out, pretend we never found it, never signed it.'

I moved towards him, catching the book between us, inhaling its leathered scent as it combined with Davian's spice. He leaned forward and kissed me, the kind of deep, lingering kiss that slowed time, that made me want to do nothing else ever again.

'It is too late,' I said, when the kiss ended, when my quick heart was still frantic and delighted in my chest. 'Because I've already said yes. And when I say yes, I mean yes.'

'I've noticed,' he said.

Behind us, Lily cleared her throat, making me laugh. I'd forgotten she was still standing there, probably waiting for a little more explanation.

But all she said was, 'OK, which one of you two is going to set me up, send me on a wild-goose chase, and then give me the key to my very own sex club so I can meet the love of my life?'

* * *

Lily forced us to go home, shooing us out of the store with

impossible-to-resist words like 'Go fuck yourselves silly.'

'But Lily,' I said.

'Seriously,' she said. 'I won't take no for an answer. We've already had a break-in. We don't need you setting everything on fire with your smouldering glances.'

She leaned in and kissed me, whispering in my ear, 'Besides, I've got a date tomorrow, so you can return the favour.'

'With Miss Hester Prim and Proper,' I teased.

Her big eyes went even bigger. 'How did you –?'

'I'll never tell,' I said. 'Thank you, Lil. For everything.'

She'd barely released me from her hug before I was tugging Davian out the door, impatient to get some part of his body naked against mine. He had the book in one hand – I had a feeling it was going to be a while before he let it out of his sight – and took my hand with the other.

'Want to sleep over at my place?' I asked.

'Again?' he teased. 'Didn't we just do that?'

'Well, if you're bored, then I'll just have to find someone else to invite home, strip naked and fuck until we fall dead of exhaustion.'

'Well, why didn't you say so?' he asked. 'That I can totally get behind.'

'I'm sorry,' I said. 'What I meant was, "Would you like to come home with me and fuck me until we fall dead of exhaustion?"'

'Yes,' he said. 'I want nothing more than to see you naked, bent over in front of me, looking back over your shoulder the way you do, with your eyes all smoky.'

'And then?' I said. My insides were already swirling with heat. I would have backed him against the wall and fucked him right here on the sidewalk if I'd thought I could get away with it.

He lifted the book, its heavy leather weight, and grinned

wickedly at me. 'Oh, I have some plans for that heart-shaped ass of yours,' he said. 'Not to mention that heart-shaped heart.'

'I'm glad,' I said. And I truly, truly was.

EPILOGUE

The art museum wasn't what I'd expected at all. I'd spent so much time in dark places lately that I'd anticipated more of the same. I thought I'd be hidden by shadows, that no one would be able to tell just how little fabric there was to my dress. Not to mention just how little there was under it.

But this was a real museum, with real museum lights. The brightness was turned slightly down for an after-hours feel, but not enough to hide anything. Least of all me, in my satin-red shine with so much of my pale skin showing through.

At least I was wearing underwear this time. Davian had suggested not, but I'd been afraid the egg he'd tucked into me before we left was going to fall out if I didn't. Apparently I could handle getting finger-fucked in a restaurant and having orgies in the dark, but I drew the line at the possibility of a sex toy falling out of me at an art exhibit.

'Ready for this?' Davian asked.

He'd stopped me in the art museum hallway, one hand on my shoulder, that creamy caramel gaze tracing my face.

That was such a huge question I wasn't sure how to answer it. So many things had happened between us in the last few days that my life felt topsy-turvy. The cops had held Wes for

279

questioning; they hadn't found any hard evidence, but they'd clearly scared him. He'd even offered to sell us the building, if Lily and I could scrape up enough money, saying he wanted to get out of town. We'd taken on our new roles as heads of the Keyhole Club behind the scenes, which, surprisingly, was far more boring paperwork and a lot less hot sex than I might have expected.

Not that I didn't have enough sex in my life. Davian kept me more than busy, and definitely never bored. I was deeply and truly in love and lust with the man who currently stood at my side, looking into my eyes. I felt like I could do anything with him, go anywhere.

So of course I knew the answer to his question.

'Yes,' I said. 'A thousand times yes.'

'You wore the perfect dress,' Davian said.

I hoped I would never stop reacting to his voice, the way just a word, even a simple word like *you*, had the power to make me wet. Or, in this case, wetter. Davian hadn't touched the remote for the metal egg, but the very fact that I could feel its presence, heavy and thick, inside me was making it hard to focus on anything else. 'And the perfect shoes.'

Wear heels, he'd said. At least six inches. So you feel like someone else, someone new, for the night.

Lily had volunteered to help me find a pair. She'd chosen these, with their patent-leather shine and eight-inch heels, the bottoms painted a dark red that matched my dress. I did feel like someone else. Someone taller, but also someone with a hell of a lot more confidence and legs that went on for ever.

'Thank you,' I said, my voice a whisper. The museum was oddly empty. We were the only ones in the long hallway. If you didn't count all of the painted and framed faces staring at us from the walls.

280

'Where is everyone?' I asked.

'What? I'm not enough for you? You need some more?' A heated tease threaded his voice as he brushed his fingertips along the exposed curve of my thigh. Both sets of cheeks prickled with heat.

'No.' I hesitated, trying to get control over the flush that ran through my body. 'I just, I meant ...' He still had the power to make me blush and stammer, and he used it every chance he got.

Davian left one hand on my hip and lifted my chin slowly with the other. Sometimes his eyes were that heated caramel of lust, but right now they were firmly golden, a gleam of power around the edges.

'It's OK,' he said, his voice serious now. 'I know you.'

'You do,' I said. There was comfort in that. And arousal. And something else that I was beginning to understand was something greater than myself. The way my heart moved when Davian so much as took my hand in his.

Davian didn't say anything else, just kept my hip captured with one hand and my face with the other, watching me. I took a deep breath, feeling the egg shift and settle inside me as I did so. It didn't help as much as I'd hoped.

Davian guided me a few steps backwards until I was leaning against the wall between two gilt-framed portraits. He pulled the remote from his pocket and toyed with it while he watched me.

Leaning in, he closed his teeth softly on the curve of my ear, his breath warm against my skin.

'I know,' he started ... and he turned the vibrations on.

I didn't hear anything else he said. My body liquefied around the solid object inside me, became a pool of heat and movement that shut off all thought. Davian's mouth moved along my ear, tongue and teeth, soft shuddering nips that raised my soft pleasure into something stronger. When he revved the vibrations, I had to close my eyes and move inwards, toward that point of pleasure in the centre of my body. Every part of me narrowed in to that single spot, focusing on the sensation. Tingles of pleasure spread outward, bringing me so close to orgasm I could almost taste it, while keeping it just out of range.

'Please,' I tried to say. Dear God, please let me come, please stop dangling me on the edge. My body clenched with want, with need. Davian still didn't release me from that place between pleasure and release. I could hear my own cries, whimpering requests for more, echoing in the empty space and I couldn't do a thing to stop them.

He turned the vibrations off, and at the sudden loss of sensation I slid against the wall, my legs shaking, my feet uncertain in their heels. I hadn't come, and I could tell by Davian's expression that he'd purposely kept that prize from me. He'd put me right where he wanted me, sweating and trembling, still full of a lust that was a long way from satisfied.

He pocketed the remote, holding me against the wall with the press of his body, angling me so I could feel his erection, pulsed and straining, against me. The thought of his cock, the curve of its arousal, pushed my lust another notch higher. I grabbed his hip, pulling him against me, reaching for his mouth.

'No,' he said, plainly, his lips barely brushing mine before he pulled away.

I wanted to howl. Or slap him. Or maybe both. Really, I wanted him inside me in all the ways he could be. Tongue in my mouth. Cock in my aching pussy. Fingers in the clench of my ass. But I was quickly learning there was no amount of begging or whining or even seducing that would sway

Davian from his path once he'd started down it.

He waited until my breaths were less gaspy, until I could ease my grip on his hip and start to stand on my own again.

'Better?' he asked.

Was I? I could barely stand, my heart was hammering lust notes in my chest and I was pretty sure even the portraits had tried to cover their ears at my moans of want. There was a metal egg of potential pleasure tucked inside me that was getting heavier even as I was getting wetter. And I wasn't sure I could walk in these heels any more.

Still I said, 'Yes,' and I knew it to be true.

'Now then, if you're ready, shall we go join the others?'

I slipped my arm in his. I *was* ready.

* * *

Inside the elevator, Davian reached into his pocket and my body tensed in the anticipation of vibrations. None came. He cast a sideways glance at me, dark eyes laughing, then pulled a key card from his pocket and slipped it into a vertical opening. He reached up and pushed his thumb against a button that I hadn't noticed before. Positioned above the regular floor buttons, it edges were barely visible where it separated from the metal. No light gave it away. No number. It was like finding a fingerhold in a rock crevice. You could look for a hundred years and not find it, unless you already knew exactly where to look.

I was getting used to seeing the world in a new light. Once, I might have considered myself to be observant, at least when I didn't have my head in a book. But now I realised that most of us were blind to the world, walking through it so filled with our own expectations that we couldn't see the things that were in front of us. And of course, that was something that the Keyhole Club took full advantage of. Assuming most of the world would never see anything more than we needed or wanted to see. What else was I missing every day? I wondered. What world moved beneath us and above us that I was still oblivious to? I couldn't wait to find out.

Davian curled his fingers around the back of my neck, drawing me forward. He didn't kiss me, as I'd expected. Instead he dropped his forehead softly to mine and kept my gaze tight with his. He exhaled softly, a gesture that seemed oddly intimate, considering the things we'd done together, but somehow it calmed my mind for a moment, allowed me to stop the vibrations of my body. I leaned against him for a long moment. This was just lust and being overwhelmed. It didn't mean anything that his breath against my lips calmed me, quieted me, prepared me for whatever came next.

Leaving his forehead against mine, his eyes closing just slightly as if in anticipation of what was coming, Davian pushed a second button, and we rushed to the top floor in a way that my body wasn't prepared for.

The weight of arousal was something I thought I'd carried my whole life, but it seemed that the deeper I got into this ... experience, whatever it was, the heavier it got. Not that it was a burden. More that my lust was solidifying its gravity in my life. It was something I was getting used to, and coming to enjoy. But there were moments, like now, flying up who knew how many storeys in an elevator to a party with the man I loved and lusted after, when I felt like I was in someone else's story, a story that I never wanted to leave.

I was grateful for Davian's presence, for the press of his forehead to mine, the curl of his hand at the back of my neck, and the soft breaths that allowed me to close my eyes

284

and remember that this was exactly where I belonged.

When the elevator dinged, I hadn't even realise we'd stopped.

* * *

I suppose there comes a moment in every woman's life when she chooses, or is pushed, to become different from what she was. Those of us who are lucky enough to have friends who know us well may get that chance when we least expect it.

As the elevator doors opened, my gaze fell on all the people who were part of the Keyhole Club. Some I knew and some I didn't yet. But the people who stood out the most were those who were part of my life, the ones who'd helped shape me and move me into this new place. Kyle, looking stunning as he always did, his arm around his new girlfriend. Lily, who was caught up in Kitty's embrace, her booming laughter echoing across the room. Stefan, who was holding court with Jay in the corner. Others who'd played a part, small or large, in this adventure that was my life.

The only person missing was Conrad. I knew Davian felt it too, from the way he took my hand, tightening his fingers around mine.

Often in my life I'd wanted to be someone else. One of my literary heroines, one of those fierce, smart women who faced her inner fears and did and said all of the right things. It took me a long time to realise that I was just like those women. Sometimes I screwed up and sometimes things seemed impossible, but the way to the happy ending is never easy. If it was easy, it wouldn't be a very good story, would it?

Bound by love and lust and a leather-wrapped book, Davian and I stepped from the elevator, hand in hand.

Hello, happy ending.